Stef Ann Holm

All the Right Angles

ISBN-13: 978-0-373-77186-8
ISBN-10: 0-373-77186-X

ALL THE RIGHT ANGLES

This edition published by arrangement with Harlequin Books S.A.

www.HQNBooks.com

Printed in U.S.A.

For Greg, with all my love and devotion.

PROLOGUE

GIOVANNI AND MARIANGELA Moretti walked hand in hand along Grove Street, an April sunset coloring the sky. The orange glow winked back at them from the windows in Boise's tallest bank building—all twenty-one stories.

The couple had eaten dinner at Moz Uberuaga's hole-in-the-wall restaurant—one of the few longtime businesses still hanging on in this part of town. Moz was a native Idahoan with Basque ancestry, and a spicy personality to match. His Firehouse Café served the best French fries in town.

"It's a nice evening," Mariangela said, her fingers tucked safely in Giovanni's own.

They both took in their surroundings, and Giovanni looked at the buildings with a contractor's eye. He was on a quest to revitalize the past.

The brick buildings that lined either side of the street had seen better days. Many storefronts were deteriorating, making the scorched "clinker" bricks more prominent—their eggplant coloring stood out against the faded gray mortar. Years of cold winter conditions, followed by baking summer heat, had left the buildings weathered. The street itself was narrow, with only two lanes. There was a time when deliveries made to this area had traffic backed up for blocks. But it had been a long time since this section of town had seen that kind of commercial activity.

The old marketplace was separated from the main commercial part of downtown Boise. The neighborhood had once been home to a thriving candy factory, a single-screen movie theater and a Mexican restaurant. The department store on Main Street had closed years ago, and in its place stood a pool hall where police were called in to bust up fights at least once a week.

"It sure has changed around here," Mariangela said with a sigh, her gaze sweeping across the boarded-up display window of the old florist. "I remember when Rosebud's had the best red roses in town."

Pausing, Giovanni frowned at the graffiti marring the closed-up entry. "I bought a lot of anniversary bouquets here."

"Now everyone goes to that big discount florist up on the hill."

Over dinner, Giovanni had discussed his reasons for wanting to take on the Grove Marketplace renovation project. But his wife had reservations, and they'd reached an impasse. He'd let the subject go, not bringing it up throughout the rest of their meal.

But now he spoke with quiet firmness, his Italian accent more pronounced than usual as he said, "Angela, this is why I want the project so badly. I *need* to bring the old downtown back, so our children's children can enjoy what we once had."

Mariangela nodded, with a wistful acceptance of what was and not what should be.

"It's too difficult, if not impossible, for Moretti Construction to get bonding on a project of this size." She gave his fingers a squeeze. "I know how badly you want it, but Giovanni…we can't."

He wasn't convinced. He was still filled with hope—if not steely determination.

He and his wife had discussed the Grove Marketplace renovation a hundred times. With a lot of new businesses coming to town, the growth opportunities were huge. An outside developer had tagged the area for a complete new look from the ground up, including a five-story parking structure and a four-star hotel.

The deterioration and decline that had begun nineteen years ago, when the supermall opened five miles away, would be halted. A multiplex theater, several restaurants and upscale shops were planned.

Giovanni had been waiting all his life to do a project like this.

His heart still swelled with pride for the old country, and all he had learned apprenticing as a carpenter there. He'd come into the world in 1935 in Naples, Italy, during oppression, but his life experiences had given him strength and resistance.

So had his beautiful wife of forty-four years. The

moment he'd set eyes on Mariangela Castelluccio, Giovanni had been smitten. She'd been eighteen when he'd married her after a whirlwind courtship. At twenty-eight, Giovanni had been ready to settle down, but not in Naples. There were too many laws governing his choices—a tangle of statutes, rules, norms, regulations and customs for the owner of a small business to follow. He wanted to make a better life for his wife by what the Americans called "free enterprise," so he'd immigrated to the States. He'd brought with him a legacy of craftsmanship from some of the best carpenters in Naples.

Giovanni wanted to use those skills to rejuvenate Boise, to help breathe life back into what had once had energy and verve. *He* could save the downtown—that wasteland of empty buildings, failing businesses and dusty ghosts of glory days past.

"Do you want to get an ice cream at Maggie Moo's?" Mariangela asked, trying to distract him from his pensive mood. She knew what made him happy, and that included something as simple as a bowl of vanilla ice cream with toffee bits.

He swallowed tightly, his love for her filling his chest and giving him a soft ache in his heart. "In a minute."

Giovanni held Mariangela's hand, her fingers slight in his grasp, her gold wedding band warm from her body heat. She smelled like a combination of his favorite perfume, spring flowers and the hint of garlic that always seemed to be on her hands no matter how much lemon dish soap she used. She didn't like smelling like an Italian kitchen, but he loved the scent that was uniquely her.

At the age of sixty-two, his wife looked better than ever, even though her raven-black hair shone with a few threads of silver now. He'd always thought she had the prettiest brown eyes he'd ever seen—their color a warm mix of walnut and golden-honey. Time had not faded the sparkle in them that expressed her love of life.

Their marriage had always been good, but they had had their struggles. Early on, Mariangela hadn't been pleased with him when he'd left her behind in Italy to get settled in America. As soon as he sent for her, he promised they'd never be apart again—and they hadn't. He had never left her at home without him, even when the babies had come and he'd had building conventions and business trips. Mariangela would bring the kids along, and they'd swim in a motel pool or visit a local attraction while Giovanni took care of business.

He was truly blessed, he knew, and he couldn't imagine life without his wonderful wife by his side.

However, in recent months, there had been a growing wedge of tension pushing between them—all his doing. He accepted the blame. He wanted this project so very badly, but Mariangela wanted him to retire.

Over cappuccino the other morning, she'd said, "But Giovanni, you don't need to get up at five o'clock anymore. You're seventy-two. You shouldn't be going up and down ladders or ducking under scaffolding. You've got a bad back and your ankles are starting to give out."

She was right, of course. His darling Mariangela usually was. She was the cement of the family, the foundation of reason and common sense that kept him glued together—emotionally and physically. But in this instance, he just couldn't let the Grove Marketplace project rest.

Throughout the years, Moretti Construction had completed some very significant jobs, but never anything this big. He'd lived in Boise long enough to want to leave his mark in a significant way, with something that would be a long-term testament to Moretti Construction's craftsmanship.

"We should take a trip home to Italy, a long visit, Giovanni." Mariangela's gentle words broke through his thoughts, bringing him back to reality.

"Yes…we should." He cupped his wife's face with his hand, his fingers calloused and rough. "But, *bella mia,* first I'd like to get this project."

He could see the disappointment in her gaze, perhaps mixed with a small flicker of ire. He'd been pushing for this too long and she was reaching her limit. But he couldn't help it.

In an almost exasperated tone, Mariangela said, "But we aren't qualified to get the bonding—you said so yourself. It'll be an uphill battle. We just aren't big enough." The compassion in her brown eyes warmed his heart, and her fingers squeezed his with a familiar reassurance he'd come to treasure. "Our life isn't going to change if you don't get the marketplace—we'll be okay."

Deep down, he knew her words to be true. Of course they'd be okay. This wasn't about their livelihood.

For Giovanni, the Grove Marketplace had everything to do with sharing his talents for others to enjoy. Doing his best and leaving his mark on an area of Boise that would flourish for many years to come.

For that, he couldn't let this rest.

He stroked his wife's soft cheek. For a second, she closed her eyes, leaned into him, and he felt her love surround him.

He almost wanted to pull out of the bidding, just to please her and make her happy, but he couldn't. There was so much more to this than he could ever explain to her. In fact, he couldn't fully explain it to himself. The desire to press forward was so strong that he blocked out caution and reason and even the quiet pleading in his wife's gaze.

With an ache in his chest, he took her hand again and drew her down the street to the alleyway. Smiling with mischief, he stepped into the alley and took her into his arms.

Giovanni planted a big kiss on his wife's soft lips, and she sighed.

"I love you, my angel," he whispered.

"I love you more." Her voice was warm now, the earlier tension gone. "Maybe we should forget the ice cream and go home."

He grinned. "What ice cream?"

Even after forty-four years of marriage, they still had that honeymoon passion.

CHAPTER ONE

THE HIGH HEELS OF Francesca Moretti's black leather pumps clicked as she walked down the sidewalk. She spoke into her cell phone, the conversation with her brother Mark carried out on autopilot because she'd had this exchange before. The generic responses she gave could have been uttered in her sleep.

Momentarily, Francesca grew distracted by a sleek summer-white suit displayed in the window of Solara, a high-end-fashion store. The neckline was plunging and required a sophisticated blouse beneath, while the cut of the skirt was fitted at the hips.

"Umm," she murmured, as Mark went on about how Dad was wanting everything done yesterday on the job. The crane had just arrived from Seattle by rail car, and the first section was assembled. They had only so much time, and the track hoes had broken ground and—

"Do you think I look better in white or black?" she asked with a smile, knowing it would irk Mark to change the subject when he was building up a head of steam on a venting spree. She didn't mean to be facetious, but they'd worked on countless construction jobs together and it was par for the course that something would go wrong, or not be ready when promised, or one of the trades would get red tagged for faulty subcontracting and not pass inspection. This was all part of the business.

But if Francesca thought she'd put a spoke in her brother's wheel, she should have thought twice. They'd bantered too many times and given each other too much affectionate grief.

"Black gives you that don't-mess-with-me-look for when you're moody."

She was about to say she was rarely moody, and that that observation was a figment of his warped male imagination, but she let his comment go since, after all, she had egged him on.

He mentioned in a casual tone, "So I heard that Legacy got another bid for a seventeen story off of Idaho Street."

That gave Francesca pause, and she no longer cared about a white suit in a shop window. "No." The word came out a mix of envy and awe.

Legacy Constructors was headquartered in Seattle and owned and operated by Kyle Jagger—a man who'd reinvented his father's multimillion dollar company into something fresh and innovative. It had become a firm to be reckoned with since Parr Jagger's death nine years ago. Kyle was the type of man who took little for granted, was ambitious and gave the impression that he deserved to be at the top. Francesca had never met him;

her opinion had been formed from what she'd heard her father say about Kyle, and plain old industry gossip.

Conversations in construction trailers provided more hearsay than a beauty salon, so she really shouldn't take what she heard as fact. Even so, one did form preconceived notions about certain successful people, and Kyle Jagger was as successful as you could get in their industry.

Legacy was Moretti's biggest competitor in the region. Her family's company stuck close to home, venturing only as far as an occasional job in Utah or Oregon. Most of their business remained in Idaho where they had the pick of smaller projects in the area. Legacy, in contrast, had sites throughout the Pacific Northwest—big ones.

But one project Kyle Jagger hadn't gotten was the Grove Marketplace. That belonged to Moretti.

Francesca remembered the day her dad had gathered the family together at Robert's restaurant. Her brother had opened a neotraditional Italian *ristorante* eleven years ago, replicating the time-honored family recipes that Francesca had grown up on. A critic for the *Idaho Statesman* had written, "If you want Italian food that sings like Pavarotti, Pomodoro is the only place to eat—*presto!*"

In grand fashion, Dad had ordered a bottle of the best Chianti, then raised his glass to toast everyone at the table. The assembled company had included her oldest brother, Giovanni, Jr., or "John," who was the family lawyer. He was a rock, the one everyone could go to to settle a dispute, whether the quarrel was simple or complex. The hearts of everyone in the family had broken for him when his wife, Connie, was killed in a car accident, leaving him to raise their son and daughter on his own.

Francesca's second oldest brother and his wife were foodies. Their mission in life was to load your plate with more food than you could possibly consume in a week, much less in one meal. Robert and Marie had opened Pomodoro, then started having babies. They were up to four—all girls with inky-black hair and doelike brown eyes.

Mark, her youngest brother, had come solo. He was by far the most handsome of the three boys, yet he never acknowledged how good looking he was. It was comical to be out with him and watch women practically walk into streetlights while gawking at his thick dark hair, brooding brown eyes and firmly set mouth. Mark was the rugged type, a guy who looked great in a torn flannel shirt and a tool belt. He worked on-site in the family business, not wanting any part of paperwork or contracts, although his contributions were invaluable in things like the bidding process.

The night her father had announced Moretti would be doing the Grove Marketplace, Francesca couldn't have been happier. She'd prayed for this for her dad. He wasn't getting any younger and she knew how much he wanted the project.

"So when does Legacy break ground?" Francesca asked into her cell phone, dragging her attention back to the present and continuing toward Pomodoro, which was on Ninth and Bannock. Wednesday nights after work were reserved for meeting her three closest girlfriends at the *ristorante* for dinner. If she hadn't been in the mood for her brother's killer *manicotti,* she might have canceled, because she did not want to hear about the latest bachelor of the day. Her friends, all of whom were actively dating, had made it their mission in life to hook her up.

"The next few weeks. Kyle's going to be on the job overseeing everything," Mark replied.

Kyle Jagger rarely ran projects outside of Seattle because he had a great crew who made sure everything got done. The fact that he was going to be personally involved with this latest project secretly impressed Francesca, although she'd never admit to that. She always tried to maintain a professional demeanor, giving compliments when they were due and keeping unnecessary criticism to herself.

She tended to be hard on herself in terms of expectations. Being a perfectionist, she'd worked hard to maintain a straight 4.0 grade average at Oregon State University, graduating with a degree in architecture. She expected nothing less than the best from herself, and admired good work turned out by others, too. Even Moretti's competition.

"I had a thought, Franci." Mark broke into her thoughts, his tone humorous. "If you ask Kyle out for coffee and find out all his trade secrets, I'll buy you whatever you just saw in Solara's window."

"How'd you know I stopped at Solara?"

"Because I heard you breathing like a sprinter, all hyper and excited about something, and that means one thing—clothes."

Francesca frowned. She wasn't a clotheshorse, but she did like to dress nicely. She rarely wore slacks to work. She kept a half-dozen pairs of heeled shoes beneath her desk in the corner office she had in the brownstone building above Idaho Street. Just because she was an architect didn't mean she had to be frumpy. She enjoyed style and flare, had a figure that could fit into almost anything…so why not?

She gave a sour smile. "I will not ask Kyle Jagger on a date to pry trade secrets out of him. You do it."

"I don't date."

"Neither do I."

"Tell that to the date squad."

Francesca cringed. The "date squad" was comprised of Erin, a CPA; Jordan, a marketing analyst; and Lily, a mortgage broker. When they couldn't set Franci up, they often combined their efforts and tried to find single women for her brother Mark.

"Do you want to join us? We're eating at Pomodoro's and I'm not sure I'm up to another matchmaking session."

"How can it be a matchmaking session when you never go out with any of the guys they come up with?"

"I don't have time."

"Me, either. I can't remember the last time I went out."

"Well, you should make time, Mark. You've got a lot to offer the right woman."

"'A lot to offer…' Isn't that crap reserved for guys named Marvin?"

Franci caught her lip with her teeth to keep from laughing. "Well, I'm here at the restaurant. Wish me luck."

"You don't need it."

Francesca shut off her phone and pulled open the door to Pomodoro. The decor was classic Italian: red-checked tablecloths, straw-covered Chianti bottles on every table, a faux grape arbor, with minilights hung from the ceiling. The rich smells of garlic and tomatoes assaulted her, causing her stomach to growl.

Striding inside, she made her way to her friends' table, aware of three pairs of eyes fastening on her, their smiles bright and broad. And they each had a frustratingly knowing look on her face.

Oh, great. They had a prospect in mind for her.

Why did she suddenly feel as if she were entering a slaughterhouse?

KYLE JAGGER LANDED HIS Piper Malibu at the Boise Airport. Though he was dead tired from a 7:00 a.m. meeting, bumper-to-bumper traffic to Sea-Tac on the I-5, then a one-hour wait for weather clearance, Kyle had to concede he'd had a gorgeous flight over the Cascade Mountains at 18,000 feet. He always packed a cooler and the stainless steel thermos his father had given him when he'd been in college. Depending on his mood, Kyle drank either hot coffee or icy cold diet cola while in the cockpit.

After picking up the truck he kept at the airport's long-term parking lot, he rubbed the grit from his eyes, then felt the bristle of beard on his jaw. He was sure he looked like hell, but whatever. He wasn't here to impress anyone. He would make a quick pit stop at his new downtown condo, then head for city hall at Main and Capitol. He needed to file something today. The high-rise Legacy was doing was pretty straightforward, but paperwork still had to be filed on time.

As soon as he took care of the paperwork, he was going to Moz's Firehouse Café for a home-cooked meal, and then he'd take a look at the Grove Marketplace.

That project should have been Legacy's, but the developer had picked Moretti. If Giovanni wasn't such a personable guy, Kyle might have been royally torked and tried a few things to sway the outcome. Giovanni Moretti could be nice as Sunday supper, but that didn't make up for the loss. Kyle had really wanted that project.

He punched the button on the elevator at city hall, catching a glimpse of his reflection in the mirrored sheen of the doors. He wore jeans and a T-shirt, briefcase in hand. His hair was still windblown from being next to the open cockpit window when he'd taxied in thirty minutes ago.

The bell chimed and the doors opened. He stepped inside and hit the second-floor button while thinking how good a cold beer and a cheeseburger sounded. Kyle had a stomach that could digest anything—an occupational necessity. In the eight years since his divorce, he'd made more trips to a restaurant than to a grocery store. He could cook, but only marginally. He had neither the time nor the inclination. It was much easier to sit and order, then read through his latest set of plans, or scroll through e-mails on his laptop.

The permit office was modern and comfortable, with carpeted floors and rows of cubicles and low counters where blueprints could be spread out and looked over.

It was late in the day and nobody was in line at the receptionist's except for a woman who wore a skirt just above the knees, with a trim jacket that fit her slender back perfectly. She stood ahead of him, one hip slightly cocked and the toe of her right foot slipping in and out of her high-heeled pump while her left leg bore the brunt of her weight—which was slight at best. The shape of her calf was killer. She must work out. He couldn't help watching the way her foot absently moved in and out of that shoe.

"We gave you the building plan," the woman said to the clerk. "Can't you check again?" Her manicured toes toyed with the front of her shoe, and Kyle noticed how smooth and well taken care of her feet were. She wasn't wearing nylons, and he found that incredibly sexy.

When a cell phone started ringing, she leaned her elbows on the counter, slipped her purse off her shoulder and dug through it for the device.

"Hello?" she answered, then listened for a few

seconds before cutting in. "Uh, that would be a no. I told you I'm not interested. I don't care what he looks like."

"How old is he, Franci? If you don't want him, I might be interested. My last date was a major dud. He called his mother three times—she was watching his cat while he was out with me. Whoever heard of a cat sitter for a couple of hours?" The clerk, who must have been in her midthirties, stopped looking for whatever it was the skirted woman had asked her to retrieve. With an eagerly expectant look on her fresh face, she waited for a verdict from the woman.

Franci put her hand on the receiver. Kyle could see her body language stiffen as she said to the clerk, "Lily wants to set me up with Carl Murphy, a man on the faculty of BSU."

"What does he teach?"

"I haven't asked. Not interested."

"Wait, I think I know him. He's a chemistry prof. He graduated from Centennial in '76. He's got to be fifty years old. What's Lily thinking?"

Clearly, these two women were old friends, given the way they were going on about some poor, unsuspecting guy.

"Lily," Franci said, "I'm at the permit office. I have to go. There's a huge lineup..." At that moment, she glanced over her shoulder, as if to invent that exact scenario. But there was only Kyle.

When her rich brown eyes met his, and he noted the way her black hair contrasted with her olive skin, Kyle couldn't readily explain the feeling of recognition that struck him. It seemed as if he knew her, but couldn't recall having met her before. She looked very familiar. The eyes, the nose. That mouth.

"I have to go," she said in a muffled voice, turning back to the counter. She flipped the phone closed, then slipped her foot back into her shoe, standing taller and squaring her shoulders, as if she meant business.

"Patty, I need that permit in short order." She grabbed her purse, ready to leave. "Can you just do it and call me tomorrow?"

"I'll see what I can figure out."

"Thanks."

Franci turned around, obviously trying to avoid Kyle's gaze, but unable to pull that off completely. She glanced his way, then paused a moment, staring. She licked her lips as if to say something, then shrugged and kept walking toward the exit, while Kyle watched.

At the counter, he couldn't help asking, "Who was that?"

"Patty" gave him a once-over, as if she were a cat and he a prime piece of tuna. Then with a sigh, as if she realized she was fishing in the wrong ocean, she said, "Francesca Moretti."

Moretti. Kyle glanced again at the exit, hoping to catch Francesca before she disappeared. Too late. She was gone.

No wonder she seemed familiar. She looked just like her father—a man he knew well…perhaps too well.

Kyle wondered what Francesca Moretti would think

if she knew the lengths her father had gone to in order to land the Grove Marketplace contract.

GIOVANNI MORETTI WORE HIS shirts Hawaiian style—he didn't tuck the tails in. He preferred to let the hem flow around his middle and disguise the ample size of his stomach. He was a big man—he admitted to weighing 240 pounds, but was probably closer to 280. But he was six-two, so considered himself evenly distributed. He liked to think of himself as solid, but his doctor had told him he was in dangerous territory. *Croca-nada!* There was no way he was giving up cheese and pasta.

Sitting behind his desk in his "office," Giovanni turned his mind from food to business. Decades ago, he'd bought this used construction trailer that was now held together by patches and memories. He could easily afford to buy a newer one today, but enjoyed the well-worn feel of this trailer.

It was inevitable that each job site ended up muddy from a water truck or a hard rain. The grooved soles of steel-toed boots collected pockets of gooey dirt, leaving chunks behind on the trailer linoleum as various foremen came in to talk to him. Once in a while, Giovanni swept up, but the gritty floor was a reminder of jobs past. Then there were the familiar smells that had been absorbed into the paneled walls. Blueprint ink, garlic from the lunches his wife brought him, sweat after a long day, the leather of his son's tool belt when he dropped it onto a desk so he could sit and talk over a cup of coffee.

These were comforts to Giovanni, and he liked them. In this trailer, many deals had been put together, history had been made. He'd brought Mark here when he was a baby. Francesca had studied for high school exams on the desk in the corner. The place was cluttered and dingy, dark and in need of new flooring. Even so, Giovanni found peace and satisfaction here. This was where it all began for Moretti Construction. To Giovanni, this trailer was a second home.

He sat behind his desk, papers stacked a foot high around him. There were all sorts of blueprints, planning and zoning reports, appraisals, and a collection of other things that to the average guy would appear to be a jumbled mess, completely disorganized. But Giovanni knew exactly where everything was, when each bill was due, what every report meant, and how to fix a mistake, should something need fixing.

He worked well in this "organized confusion." It was his way of doing things. Nobody understood that except Franci, his baby girl. When she'd been born, after his three sons, he'd thanked the good Lord for blessing him with a daughter. She was the light in his eyes, the smile on his lips. He'd spoiled her when she was little, often buying her a new dress for Mass when she wasn't expecting it. He recalled the day of her Confirmation, with her in that white organdy dress with the veil and wreath on her thick crown of black curls. She'd walked with measured steps, just the way they'd practiced, holding her candle and approaching the altar. He'd never been more proud.

She'd developed into a bright and beautiful young lady. By now, at thirty-four, she'd accomplished more than he had in his entire lifetime, and he found his chest puffing with pride whenever he thought about all that she had done for the community…about all that she could still do. She was ambitious. And fearless. He loved that about her. Perhaps it was growing up with three older brothers that had taught her never to be afraid of anything. She plunged in without looking—and at times, he'd worried about her. Such as when he'd taken the family on a vacation when Franci was just out of diapers. She'd jumped into a motel pool—the deep end—without fear that she'd drown. He'd been halfway out of his lounge chair when he saw her legs scissoring and her arms thrashing in the water to stay afloat, something she'd seen her older brothers do.

Since then, Giovanni had learned not to hold his daughter back, but to let her go. He'd watched her swim through high school, graduate with honors, then continue on to college. Sometimes she put too much pressure on herself. With chagrin, he realized she got that from him. He expected a lot from himself. It was the Italian way—to exceed personal expectations.

Perhaps the whole family took after him….

Robert was the most laid-back of the bunch, happy to be in the kitchen and creating new flavors for the family to try. Despite having four daughters, and a house full of good-natured chaos, he rarely broke a sweat or got addled about anything. His wife, Marie, God love her, was the queen of patience. Nothing fazed her. She smiled all the time.

Now if only Giovanni could see Mark and John settled and happy with women in their lives. And Francesca with a great man.

Poor John had had a good wife, the love of his life. But she'd been taken from them in a car accident, leaving John devastated. Only this year had he begun to move forward again, without long stretches of silence and sadness. Thank God he had the children to raise.

Mark, on the other hand…! Giovanni's number-three son was as easygoing as they came. He was a Moretti through and through—and nothing short of an Italian Adonis. Women followed him like sheep to a herder. Mark had had several girlfriends in his life, but nothing really serious. He'd never lost his heart. He did lose his head in construction, though. He could spend hours building something, and forget about time and everything around him. He had the "Moretti hands," the ability to make something from nothing. It was a gift.

Giovanni heard the last bubbling perks from the coffeemaker that sat on a filing cabinet. He kept that fake stuff on hand for contractors who didn't want the calories. And for himself he had cream. The real thing. Nothing powdered. Giovanni loved a good cup of fresh-roasted coffee, heaped with cream and just a half spoon of sugar. And, of course, a sweet-dough pastry for breakfast. Since he was supposed to be watching his waistline, he'd packed a banana along with Mariangela's hazelnut cinnamon rolls.

He was drinking a cup of coffee when the trailer door opened and Franci came inside with the permits he'd needed from city hall.

"What an ordeal this turned out to be," she sighed, juggling a briefcase and the papers, her leather purse straps thrown over her shoulder. "But I got them."

"I knew you would." Giovanni rose and cleared off the chair for her. He set the papers and envelopes that had been resting there on the corner of his desk—he'd get to them later. Mariangela never understood why he didn't hire a secretary to work in the trailer, to answer the phone, to sort and file paperwork. Simply put, he didn't need the intrusion. He was hands-on, and liked doing things his way or no way.

Franci sat in the chair, crossing her legs. She wore a fitted white suit and black pumps. "You get yourself something new?" he asked. His daughter was high-fashion, and he wondered if all those dresses he'd bought her as a little girl had started her habit of almost always wearing a skirt or dress.

After glancing down at the stylish jacket and skirt, which fitted her figure perfectly, she met his eyes. "I got paid on the Carmichael building remodel. They loved the drawings—giving me a bonus because I went the extra mile."

"You look good."

"Thanks, Dad. You don't," she added bluntly.

"Never mince words, do you, Franci?"

"No." She waited for his reply.

Truth be told, he hadn't been feeling up to snuff lately. He'd been having some heartburn. He wasn't one for popping antacids, but now he always carried a roll in his pants pocket. He was trying to cut down on spicy food, but it didn't seem to make much of a difference. He attributed his recent bout of not feeling up to par to the stress of the job and dealing with the developers.

But even worse, having to make that phone call to—

"You look overworked and tired," she stated. "How're you feeling?"

"Good."

"Why don't I believe you?"

"I don't know." He changed the subject, talking about the project and what needed to be done. He was filling her in on details of the crane's progress when his daughter suddenly cut in.

"Mark told me Legacy got a seventeen story, and Kyle Jagger's in town running it."

Giovanni didn't let on that the mention of Kyle's name made his heart squeeze a bit and start to beat faster. "I think the building will be a great addition to Boise. That hole in the ground has been sitting there for a year. It's about time somebody took on the project, and Legacy will do a great job."

"No doubt…" Franci mused, her eyes clouding over as they often did when she became lost in thought. He couldn't guess what she was thinking, so didn't try.

But after ten minutes of her being distracted as they went over a set of plans, he finally asked, "What's on your mind?"

She pursed her lips. "I saw someone in the permit office last night and he's been on my mind. It's just been a little irritating, that's all."

"Who'd you see?"

"I don't know." She rolled her eyes as if annoyed with herself. "Some guy."

Giovanni smiled, feeling a spark of hope. His daughter hadn't had a serious relationship in years. There had been two men that he knew of who had captured her heart. Paul DiMarco at Oregon State. Giovanni had met the guy a few times and thought he was nice enough. He'd thought she was going to marry Paul, but she hadn't. Instead, she'd announced one day that he wasn't for her and she'd wished him the best.

The second man he knew simply as Eduardo. She'd dated him when she'd studied in Florence, after graduating from college. Their courtship had been a whirlwind one, and Giovanni had even worried she might do something like have an impromptu wedding and not include the family. But she hadn't. She'd come home from Italy not wanting to talk about the breakup. Not even Mariangela could get Franci to say much about Eduardo.

Inwardly, Giovanni sighed. It would take quite a man to get, and keep, his daughter's interest. Francesca Angela Moretti had high expectations.

"What made the guy catch your attention?" Giovanni asked, taking a sip of coffee.

"Nothing. Nothing really." She tossed her head as if to shake off the thought. "I don't know why I even brought it up. I think the date squad is getting to me. I actually thought about letting them fix me up to get them off my case. Maybe I will. Even though I'm pretty picky."

"He'll have to pass my inspection, too," Giovanni stated with a wink.

His daughter smiled. "Well, it'll be very hard for any man to measure up to my dad."

A broad grin creased Giovanni's face. He sure loved his daughter. She'd always be his little girl.

CHAPTER TWO

WHEN ROBERT MORETTI dreamed, it was always about food. A sausage on the table, balls of cheese, bowls of plump red tomatoes, a bottle of the best wine, heads of garlic. Dreams with food—it was the burden of being Italian. He lived and breathed *la cucina.* Put him in the kitchen and he became an artist, transforming simple ingredients into favorite dishes.

These dreams became a reality as he prepared for a special event. When his dad wanted to throw a party, he did so with style, and he always hosted the event at Pomodoro.

Tonight Robert had gone all out, closing down the restaurant to the public and putting on a spread fit for royalty. He'd been preparing a feast for his family for days. Beef and lentil soup, broccoli florets with lemon olive oil, polenta, rack of lamb with mint-basil pesto, penne and sauce, red snapper with parsley vinaigrette, chocolate ricotta pudding and limoncello cheesecake squares.

The aromas coming from the kitchen filled the *ristorante* with a delicious combination of mild and spicy, delicate and sweet. Guests were arriving, and Robert was still running around like a madman in the small kitchen, sweat dampening his brow as he tempered flames on the commercial stove, checked bubbling sauces and tossed salt into boiling water.

He couldn't imagine doing anything else with his life. Years ago, when he'd told the family of his intention to open a restaurant, he'd expected a few jokes—especially from his oldest brother, John. But nobody had said anything remotely critical. Instead, Robert's announcement was met with enthusiasm and support. He'd taken to cooking while in middle school, and realized he had a gift for putting ingredients together. His family realized it, as well.

Robert glanced over the shoulder of his white chef's smock to check on his sous chef, who was pressing garlic and chopping more onions. They traded information, making sure they each knew what the other was working on.

After about twenty minutes, Robert popped his head out the revolving kitchen door, skimming his gaze across the crowd. He saw his wife at the hostess station, greeting people as they arrived, and he noticed his sister in the corner with their dad.

Franci looked great with her hair twisted on top of her head. Dangling earrings sparkled from her earlobes, and she wore a matching choker around her neck. Her brown eyes shone in the soft candlelight, as did the glass of red wine in her hand. She wore a body-hugging black cocktail dress and high heels, which made her height nearly six feet. She was a stunner, no doubt about it. She worked long hours, and didn't give herself enough relaxation time to enjoy all that she'd accomplished. A definite overachiever.

Robert was glad he wasn't so uptight.

Spying his wife again among the guests she'd shown to a table, he smiled, just as Marie briefly turned and caught his eye. She grinned at him and his heart warmed. He was in love with her just as deeply today as when he'd asked her to marry him.

Che bella! he thought as he turned back to his hot kitchen.

EARLIER IN THE DAY, Francesca and her father had agreed not to talk business at the party—a celebration for landing the Grove Marketplace project. But an emergency had erupted late in the afternoon, and both of them had been trying to get it taken care of with minimal impact on the schedule and without incurring hefty costs.

While digging the piers for the building's footings, the excavator had hit the water table, which proved to be three feet higher than the engineers had told them it would be. They'd had to stop digging and bring in pumps to dewater the hole.

"Even though they're pumping," Giovanni said while grabbing a prosciutto roll off the antipasto plate, "it's going to put us two weeks behind."

Francesca remained optimistic in spite of the setback. "Yes, but the developers have agreed to pay the equipment cost and any cost overruns."

"It's not a good sign," her father proclaimed. "Already we have trouble. I'm going to light a candle."

Whenever a situation became too stressful, her father's answer was to light a candle at Saint John's Catholic Church.

Francesca's upbringing had been very involved with the church. She'd gone to the parish school, studied catechism and regularly attended Mass. As she got older, she'd drifted away from the many activities. While she was still a firm believer in the foundations of her religion, she'd questioned the legalistic ways of the church. Out of curiosity, she'd gone to her friend Jordan's nondenominational Christian church a few times and found it not at all what she'd expected.

She was used to robes and incense, Latin phrases and rituals. Instead, she'd encountered a pastor who wore a white shirt without a tie, and a charcoal-gray suit. He didn't stand behind a pulpit and read directly from the Bible. They'd sung songs with a praise band—drums and guitars. It was definitely different than what she was used to, and she'd enjoyed it.

"And I'll light a candle for Mark." Her father's voice brought Franci out of her musings.

"Mark? What's the matter with him?"

"Nothing that I know of." Giovanni ate the prosciutto in two bites, then snatched up another. "Backup. Just making sure he's not going to get hurt on the job."

Francesca nodded, a thought crossing her mind: *Did Dad ever light candles for me as backup?*

She knew he loved her dearly, but sometimes her good-hearted father grew frustrated with her. It wasn't as if she *liked* being so picky about things. It was just who she was.

"How many people do you think will show up?" she asked, gesturing with the wineglass in her hand. She'd been savoring the taste of the cabernet. Robert always served the best reds.

"We invited two hundred, but you know how these things are."

"Mmm," she responded noncommittally as she glanced about the crowded restaurant. She recognized a lot of the faces, but more than a handful were new. Moretti Construction had their favorite contractors, but new foremen were being hired all the time.

Her mother, dressed in a lovely matching skirt and blouse, was talking to an electrician's wife. Mariangela had always fit into her husband's world and was never timid about speaking to people she didn't know. Francesca admired that about her mom. Having been born and raised in the old country, she could have been docile and submissive. But to the contrary, Mariangela had a lot to say, and Francesca knew her father asked her mother's opinion about a variety of things regarding the business.

Her parents' marriage was solid and loving. Watching them together was like watching a romantic movie from the 1940s, only in Technicolor. Giovanni was an old-school gentleman, and Mariangela had always prided herself on her role of wife and mother.

Though she usually didn't feel bad about being single, Francesca wished she could meet a man who would give her the kind of love her mom and dad had. She'd thought she'd found him in Eduardo…but no. That breakup had been the cause for her reticence about getting involved now.

Francesca wasn't a flirt, didn't go to nightclubs with the girls. She preferred to stay home, read, listen to music or paint. She enjoyed watercolors. Her list of pleasures was short. She hadn't always been so standoffish, but after being burned several times in the relationship department, she'd let her personal life simmer down, and had withdrawn from the dating market to lick her wounds. She was completely healed now, and lately, she'd been thinking about letting the date squad set her up. Then again, she'd rather do her own shopping where men were concerned.

Panning her gaze over the groups of men and women socializing and conversing, Francesca stopped short, focusing on one man in particular. The one she'd seen in the permits office at city hall. Her heartbeat started doing strange things, and it felt as if her breath caught in her throat.

What was *he* doing here?

She'd heard that Allied Plumbing had hired a new foreman, but she'd yet to meet him. Dealing directly with subcontractors wasn't part of her job. If she knew someone, it was because he or she happened to come into her father's trailer while Franci was there.

"Is that the new Allied foreman?" she blurted out, then bit her lip. She should have had a little more tact, but there was something about the man that made her stand up and take notice. That was rare.

Giovanni followed her line of vision, then paused. "That's Kyle Jagger," he finally said in an even tone.

So this was the infamous Kyle Jagger, inheritor of the now hugely successful Legacy Constructors. He was nothing like Franci had expected. Many years ago, she'd run into his father on several occasions while doing business in various parts of town. Parr Jagger's Scandinavian features had been weathered and his face drawn. His hair had been pale, his eyes a watery blue. She'd thought he was pleasant, but had never really had the chance to get to know him.

His son was completely dissimilar—dark and handsome, tall and broad-shouldered. She couldn't tell his eye color, but she noted how the restaurant lights played across his dark brown hair and gave it a burnished shine.

He wore a black suit with a tie, too formal for the occasion, but it looked as if it had been tailor-made for him. His crisp white shirt showed no signs of wrinkles. In fact, nothing about the man seemed flawed at all. He was very polished, very put together in a *GQ* sort of way—completely unlike how he'd been dressed at city hall.

Clearly, he was very confident—if not downright arrogant—showing up at a Moretti party uninvited.

"He's got some nerve, doesn't he?" Francesca couldn't help the note of disbelief in her voice.

Music played in the background through Pomodoro's speaker system—some Italian ballad that Francesca was able to tune out as she stared at Kyle.

Her father's resonant voice cut through the soft laughter and conversations that drifted through the room. "I invited him."

Francesca turned to her dad. "What?"

"It's just good business to have him here."

The savory smell of roasting garlic that, earlier, had been whetting Francesca's appetite, now lost its appeal.

"I don't see why. We're never invited to Legacy's parties."

"Somebody has to start somewhere."

Mariangela joined them, and Francesca was at a loss as to what to say next. To speak further would tip her father off that Kyle Jagger interested her beyond simple curiosity. She dropped the subject, but throughout the dinner Robert had painstakingly prepared, she found her gaze gravitating toward Kyle.

They were seated on opposite sides of the restaurant, and the man was totally unaware of her presence. With an internal groan, she wished she were unaware of him. Even the way he ate attracted her attention.

His hands were large and tanned. The way he buttered a slice of warm bread had her following his every move, especially when he brought it to his mouth for a bite. He spoke while stabbing food onto his fork, then raising the implement as if it were a casual prop for him to hold while he commented to the man seated beside him. When he finally did take a taste, his eyes and mouth showed a real appreciation for her brother's culinary talents.

Low light picked up the metallic glint from his wristwatch as he brought a wineglass to his mouth and drank the rest of the contents in one long swallow. She'd secretly watched his Adam's apple, a flush fanning across her skin.

When dessert was being served, Giovanni rose from his table to make an announcement. Francesca had never been happier for a distraction.

"Thank you for being here with us tonight." He stood proudly and grinned ear to ear. "Moretti Construction wouldn't be what it is today without your hard work and dedication."

Applause broke out, and several wineglasses were lifted.

Her brother John, who'd been rather quiet all evening, caught her gaze and smiled. She smiled back. Franci ached for his loss, and was glad he'd come out for the party. He was a wonderful man, so giving and with such a great heart. He could be reserved, even aloof, but she loved him just as he was. She knew that the real John, the one deep down, had more warmth and character to him than he ever let anyone see. It was tragic that that part of him had died with his wife. Franci prayed he would find someone else when he was ready.

"The Grove Marketplace will immortalize Moretti Construction for years to come," her father continued. "I'd especially like to thank my son Mark for his input on the technical aspects of our bid."

In acknowledgment, Mark lifted his chin slightly, a half smile on his mouth. Even without trying, he could warm the heart of even the most cynical woman, he was so handsome.

"My son John," Giovanni said next, panning the crowd until he found his eldest boy. "John's efforts with the legal end of things made sure we weren't going to get ourselves between a rock and a hard place."

One of the drywall subs teasingly said, "You mean between Sheetrock and a steel wall."

Laughter rose.

Her father took it with a smile. "And thanks to my son Robert, God love him, who has a talent for cooking that he sure didn't get from me."

More laughter sounded.

"And lastly—" Giovanni's baritone voice lowered with emotion "—my beautiful daughter, Francesca, without whom I wouldn't know my left hand from my right. She thinks ahead of me, knows what I want and gets it done without me having to ask. *La bella figlia ed il mio amore.*"

Francesca's heart melted. *My beautiful daughter, my love.*

Her dad kissed his fingertips, then extended his hand toward her.

She blushed at the unwarranted attention. She'd just been doing her job.

She felt everyone's gaze transfer to her, and grew painfully self-conscious that a certain pair of eyes were on her. She could hardly breathe, much less take even a quick peek to verify what she felt right down to her toes.

Thankfully, her father wrapped things up. "I know each and every one of you takes pride in what you bring to the project. I want to show my appreciation to all of you by saying *salute!*" He lifted his glass and drank a toast to those gathered for the evening.

Francesca could hardly lift her glass to her mouth. She sucked air into her lungs, still feeling that one lingering gaze. She dared herself to dart her eyes toward the table on the far side of the room, sucking in a gasp as she made contact.

Kyle Jagger was staring at her intently.

KYLE HAD BEEN AWARE of Francesca Moretti all night long. She'd been sneaking glances at him and didn't think he'd noticed. His ability to sense that someone was looking at him was highly tuned. He could feel a gaze on him across a crowded room. Maybe that trigger came from years of experience at subcontractor meetings, where everyone tried to read you like yesterday's news, trying to figure out what angle you were coming from. Kyle had a pretty good poker face when he needed one.

He'd kept tabs on Francesca throughout the evening, noting the way the fabric of her dress clung to her body. She had curves in all the right places, and a smile that shot straight to a man's gut. He'd watched her talking to her father, the way she'd laugh or add something and wait for Giovanni's reaction. Kyle had pretty much guessed they were talking about him when her gaze shot straight to him in midconversation. For whatever reason, he'd taken that second to look away, but he'd felt the burn of her eyes.

He tried to remember the unique brown color of those eyes. He recalled them being warm and soft, with thick lashes and a nice arch to her brows. Her sensuous lips were luscious tonight, painted a rich shade of raspberry.

On several occasions, he'd been tempted to walk up to her and introduce himself. But he found he was rather enjoying her attempts at being nonchalant while stealing looks at him. Knowing a beautiful woman was interested in him always piqued his attention.

Kyle had been divorced for eight years now, ever since his ex-wife had cheated on him and he'd figured out she was having an affair. Hailey had long since broken up with the "boyfriend," and wanted him back, but Kyle had moved on.

In hindsight, he had never questioned his love for her, but compatibility-wise, they hadn't been an ideal match. He'd been young when he married and he hadn't really thought things through. Hailey had been really attractive, outgoing and incredibly sexy. But it just hadn't worked out, and Kyle was no longer regretful about it. Things happened for a reason.

At the time, he'd been pretty broken up about it—an ego thing. Any man would question himself if his wife strayed, and Kyle was no different. In time, he'd been able to see that some of the blame lay at his feet. He'd been always absorbed with work and didn't take enough time to tell his wife how much he loved her.

Inhaling, Kyle thought, *water under the bridge.*

There was nothing he could do about it now. He didn't date very often. He continued to work quite a lot, but there was more to life than that. Namely golf.

Kyle was a weekend golfer. Being on the course was the best way for him to unwind. He liked the outdoors, enjoying the warm summers and cool winters of Idaho, compared to the wet climate in Seattle. He also liked to ski. He'd gotten into it only last year, and was looking forward to the upcoming season.

He'd decided to take more personal hours for himself lately, to not be so involved with the corporate side of things, and to let go of a lot of the stuff he couldn't control. Kyle needed to make the effort to strap on a bag of tools sometimes and get real with what he did for a living, instead of sitting at a boardroom table all day, fielding phone calls, trying to fix the next-to-impossible as he watched mistakes make a ding in the company assets. It was that zero-to-one-hundred-miles-per-hour stress that had probably killed his dad. But that was something Kyle didn't dwell on.

Earlier tonight, he had spent some time talking to Mark Moretti, the youngest of Francesca's three brothers. He knew Mark from the trade, having run into him a couple of times over the years, and respected him. The guy liked being on the job site. Kyle and he had a few things in common.

Kyle didn't socialize much, within the industry or out; the bar scene just wasn't his thing. But he and Mark had talked about taking a Saturday and playing eighteen holes at Shadow Valley. Kyle looked forward to sinking some chip shots.

People were beginning to leave the party, but Kyle had no desire to head to the condo just yet. There were some nights when he just wasn't in the mood for quiet or solitude, and he didn't feel like looking at blueprints and files he needed to review.

Besides, why go home when he felt a pull toward a certain someone here?

He finished the last of his black decaf at the bar, where he'd spoken briefly to Giovanni before his host had excused himself to move on to other guests.

With a cursory glance around the restaurant, Kyle spied Franci exiting the ladies' room, wisps of black hair framing her face as if she'd tried to tame them, failed and had given up.

She spotted him, and he could see her hesitate—was she changing directions or heading his way?

He took the decision out of her hands, rose and went straight toward her, his arm extended.

"I'm Kyle Jagger."

"I know," she replied, standing taller.

He liked her taller-than-average height. He was six feet four in his bare feet, and she came up to his nose in those sexy black heels.

"Yeah, I figured you did, from the way you were watching me all night."

If he'd put her off-kilter, she didn't show it.

"I was glancing." She shrugged and took the straightforward approach, something he admired.

"Watching. Glancing. There's not much of a difference."

"I was interested because I was surprised to find you at a Moretti party."

"I was invited."

"My father said it was a business decision, but I don't see how Legacy and Moretti could have business together. Your company handles things on a sterile corporate level, while Moretti still offers personal customer service." As soon as the words were out, she winced. "I'm sorry, it's just that Moretti is a very old-fashioned company."

The decisive way she spoke had him reining in his inclination to tell her just how deep the Legacy and Moretti tie ran. If he didn't have a gentleman's agreement to keep certain information to himself, he might have set her on her heels.

"You're right—we don't. Not really," he added, just to sound a little disinterested, since that's what she was looking for. "But I'd heard really great things about this restaurant and I wanted to give it a try. Why not combine business with pleasure?"

She frowned, a cute pout forming on her lips, as if she weren't all that impressed with him. Briefly, he wondered if he could say something that would get her pulse to turn over.

Most women he encountered practically threw themselves at him, even when there was little interest on his part. He wasn't into looks as much as he was into brains. Maybe he was in a minority, but he liked a healthy discussion *and* pleasing features. There was nothing better than having a good conversation with a woman who looked you in the eye when she asked questions, or offered her opinion.

Talking with Franci was a good opportunity for Kyle to see what she was really like. He hadn't wanted to pry information out of Mark, other than to ask if his sister was involved with anyone—and he'd posed the question in a way that didn't tip Mark off to Kyle's personal interest.

He could already tell Francesca was headstrong, but she had heart, too. That was evident in the way she'd spoken with her father, her hand sometimes falling on his shoulder or sleeve to reassure him, to make a gentle point or just to convey affection.

After being married to a woman who hadn't been very affectionate, or willing to communicate on a deep level, Kyle realized he craved that. He would need understanding and compromise in his next relationship.

He'd witnessed how Francesca carried herself, and

was pretty sure she was genuine. Women in her position were either there for a power trip, or else loved what they did. She clearly had the heart for her job and a passion for her family.

"How'd you become an architect?" His impromptu question threw her off balance, judging by that glint of light in her eyes.

"The usual way. I went to college."

"You know what I mean—why architecture?"

The cut of her dress afforded him a marginal view of the swell of her breasts. She had perfectly flawless olive-toned skin—that ethnic Italian complexion. She wore very little makeup, and didn't need it. He thought she was absolutely stunning. And she smelled really nice.

"I like to design things. And draw." That's all she offered, but he knew there had to be more beyond her brief response.

The instant she shifted her weight from one high-heeled foot to the other, evidently aware his peripheral vision had strayed toward her cleavage, he refocused on her face. "So do you like your job?"

"Very much."

"Ever design something just for the fun of it and not for the money?"

"My Barbie house when I was ten."

He couldn't help laughing.

She added, "Of course, there have been other things."

"And they were…?"

"Why the inquisition?"

"Maybe because I'd like to get to know you better."

Tilting her head, she silently studied his face.

He folded his arms across his chest. Getting her to talk about herself was like pulling nails out of concrete. She could have been more forthcoming, but wasn't giving out any more information than she had to.

Recalling how free and easygoing she'd been on the phone at city hall, he regarded her with frank assessment. While he doubted it, maybe she was uneasy around the opposite sex. "So if I were to invite you to dinner, what would you say?"

The color on her cheeks darkened to a deeper shade of pink. "Excuse me?"

"I was just curious how you'd respond if I asked you to have dinner with me."

"Most likely—no," she said, her voice raising in pitch in spite of her best efforts. "We're not exactly friends."

"But that's how friendships begin."

"Not in this case. Remind yourself that Legacy is no friend of Moretti's."

"Not true. I consider your father to be a good man."

She managed a polite smile, but it was evident she didn't know what to make of their exchange. "Thank you. I think so, too."

"It was nice to finally meet you." He turned, then paused and called to her over his shoulder. She stood there unmoving, looking like a dark goddess with her rich black hair and beautiful lips.

"Franci?"

"Yes?"

"Do you golf?"

"Uh, no."

With a smile, he said, "That's too bad, but there's always lessons."

"Only if you want to learn how to do it."

His laugh was amused. "I'm sure I could teach you a lot about most anything."

CHAPTER THREE

FRANCESCA LOOKED INSIDE boxes of old Barbies, stuffed animals, art notebooks and outdated clothes she'd been too attached to to donate to a thrift store. She'd never wear that pleated Ra-Ra skirt from 1991 again, but she'd spent what for her had been a fortune on it, and had worn the skirt like crazy that summer.

She stood on a folding chair inside her old bedroom closet at her parents' house. The closet was a catchall for things she hadn't moved with her to college, then abroad, then back to Boise and finally to her modest house in the North End. Her mom and dad had lived in the same home for over thirty years—the mortgage having long ago been paid off—and her bedroom was pretty much how she'd left it after high school graduation.

The twin bed purchased at Sears, with its lavender chenille spread, looked as if she'd just made it this morning before heading to school. The pink-and-purple floral wallpaper had faded a little, but Pookiebear still rested on the bed. Her senior year boyfriend had won the stuffed animal at the Idaho State Fair, and she still had it after all these years, even though she had lost touch with Tom Hansen years ago.

Reaching higher, Francesca nabbed a brown box and brought it down, sitting cross-legged on the carpet to look through the contents. She found the journal she'd kept during her turbulent teenage years, including the summer when she'd grown several inches, and then felt like a giant entering the tenth grade. She skimmed a few of the entries, smiling with remembrance over how awful she'd felt life had been at the time, with her being so tall and thin. Now she didn't mind a bit. The gangly girl had taken on shape as a woman, and her curves had rounded out.

She dug deep inside the box and came across school annuals and report cards. Glancing at the grades, she was happy to see all those straight A's. So much for Kyle Jagger teaching her "a lot about most anything." She wasn't stupid and didn't need an education from him.

Then again, she had a feeling there was a subliminal message in his comment—and in that regard, no doubt, he was highly skilled.

She continued to rummage through all sorts of mementos until she found what she was looking for.

"Aha!" she exclaimed.

"Aha, what?" Her mother's voice carried from the bedroom doorway, where she'd just appeared.

"This." Francesca held up a sketchbook. "My drawings from Tuscany. I knew I'd find it somewhere. I'm doing a remodel and have a certain portico in mind, and I knew I'd sketched the perfect one once before."

Mariangela entered the bedroom and sat on the bed. Her dark hair shone like black silk. She wore a pair of black capris, a green V-neck T-shirt and chunky jewelry on her neck. Her toenails were painted pink, but her fingernails had a clear coat on them. The only jewelry on her hands was her wedding ring, a simple gold band. Over the years, Dad had told her he'd buy her a ring with a diamond, but Mom had declined saying that this was the ring he'd put on her finger the day she'd taken her vows, and she didn't want any flashy upgrades just because they could afford something bigger now.

Aging suited Mariangela well, and Francesca thought she was still very pretty.

"Franci, *bella,* have I told you lately how proud of you I am?"

"Thanks, Mom." She thumbed through the drawings and was reminded of the places she'd visited, the Italian architecture that was so rich in history she'd had to put it on paper.

As she viewed her old artwork, she remembered what it had been like when she'd gone to study in Italy. The hopes and dreams she'd had for her life. Meeting Eduardo for the first time.

Francesca rose to her feet to sit besides her mother. She put her arm around her, then laid her cheek on Mariangela's shoulder.

"Mom? What did you see in Dad when you first met him?"

Without thought, her mom replied, "He was a gentleman. He wasn't a man of means, but he had integrity."

"Tell me again how you met him."

"Let's see…it's been so long ago, I may forget the details."

Francesca lifted her head and settled back on the pillows after shoving Pookiebear aside. "You have a great memory."

As if recalling a special moment in days gone by, Mariangela got a far-off look in her eyes as she settled in next to her daughter. "I was working as a clerk in a millinery shop. It was up to me to make sure my father knew when he had to come home for dinner. He was notorious for forgetting the time. I got off work and headed down to the wharf to look for him."

Grandfather Castelluccio had been a fisherman.

"He wasn't on the boat, so I searched the seawalls, where all the bearded men sat smoking their clay pipes and looking as if they were waiting to be photographed for a travel poster. I couldn't find him and I gave up, assuming he'd gone home." She fingered the lace around a pillow's edge. "I headed there myself. I had to walk past the Odysseus Hotel and the café where they served the best cappuccino in Napoli. Your father was there, and he saw me in my skirt and tall shoes—can you imagine I used to wear heels?"

"No," Francesca said with a smile. Mariangela dressed for comfort now.

"In any case, your father came outside and called

after me. He said he had a hunch that the sun rose and fell at my feet, and he wanted to know if I'd share his company at sunset so he could see for himself."

"That's so sweet. You were immediately taken by him."

"Not at all. I thought he was bold as brass to make such a statement, but his eyes…oh, they were so kind. He wasn't like any man I'd ever met, and while he'd spoken words like poetry from a B-movie, I overlooked that. He did have manners and he was a gentleman—that was apparent to me that night when he came to call on me. He brought my father a box of cigars and my mother a box of pastries."

"So you fell in love with him that night?"

"Actually, it was a few days later, when I realized Gina Tucci had big designs on Giovanni. She was the ticket girl at the movie house and had a behind on her like double mandolins. He said she wasn't his type, but she made the best *spiedini* he'd ever eaten. I was no slouch in the kitchen, so I prepared him a dinner he wouldn't soon forget. We were engaged a few weeks later."

Francesca dragged in a slow, deep breath as her thoughts became introspective. Sometimes she was fine with being single. She earned a good living, took care of herself, liked the solitude of her home and watching late night television if she couldn't fall asleep. She could come and go as she pleased, head out of town for much-needed relaxation—although she hadn't done that in forever—and her house was always organized the way she liked it. But there were some days when she wouldn't mind sharing the breakfast table with someone. And it wouldn't be a big deal to throw in laundry for two, to shop for groceries with an extra person in mind, to snuggle deep in the covers on a cold wintry day and just talk…or kiss.

Francesca rarely thought about Eduardo anymore. He had been her European fling; they'd spent days on the beaches, drinking wine and reading poetry, riding the Vespa around the scenic countryside. Looking back, she couldn't believe she'd been so carefree. She'd long ago rebuilt herself emotionally, and recovered. Now she tried to dwell on what she did have rather than on what she didn't.

But at thirty-four, she wasn't getting any younger.

"*Bella mia,*" her mother said softly, "you'll meet someone when God is ready to give him to you."

"You think?" Franci snorted with a half grin. "I don't know about that."

"Have faith. Just in case, I'll light a candle."

After a long silence, Francesca gave a conciliatory sigh. "Maybe you'd better light two."

When she left her parents' house that night and headed home, Franci was full from having eaten too much ziti and sauce, too much bread dipped in olive oil, and two glasses of wine. Her mother's solution to anything troubling was heaping bowls of pasta and garlic-studded tomato sauce. Food could solve the world's problems.

Thank goodness Mom hadn't mentioned their midafternoon conversation to Dad. As the pasta had been passed, Francesca had a horrifying recollection of the day she'd gotten her period, at age thirteen. She'd called her mom into the bathroom, and Mariangela had dramatically put both hands on her cheeks and declared she was no longer her baby girl. Francesca begged her not to tell Dad, but she'd heard her mother dashing toward the kitchen saying, "Giovanni, she's a woman now!"

Why was it Italians never took a private squabble out of the house, yet broadcasted personal information in the kitchen as if it were a free-for-all?

Remembering that she needed to buy skim milk, and a greeting card for Robert's birthday, Francesca clicked on her turn signal and pulled into the parking lot at the grocery store.

As she stepped out of the car, moths flitted about the lights and she noticed a man shoving his shopping cart into the collector; he appeared to be about her age, but only as tall as her mother. Before getting into his car, he gave her an interested smile that she pretended not to see.

Franci's problem wasn't getting a man's attention, it was mustering a response. Heading into the store, she didn't think she was that hard-nosed about potential dates, but these days nobody seemed to appeal to her.

Except for—

She wasn't going to think about *him.*

With a spontaneity she normally didn't have, Francesca fished her cell phone out of her purse and hit an autodial number.

"Hello?" Her friend Lily answered on the third ring.

"Hey, it's Franci."

"Oh, hi. Can I call you back? I'm watching my favorite—"

"Set me up," Francesca declared, her heartbeat hammering in her chest. "Make sure he's tall and not stupid. I don't care if he's bald or even a little hefty. But teeth—he's got to have nice teeth. Oh, and a job. I guess that goes without saying, or maybe not. You can give him my cell number, but don't tell him what I do for a living. It intimidates some men. And, well, I guess that's all. Just do it before I change my mind."

KYLE'S CONSTRUCTION TRAILER had two sets of iron stairs leading to the entrances. It had three rooms, and thermostat heating and air so that the temperature was always comfortable. The vinyl floors and white-paneled walls were pretty standard, but the chrome-and-glass desk he worked at was not.

He sat in a black leather chair, going over reports and fielding incoming phone calls that never seemed to end.

His cell rang once more and he picked up. "This is Kyle."

The project superintendent's voice was loud over the construction noise. "Our safety fencing never showed up this morning."

Eighty rolls of orange plastic safety fencing had been scheduled for delivery to the job site, but nobody had seen it.

"Any idea what happened to it?" Kyle questioned, thumbing through invoices and trying to take care of two things at once.

"Not yet. I've been dealing with the concrete guys. One of the trucks ran over a pump line and busted it. We've got a mess."

"Okay. I'll call on the fencing."

A moment later, Kyle had the company on the phone.

"This says we made the delivery," the man insisted. "Yesterday afternoon."

Kyle drank a swallow of coffee, not caring that it had long since grown cold from when he'd poured it into his cup an hour ago. "Who signed for it?"

"Mark Moretti."

Kyle released the invoices, sat back in his chair and gave the call his full attention. "When?"

"Just like I said—yesterday afternoon."

"Mark Moretti doesn't work on my project."

"Wait a sec." The phone was set down, then picked up a few minutes later. "Sorry, it looks like we delivered one hundred and ten rolls to Moretti Construction, plus your eighty rolls. The trucking company delivered all one hundred and ninety to the Grove Marketplace. I can get your order picked up, but not until late tomorrow."

Kyle sat up and shoved his coffee cup aside. "No. I'll get it."

"You sure? It was our mistake. Maybe I can pick it up sooner. I'd have to make a couple of calls."

"I can take care of it."

As soon as Kyle disconnected the call, he made another one, this time to Mark Moretti.

"Mark—it's Kyle Jagger."

"Hey, what's up?"

"My safety fencing got delivered to your job site by mistake. I'm going to come pick it up."

The sounds of heavy equipment droned in the background as Mark spoke. "I thought that looked like a lot, but I just haven't had a chance to check it out. Come by anytime."

"I will." Kyle ran a hand through his cropped hair, then said, "Is your architect around?"

"Yeah. She's in the trailer. Why?"

Kyle didn't respond. He clicked off the phone and went to find the keys for the Legacy flatbed.

FRANCESCA WAS HAVING a hideous day. It wasn't even lunch yet and already she'd had to contend with a measurement error in the plans and she'd had to redraw her design. Her 3:00 p.m. appointment at the lighting showroom had been canceled until early next week. She'd left her window catalogs at Bella Design, her architectural office. She'd really wanted to get her dad's opinion on what type of skylights he thought would be best for the top floors. They already had one tenant secure—a bistro restaurant—but the rest of the upper floors were yet to be leased and she wanted to make sure she kept the same look throughout.

The white work desk she kept in her dad's construction trailer was marginally organized. When she passed through his doors, she deliberately left her preference for a neat and tidy workspace behind, otherwise she'd go insane.

Her desk seemed to be the catchall for junk mail, glossy catalogs with everything from lights to backhoes, sample fixtures and sample tiles. Doughnut boxes, always with one doughnut left—the plain kind, since the glazed and chocolate ones, and the French crullers, flew out of the box fast.

Today even a dried-out plain doughnut seemed appealing. Her stomach rumbled with hunger.

She was just about to take a bite and wash it down with a diet pop when the door opened and in came Kyle Jagger as if he owned the place.

He filled the doorway, tall and broad, wearing a pair of Levi's that hugged his hips. His black T-shirt was tucked in, the laces of his work boots cinched tight. A Blackberry was clipped to his belt. It rang once and he pushed a button; the phone went silent.

He didn't wear a hard hat but he was ready for business, and as she lowered the uneaten doughnut back into the box, she wondered just what kind of business he'd have with Moretti Construction.

She was suddenly nervous, but not in the way she'd be if she were waiting in the dentist's chair. This nervousness was like being pleasantly flustered when presented with something unexpected.

Franci immediately grew annoyed with herself and ignored the feeling.

Keeping the tone of her voice neutral, she asked, "Can I help you?"

"Only if you're ready to sign over the Marketplace contract to Legacy."

His gall made her jaw drop.

Kyle's mouth quirked into a half smile. "Just kidding."

Francesca didn't laugh.

He slipped his hands into his pockets, drawing her attention to his flat stomach, and the way he stood—as if he knew that every woman who'd ever looked at him was consciously aware of her femininity when in the presence of such a masculine man.

Franci swallowed, popped the tab on her diet soda and took a cool drink to wet her dry throat. But she'd need a lot more than ice-cold pop to lower her body temperature where Kyle was concerned.

"So what are you doing here—really?"

"Gem State dropped off my safety fencing with yours. Your brother signed for an extra eighty rolls that belong to Legacy."

Mistakes like this happened every once in a while. For a brief moment, she felt bad she'd kind of skewered him with her gaze.

He came toward her, leaned his hip against the edge of her desk and sat on the corner as if he belonged there.

Then again, maybe she wasn't feeling all that bad.

He was arrogant, cocky, confident, rude, overbearing, self-assured, and better looking than a pair of Gucci boots….

With a frown, Francesca shook her head. Where had that last thought come from?

She sat taller and shuffled some papers—anything but meet the gaze that was fastened on her. When she couldn't take it any longer, she addressed him. "Did you need me to call Gem State and get that fixed for you?"

Not that calling a fencing company was her job, but she wanted to get rid of him. The way he stared at her made her feel as if she were sitting here in only her underwear.

"Nope. It's already been taken care of. Mark had your guys load the rolls onto my flatbed. I'm good to go."

Then why didn't he leave?

After an agonizingly long moment of smelling his scent—a clean soap and probably an expensive salon shampoo—she blurted crisply, "Is there anything else?"

"I brought you something."

Curiosity made her ask, "What?"

He stood up slowly, went outside for a second and returned with a brick. He laid it on her desk.

Her brows knitted with confusion. "A sample? We've already pretty much narrowed our choices down to two."

"No. Read it."

She did. The brick had BOISE printed on it in stamped letters and now that she took a closer look, she realized it wasn't newly fabricated. It was quite old.

"They excavated a bunch of these from our job site. They're from the trolley tracks."

The old Boise trolley lines had been buried under asphalt years ago, when automobiles became the norm. The brick had to be a hundred years old.

How did he know she liked to collect historic architectural pieces from around Boise? She marveled at the turn-of-the-century construction. Most people who met her expected her home to be decorated in a sleek and modern style. On the contrary, she was an antique junkie. She liked to surround herself with things from the past. Her foyer had a prism-glass chandelier taken out of a soiled-dove house that had operated off Broadway back in the 1880s.

She gave Kyle a heartfelt smile, feeling as if she'd just let him see a piece of her she really wasn't ready to reveal. But she couldn't help it. "Thanks. This is really great."

"I thought you'd like it."

"I do. Thank you," she repeated.

"Consider it a peace offering."

"For what?"

"Pomodoro. I could tell I was pissing you off."

Franci's eyes narrowed, the warm fuzzy feeling dissipating as if a coastal fog had just blanketed her. She definitely didn't want him reading her so closely—and being right. "No, you didn't. I was perfectly fine with our conversation."

"I didn't think so."

"Well, you thought wrong."

Kyle laughed, the inflection in his tone as clear as an August sky. He didn't believe her. She pressed her lips together and picked up her pen. "I have to get back to work now. Thanks for the brick. I like it, and that was nice of you to think of me."

Did he think of me the way I've been thinking about him?

"No problem." He was still smiling that knowing smile when he left the trailer. As soon as the door closed, Franci winced.

She grabbed the stale doughnut, took a bite and told herself there was nothing to get worked up about. Kyle Jagger was just a guy who'd happened to stop by the office. Lots of guys came in here all day long.

But as she chewed, she conceded that none of them smelled as good as Kyle. Nor looked half as great.

GIOVANNI MORETTI DIDN'T throw his weight around in Boise, but he had construction connections and received favors without even breaking a sweat. Those fortunate enough to know him couldn't agree more that his heart was pure gold. He could come across as blunt if there was a deadline looming and things had gotten messed up and there were delays. But even when he was being blunt, he always spoke with laughter and good humor, making lemons out of lemonade.

Father Mike Kowalsky knew firsthand, and many times over, just how generous Giovanni could be. And not only in the offering plate. It mattered not that Father Mike was Polish and Giovanni was Italian. They both spoke the language of charity and sacrifice.

As Catholics, they had their values firmly committed to a higher being.

Seated across from the priest, who ran on adrenaline and faith, Giovanni propped his fingertips together over his ample stomach. "I'll get a crew on it," he said.

"Are you sure you can spare them?" the priest asked.

Giovanni didn't feel a twinge of pressure; he waved off Father Mike's concern. "I can pull the painters off my Curtis Road job. I think they're almost done, anyway. They'll put some guys on it at the end of the week, and I'll make sure they're paid extra."

"That's generous of you."

To Giovanni, it wasn't being generous. It was being Christian. God had blessed him with many things, and this was his way of giving back. Few knew just how much Giovanni Moretti did for the Boise community, and that was how he liked it. He wasn't comfortable with accolades or notoriety. If he found out someone was in need, he took care of it, quietly.

This latest benefactor was the Catholic church he attended, and the new gymnasium he'd donated money for, to help it get off the ground. His kids had attended this school and he wanted to keep it going for generations to come. The newly constructed gym needed to be painted, inside and out, and Giovanni was on it with his construction company. Lending a helping hand made him feel good.

"The church appreciates all you do, Giovanni," Father Kowalsky declared.

The church office was pristine and simple. It smelled like leather-bound books, beeswax and the faint smell of assembly-line lunch wafting in from the school cafeteria.

Giovanni rose to his feet. The priest extended his hand and he shook it.

Before Giovanni left the church, he tucked several large bills into the collection box.

As he stepped outside, his cell phone rang. It was Mark.

"Dad, where are you? We have a meeting in ten minutes."

Fumbling with his sunglasses, Giovanni replied, "I've been talking to Father Kowalsky."

"Confession?" But Mark's tone was laced with humor, as if he knew full well why his dad had been at the church.

"Yes. An hour's worth and one crew of painters."

Mark laughed, then clicked off the phone.

Giovanni smiled as he got into his truck and turned the diesel engine over. He was feeling really great. The air was fresh, the sky blue and the white clouds were high. He knew Mariangela was making a big dish of pork chops *alla pizzaiola,* and after dinner, he'd sit on the patio with his beautiful wife, hold her hand and drink a glass of the imported wine he'd bought today.

As Andrea Bocelli's voice floated through the truck's speakers, Giovanni thought life couldn't get better than this.

CHAPTER FOUR

"REMEMBER THAT SHOW *Felicity?*" Jordan asked, after taking a sip of her lemon-drop martini, then licking the sugar from her lips. "I just read that Keri Russell is thirty-one. If she's gotten that old, then we're ancient."

"Thirty-four is not ancient." Francesca sat on a tall bar stool, rock-and-roll music echoing around her. It wasn't their regular weekly get together at Pomodoro. An emergency girls' night had been set up at the restaurant-distillery called Bardenay—all because of Franci's call to Lily yesterday.

As she uttered the statement about her age, Francesca staved off a wince. In truth, thirty-four was pushing things for any woman hoping to marry and start a family. She'd thought about the time lines. If she met the man of her dreams today, dated him for a year or two, then got married and became pregnant right away, she'd be in her late thirties when she had a baby. Doing the math, she'd be almost sixty when her son or daughter was twenty. She hated to accept it, but that would be ancient....

Francesca swirled a warm triangle of pita bread into

an olive dip. They'd ordered a Mediterranean appetizer along with four martinis—two lemon, one sour apple and one ginger.

Not even the relaxing affects of a lemon-drop martini could change the facts. Francesca wasn't getting any younger.

Lily leaned closer. "We *are* getting older. Let's face it, women in their midthirties are competing with women in their twenties, and we aren't coming out on top."

"Who said?" Erin asked. She was the shiest of the group, a slip of a woman with soft red hair and a pale complexion.

Defending herself, Lily replied, "I read it somewhere."

Fighting off a giggle, Jordan said, "The *Enquirer?*"

"I forget where." Lily was about five feet eight inches tall and built very generously in the chest—God's gift and no silicone enhancement. She rarely had trouble finding a date for Friday night, but men were mostly interested in talking to her chest and not getting to know the real her.

Francesca had had twenty-four hours to calm down about the whole setup thing, and now wished she hadn't called Lily during a weak moment.

Today she was doing much better. She'd been far too busy to spare a thought for any man, not even the good-looking guy who'd come into the trailer to ask her father a question. Francesca had barely given him a glance before taking off for her own office to finish up a project she had to present tomorrow at 8:00 a.m.

She'd told herself she had a one-martini limit tonight. She had to be fresh in the morning to meet with her clients. But already Jordan was ordering another round, and as the second hot appetizer of the evening was being delivered to their table, Francesca knew that Lily was gearing up to deliver her thoughts on dating.

"So, we all know why we're here," Lily said. Her ebony hair was swept into a neat ponytail and her white blouse looked as fresh as when she'd buttoned it that morning. "Franci wants me to set her up, but three heads are better than one, so I needed input from all of you."

"We really don't need any input," Francesca prompted, the pita bread suddenly feeling like a lump in her stomach. At this point in her life, it was almost useless to hold out hope of having the whole package—a husband and kids. She was almost past her prime, and she hadn't met the right man. "I've changed my mind. I don't need to go out with anyone."

"No way," Lily retorted. "You've never called before to ask me to fix you up, and I'm not letting you off the hook. We're all in this together."

"Then you go out with someone," Francesca said, drinking the last of her martini and suddenly glad another was on its way.

All three of her friends practically groaned at the same time.

"What do you think we do every Friday and Saturday night?" Erin asked.

Lily added her two cents' worth. "We don't just sit at home in our bunny slippers like someone else we know."

"I don't have bunny slippers," Francesca countered. "They're those pink ones from Victoria's Secret."

"Probably the only thing you have from that store." Jordan gave a light laugh, her golden-blond hair shimmering.

Francesca scowled. Too bad they were right. She shopped for her underwear at the Gap—the comfortable cotton stuff that fitted her like a glove. Nobody had seen her stripped down to a bra and pair of panties in...like, forever.

"Well, we do go out," Erin said simply.

Studying her friends, Franci spoke with all seriousness. "If you're going out all the time, how come nobody has a steady boyfriend?"

"Because men our age can be jerks," Jordan stated.

Erin quietly added, "Or gay."

"Oh, come on. Boise's filled with men. I see men every day in my job and they come in all shapes and sizes and...well, they're just all over the place." Francesca neglected to add that she didn't find ninety-percent of them worth their weight in tools. It wasn't that she was snobbish about carpenters, she just didn't find many of the tradesmen who frequented the trailer all that appealing.

If she had to think about necessary attributes in a man, which happened on occasion, Francesca did have a type that she preferred.

He had to be clean-shaven. A must. There was just something so nice about kissing a man without facial hair. He had to be smart, or at least educated enough to know the basics, while having a sense of humor. Contrary to what men assumed women wanted, they did like a man who could make them smile and laugh.

Men who wore jeans were fine with Francesca. In fact, she preferred jeans over a suit. If he could cook—big points. Francesca was comfortable in the kitchen, but didn't cook a lot. She ate out at Pomodoro, or at home with her mom and dad, more than she cared to admit.

"So if you see so many men, why aren't you dating? And if you don't want to date any of them, why haven't you thrown some our way?" Lily said matter-of-factly, after taking a drink of her ginger martini.

"Nobody asked me."

That was true and they knew it. Nobody came to Francesca Moretti and asked her for dating advice or help.

"Because we have our own methods," Jordan clarified.

"How come they aren't working?" Francesca asked.

"Who's to say they aren't?" Jordan popped a shrimp into her mouth. "I have a date this Friday with a very interesting man who looks like George Clooney in his photo."

Erin spoke up, clearly in awe. "She's Internet dating. I'd never have the guts."

Francesca glanced from one to the other. "I heard that can be dangerous. Guys post pictures that aren't even them, or photos that are ten years old."

"Dean assured me his photo is current, and I talked to him last night for three hours on the phone. He sounded great. We clicked and I can't wait to meet him." An excited glimmer filled Jordan's eyes. For a marketing analyst, she clearly had been mulling over the marketability of this Dean guy, and was sold—sight unseen.

"Good luck," Lily said skeptically. "I tried the online thing and it was a disaster. Maybe I just wasn't doing it right. I believe in the referral method. Only date a man that you've had checked out by a friend, or a friend's friend, or a friend of a relative or co-worker, and they've seen him in the flesh. That way you know what you're getting." Turning her attention toward Francesca, she said, "With that in mind, I do have someone who I think would be perfect for you."

"Not that Carl Murphy. I told you—not interested."

"No, not him. This is someone else. He's really great."

A combination of curiosity and dread mixed in with the sweet, lemony swallow of martini sliding down Francesca's throat. She dared to ask, "Who is he?"

"Rick James."

"Isn't he a singer?" Erin asked, biting a shrimp off one of the bamboo skewers.

"Yes. But, Franci, don't bring that up to Rick. He's sensitive about the comparison. Rick's more classical than soul. He likes to go to the Morrison Center."

Erin's expression grew thoughtful, as if contemplating the sum of debits and credits a man like Rick James could possibly have. "A sensitive man. He could be a keeper. I've always wanted a guy to be comfortable going to a chick flick with me."

"What's he do?" Jordan examined her fingernails. She wore acrylic ones that were always perfectly French-manicured.

"Same as me. Mortgage broker. He's got an office in Eagle and he does very well."

"How come *you* aren't dating him?" Francesca asked.

Logically, if he was so great, why hadn't anyone snapped him up? There had to be hidden things in his closet, for sure. Franci had run across this before. A guy looked great on the surface, but as soon as you kicked a tire or opened the window of his past—baggage. Red flags the entire length of a football field.

"He's not my type," Lily replied easily. "I like a man who's into outdoor activities. Rick is more the indoors kind."

"A couch potato?" Erin suggested.

"Not exactly…he's into reading. He's in a book club that meets at Barnes and & Noble once a month. And he's also in a wine club and he goes to all those cooking classes at Kandor."

Nothing Lily was saying made Francesca balk and dismiss the man sight unseen. Lily was a weekend warrior. She let out her pent-up energy on her mountain bike and in-line skates in the summer, and in the winter, on snowboarding and snowshoeing. That Rick wasn't into all of that didn't bother Francesca. She did like the fact that it appeared he was secure enough in his masculinity to take cooking classes. Nobody would ever find her snickering at a man who liked to cook. After all, her brother was a chef and earned a good living doing what he loved.

What did give Francesca pause was the book club aspect. She never picked up a book. No time…or perhaps no inclination. She didn't watch a lot of television, she just preferred to listen to music in the evenings and draw.

She caught herself asking, "What does he look like?"

"He's blond with brown eyes, on the tall side—I'm thinking like six feet. He doesn't have a killer body, but don't let that stop you. He's not fat, just a little thick around the middle. I think he has a great sense of humor and he seems to be happy with himself, and his business is really doing well." Lily folded her arms beneath her breasts. "I think you should give him a try."

"It sounds like you want her to take a test drive on him," Erin said, her brows lifting.

Jordan replied bluntly, "Some women wouldn't complain about doing that no matter what the man looked like. Some women are trying to ruin it for those of us who don't sleep around."

"Has he gone through a divorce?" Of the three women who comprised the date squad, Erin was the only one who'd been married and divorced, and it was usually the first question she asked about a prospective date.

"Yes."

"Good," she said. "I know I always say this, but it's not a bad thing that a man in his late thirties has been married before. It's almost better that he has. This way you know he's not commitment phobic."

"Hey, just because none of us have been married doesn't mean we're commitment phobic," Jordan said after taking a drink. "I don't mean to sound awful, but Erin, your marriage didn't last and I don't think that has any bearing on you being more datable than me, even though I've never been married."

"Women are different than men." Erin stood her ground. "When a man is that old and has escaped the marriage noose, it means he's a momma's boy."

Francesca felt the niggling start of a headache rise up the nape of her neck and settle at the base of her skull.

Divorced.

Momma's boys.

Deans who looked like George Clooney.

What happened to the days when a man looked at a woman and swept her off her feet, just like her father had done with her mother? Francesca envied her parents' romance, had wanted the same for herself, but the longer she was single, the more she was resigned to never having that happen for her.

It was okay—truly. Or so she told herself. She led a busy and productive life. She didn't lack for anything, she was just lonely sometimes. For the most part, she was happy with things just as they were.

Except for days like yesterday, when it seemed so quiet in her house. She could hear the faint ticking of the wall clock in the living room as she sat on the sofa and drank a cup of tea, her sketchbook in her lap. As she'd walked down the hallway to her bedroom, she'd been painfully aware she lived alone.

Gazing at her nearly empty martini glass now, she admitted a painful truth to herself. With all that kept her occupied in her life, she was missing the one thing she wanted the most: a family life like she'd had growing up a Moretti. To have the culture and closeness of her parents and siblings. To be in a home that smelled good from Mom's cooking, and from the fresh sawdust in Dad's garage as he built a cabinet for the living room stereo. To have the happy barking of a dog, such as Mugs, the family pet joining in on every excited occasion.

The way Francesca lived, she might as well be cloistered like a nun.

With that thought, she smiled—a crooked smile, she knew. It wouldn't kill her to meet this Rick James for coffee. The worst that could happen was she wouldn't find him attractive or interesting.

"Okay." The word that left her lips sounded as if it was being spoken by someone else.

Three sets of eyes leveled on her.

"What?" Lily asked.

"I said okay. I'll go out with Rick. Give him my number and tell him I look forward to hearing from him."

Erin, normally on the reserved side, broke into a broad grin. "Well, I guess there's hope for all of us if she's going to go through with it."

Franci was about to say something to the contrary,

but she bit her lip. With a curve lifting the corners of her mouth, she murmured, "Yes, maybe there is."

KYLE WAS RUNNING LATE and the meeting started in two minutes. He gave his watch another quick glance, as if that would buy him some much-needed time. If he hadn't gotten caught up in a phone call with the building inspector, he would have left his trailer fifteen minutes ago.

Downtown parking was a pain during business hours, and he went around the block several times before finding a spot. Gathering his briefcase, he slipped some coins into the meter, then took off running.

When he entered the meeting hall, he stood in the back after closing the double, metal-hinged doors softly behind him. A woman at the podium was discussing historic preservation and what Boise needed in order for the city to be revitalized.

Since the seventeen-story building he was constructing was located in the historic preservation zone, there were certain rules and guidelines he had to follow. This meeting was mandatory for his company.

Glancing at the backs of the heads of those in attendance, he tried to see if he recognized anyone. The ceiling lights weren't the greatest and he couldn't spot anyone he knew.

His mind wandered as the use of fascia was brought to the table. He had a million things to do, and not enough time to get to most of it. His life was all chaos and disorganized paperwork. If he was smart, he'd hire a secretary who could filter out the clutter on his desk in the trailer.

When the speakers changed, Kyle took the opportunity to sit down, folding his arms over his chest and inhaling deeply. He fought off the urge to get a set of revamped specs from his briefcase to review the changes and make sure they had been redone correctly.

But he resisted. He was here for a purpose and that was to make sure he followed the city's architectural guidelines, even though he really didn't see the point, since his plans had already been approved.

An hour later, the meeting broke up, and Kyle was on his feet and heading toward the exit when he spied a familiar figure ahead of him.

His eyes lowered to the nipped-in waist of the woman's suit jacket and the snug fit of a skirt that fell just above the backs of her knees. She walked with grace and assuredness, a fluid stride that had his attention before he even figured out who she was.

Francesca Moretti.

Her very name conjured up images of a sultry beach on the coast of Italy. Wine and cheese. Silver moonlight shining on her hair.

Those inky-black locks were twisted up at the back of her head and anchored by a hair claw. She clutched the handles of a briefcase as if it were a designer handbag—very confidently. It was clear she had listened to every word of the meeting and was determined to incorporate the information in her project. He hadn't felt the same dedication. His thoughts had drifted in ten different directions, from the status of the latest steel order to picking up his dry cleaning before the store closed. And now they converged on one target: Francesca.

With several long steps, he was by her side.

"Hey," he said in greeting.

Her chin lifted and she looked at him. "Oh, hi."

If she was surprised to see him, she didn't show it. He would have welcomed any sign of interest, but she had a way of masking what she was thinking that sort of bothered him. Most women, when they met him, laid their cards on the table, and he had no problem reading their train of thoughts—usually an open invitation to him asking them out. Sometimes he did. Most times he didn't. With Franci, he had no clue about what she thought of him.

Maybe it was time to change that.

"Long meeting," he said, opening the door for her and accompanying her down the hallway.

"It was," she agreed. "I had to come for my dad. He couldn't make it. I don't like attending these things, but the building department has gotten so stringent."

They were talking about nothing, when he really wanted to ask if she knew just how good looking she was in that expensive business suit. The lines of the jacket hugged her body perfectly and the collar rested low against her throat, with just a slice of pink blouse showing. She looked good in the charcoal-gray outfit. Her heels had to be four inches high, and they accented the shape of her calves. He noticed she wasn't wearing nylons today, either. She seemed not to favor them. He liked that, thought it was sexy she went with bare legs.

She checked her watch. "The rest of the day's shot," she said, more to herself than him.

He knew the feeling. It was too late to go back to the trailer and be productive, but too early to wrap things up and head home.

Outside, the day was bright and warm. As they headed down the concrete steps to the sidewalk, Kyle noticed a vendor on the corner hawking hot dogs from an umbrella-covered cart. The savory smell wafted in the air and made Kyle's stomach growl. He noticed Francesca inhaling slightly, as well, then licking her lips.

"You want one?" he asked.

She was poised to decline; he could see it almost immediately in her brown eyes.

Putting a hand on her shoulder, he said, "Have one. And then let me show you around my job site. In fact, I want your opinion on something."

"My opinion?"

"Architecturally speaking."

He hadn't planned on saying that, but he hoped she'd take the lure. It wasn't every day you invited a competitor to check out your project and view your drawings. But while she was looking around, he'd be looking at her and admiring her curves and angles, which were better than any curves and angles being erected in steel.

After a long pause, she said, "Sure. Okay." After

she'd placed her order for a dog with mustard and relish, she added, "But just so you know, I'll give you my honest opinion."

"I wouldn't expect anything less."

That said, he racked his brain to come up with a potential flaw in a set of plans that were already perfection.

CHAPTER FIVE

FRANCESCA LIKED TO THINK of herself as a smart, intuitive woman. Pulling the wool over her eyes was next to impossible. Some would say she was a chronic skeptic, doubtful and distrusting until she had all the facts. She considered having reservations about things too good to be true to be a wise thing.

She was drumming her fingers on her waist, her arms crossed, almost as soon as she entered Kyle Jagger's construction trailer.

Within a matter of minutes, she knew she'd been set up.

"Where're the plans you wanted me to look at?" she asked. She'd already given the desk a sweeping glance and there weren't any plans to be seen. Odd, since trailers were usually full of them.

What she had noticed during the short ride over in his pickup truck was that he had numerous plans rolled up with rubber bands resting sideways on the cab's floor. He'd even apologized about the mess and moved them out of her way.

"Let me show you around the job site first," he

replied easily, as if he hadn't detected the lift of her brows and her dubious posture.

Francesca wasn't sure what to do. She'd left her car behind in her office parking garage, as the meeting was nearby. Kyle's building site was not within walking distance to her office, and the only way back was in his truck.

She grew upset with herself for being tempted by his appeal and the pleasant idea of being in his company. So tempted that she'd bypassed her level head in favor of a hot dog and his disarming smile.

After all, the afternoon was still young. She could have gone home and put in a load of laundry.

One look at Kyle and she knew she had to be delusional if she'd rather wash her clothes than spend time with this man.

Kyle's dark brown hair had been recently cut and just reached the top of his ears. He wore a pair of jeans and work boots, and an open-collar polo that had the company logo embroidered on the front pocket. The shirt's bleached whiteness gave his skin tone a polished golden hue that looked natural and healthy. She'd gotten her first really good look at his eyes while standing outside the meeting place, on the street. They were a deep green-gray. Her study of them was short-lived because he'd slipped on a pair of aviator-style sunglasses.

"Come on," he coaxed now, his smile the perfect lure.

If Kyle was any more handsome, he'd have to be illegal. Why was it he could attract her attention more than any man she'd met in, like, forever?

He wasn't all that likable. Okay—maybe that thought was wishful thinking on her part. He *was* personable, and she admired how he carried himself.

Francesca reminded herself that she had to hold on to reservations about him because, after all, he'd tried to outbid them on the Grove Marketplace so his company could land the project. She wasn't up to flirting, much less dating, a competitor. Things would be too complicated. She'd have to watch everything she said, making sure to keep business confidences within the family.

But she was here now, and admitted she felt curious about what he was working on. She'd done a little snooping, and the seventeen-story project he was getting off the ground was state of the art, while being true to historical preservation, plus energy efficient.

There couldn't be any harm in seeing what made a Legacy project so great.

"All right," she replied.

Kyle's strong hand touched her shoulder, the contact instantly heating the skin beneath her jacket and starting a fluttery feeling in her stomach.

His eyes held hers as he asked, "Can you get around okay in those shoes?"

After years of visiting her dad's job sites in business attire, Franci was used to walking on planks or picking her way across rough ground while wearing a pair of sleek pumps.

It took her a moment to find her voice. "Of course."

"Just making sure." He lowered his arm and grabbed

a set of keys. She fought against missing the intimacy of his touch. "I wouldn't want you to sue me if you broke your leg or something."

"I could run up a flight of stairs in these." She glanced at her shoes, noticing Kyle was looking at her legs. She smiled and added, "And I have." Taking a step toward the door, she asked, "Where are the hard hats?"

"Honey, we don't need any." With a crooked grin, he opened the door for her. "Everyone's gone home for the day."

Franci wasn't sure which unsettled her more—the fact that he casually used an endearment and she couldn't remember the last time a man had done so, or the idea that only she and Kyle would be at the monstrous construction area.

Before leaving the trailer, Kyle grabbed a beat-up thermos and two foam cups. He led her through the building, which was still open to the elements. Materials were stacked on various floors, and a variety of debris littered the trail as she followed Kyle.

"Watch that," he'd caution, leading her in a different direction so she wouldn't run into a pallet of supplies. "On your left," he'd say while passing scaffolding.

She was an old pro at dodging the obvious, but it warmed her heart nonetheless that he looked out for her well-being.

The concrete for the Legacy project had been poured and the shell and core completed. The building was an ambitious undertaking, complex in certain ways, yet simple in others. Even with just the basics in place, she noticed the quality construction and was able to envision how interior walls would be fleshed out.

"Who was your architect?" The question was more from personal interest than probing the competition; she'd neglected to dig up the information on her own. She didn't recognize any signature features that several of her architect friends in Boise used, but the project was still in early stages.

"Pete Ivy. He's out of Seattle."

"Nice lines. I like the height and how he built out the walls on the corners."

"He's a great guy. He's got a boat and often takes a group of us out to the San Juans to do some fishing. Too bad I don't like to eat fish."

Francesca laughed, a good-natured sound that echoed off the concrete floor. She hadn't been prepared for Kyle to admit something like that, and she thought it both cute and sweet. His statement immediately softened her toward him. Then she shook her head, attempting to clear the romantic fog that seemed to be clouding her reasoning.

The only response she could think to say was, "You haven't tried my brother's *tonno alla griglia.* You'd love it."

Kyle gave her a grin over his broad shoulder. "I can't even say it. How could I love it?"

Francesca stepped over a box of metal fittings, her high heels clicking on the hard floor. With slow enunciation, she repeated what she'd said, then translated, "It's tuna steaks with basil."

"This guy eats no tuna, not even from a can."

"What did your mother make for you in your grade school sack lunch?" she asked, more than mildly amused by their conversation and the ease with which they'd fallen into it.

"Raisin bread and American cheese with margarine spread."

Francesca grimaced. "Yuck."

"Ever tried one?"

"No."

"They're good. I'll make you one sometime."

The comment sobered her. There was no point in even taking the thought further. She wouldn't entertain the idea of eating a cheese sandwich with him, so why did her heart slam against her ribs in response?

Dusk was casting the building core in shadows and making it a bit more tricky to navigate. Kyle took her to the strong-steel, yellow grids of the seventeen-story crane's erected base. Though the elevator shaft was exposed to the elements, the platform inside would be stable, Franci knew. The whole idea of a temporary elevator could set her pulse racing, however. She blocked out images of those cheap carnival rides at the Idaho State Fair, the squeaky nuts and bolts holding them together. Francesca had a marginal fear of heights, nothing terribly paralyzing if she didn't overanalyze being high up in an elevator that could be disassembled and driven away on a flatbed semi.

She stopped short of the elevator gate as Kyle opened it. "What are you doing?" she asked, her knees locking.

"I'm showing you the site."

"I thought that's what we've *been* doing."

"You can't get a good feel for it down here. Come on."

Kyle extended his hand to her, but she held on tight to the strap of her purse, which was snug against her shoulder.

When she didn't move, he set the thermos and cups on the elevator floor, then took her by the shoulders and maneuvered her inside.

"I've got you," he assured her, his hands staying on her shoulders while he stood behind her.

Francesca had no time to consider the growl and rumble of the equipment as the platform lurched upward. All she could think about was how warm and reassuring Kyle's hands were, and how she hoped it would take forever to get to the top.

THE VIEW FROM THE TOP of the world in Boise was nothing like the view from Kyle's downtown Seattle condo. There he could see the harbor and ferries, the yachts and cargo ships, and the glittering rays of the afternoon sun. Here, if he glanced around in a full circle, he saw mostly trees. No wonder Boise was nicknamed the City of Trees. In the summertime, he had to admit it was a stellar setting with so many thick green leaves, and the way the skyscraper windows mirrored vibrant colors from planters.

To the south was the distinctive blue Boise State University football field. If you lived here, you most likely were a Bronco fan—especially after their big win in the Fiesta Bowl. To the north of the stadium was a sweep of trees that lined the banks of the Boise River. Farther to the west, the city fanned out and melded into suburbia. Going north was Bogus Basin, a ski resort and campground that made for year-round use. In the distance, the foothills were dotted with expensive houses, but the landmark Tablerock Cross was still prominent.

Nightfall was casting its veil over the city, a twilight blanket of silvery-blue, with a fan of orange on the horizon. The wind blew softly, and even up here it smelled like freshly cut grass. Above them, the American flag whispered from its tie-down atop the crane, a crisp sound of fabric moving in the breeze, with the occasional clink of metal.

Kyle had built a lot of buildings, and this seventeen story was no more special than any of the rest. But the steel frames and the structure that surrounded them felt different right now because this was the first time he'd ever brought a woman this high to see things as he saw them.

Oftentimes, he came up to the top of a site to wind down after a long day of phone calls, meetings and endless talks with his foremen and the subcontractors. He'd stand on the crane platform and look at the city below, watch how traffic moved and how the people ebbed and flowed on the sidewalks. Lights would illuminate the storefronts, car headlights would come on, and the scent of the air would change. Restaurant stacks billowed smoke from charbroiling steaks, and cooking aromas wafted from vents.

Francesca's shoulders began to relax under his touch, but he was reluctant to let go.

Her resemblance to her father was uncanny, but she was nothing like him. Kyle liked how she could laugh at something he said, how she let him take the lead and be gallant without giving up her identity as a businesswoman.

It wasn't as if Francesca carried herself differently. Kyle knew from their brief meetings that she had passion, a strong work ethic and a love for what she did. But something about her marked her as an overachiever.

Many of the women he knew today were beyond independent in their quest to have it all. He hoped that, deep down, Francesca had an old-fashioned side to her.

His ex-wife had eventually put her work first and him second. Not that he blamed her. He'd been so tied up in rebuilding his company that he'd neglected to be the man of the house. Kyle had to own part of the responsibility for Hailey having had an affair. He hadn't been there for her emotionally. Still, that was no excuse to be unfaithful.

It had torn him up inside when he'd found out about her affair. He hadn't accepted that she'd actually do such a thing to them, so he'd turned a blind eye. Until one night she'd come home hammered from an evening out with the girls, and she'd spilled her guts, then asked for a divorce. She lasted about six months with the guy, they broke up, then she'd come back to Kyle and wanted another chance. He'd said no.

He didn't look to his past to create his future. In that six months, he'd reconciled a great many things. He'd confronted a few of his inadequacies, some of the traits he hadn't liked that he'd inherited from his father, and a couple of bad habits that he had to own had probably caused Hailey to start seeking the attention of other men.

In any case, it was done and over. He'd moved on. In the eight years since, he hadn't wanted to get seriously involved with anyone. He'd dated, but nothing lasting. One woman had been really great, but she had a one-year-old son and was in a bitter battle with her ex-husband about visitation and child support. Kyle hadn't wanted to get involved with that. So he'd let that relationship fizzle before it had a chance to heat up.

Kyle followed Francesca's line of vision now and smiled. "How does it look from up here?"

"Wonderful. Amazing." Her awed declaration was clearing in response to seeing the Grove Marketplace. The complex looked entirely different from this angle. The girders for the new part were in place and the skeleton looked strong and steady, the rust-colored iron almost glowing in the last remnants of the sunset.

"Yeah, I thought so. But don't ever tell your dad I said that."

She laughed softly. "No, I think I'm going to tell him."

Kyle smiled. Her skin was warm through the fabric of her suit jacket. Strands of her hair had worked free from the upswept do as the light breeze caressed them, and cradled her neck and shoulders. He was tempted to touch them, to splay his fingers through them, then trace the outline of her collarbone.

A jolt of something indefinable affected his pulse, making it pick up as if he'd been running a marathon. He didn't care to examine why or wonder further about his reaction toward this woman.

There would be complexities. If she knew how deep the ties were between him and her father, she'd probably throw him off the crane. And he didn't feel like landing with a splat on the concrete seventeen stories below, so he let go of the heat that seemed to be pooling low in his body.

He dropped his arms, reached for his thermos and poured two cups of hot coffee. The thermos was ancient and kept anything inside as warm as a furnace pretty much all day long.

"Here." He offered her a cup and she took it.

"Thanks." After a sip, she said, "So, do you do this a lot?"

"You're the first," he replied.

A blush worked its way up her neck. "I mean do you come up here a lot?"

He'd known what she meant, but wanted her to know she was special. "I try to every day. Don't you ever ride to the top of your crane?"

"Not often. I kind of have this height thing." After she

made her confession, she gazed straight ahead, as if not wanting to meet his gaze.

"Yeah, you're tall," he teased. "What are you—six feet in those shoes?"

Glancing at the black pumps, with their sexy cut and tease of toe cleavage, she remarked, "Probably more like six foot two in these."

"They're nice," he commented, referring to her legs and not the shoes. She had limbs that didn't quit and calves that were sexy and shapely.

She grew conscious of where his eyes had fallen as she took another drink of coffee. Asking him a question, she tried to take his mind off her legs. "So, where do you spend the majority of your time?"

"Seattle. I have a downtown condo off of First Street."

"I'm sure the view there is spectacular."

"It is."

He enjoyed the smell of her as the wind brought him a hint of her perfume. "So how close are you and your brother?" Kyle asked.

"Which one?"

"Mark."

She inched her chin higher. "Why? Is there something I'm not supposed to tell him, too?"

Kyle shrugged. "Not at all. I was just asking. He and I are going to play some golf."

"You are?" She practically blurted the words.

"Yeah. Is that okay?" He smiled as he asked.

"I don't keep tabs on him. Do whatever you want."

"If I buy him a beer after we hit eighteen holes, do you think he'll tell me anything I want to know about you?" Kyle enjoyed the way she scowled at him, then smoothed out her expression as if she wasn't worried.

"Ask him anything you like, but you might as well ask *me,* so you get the information right. I have nothing to hide."

Kyle studied her a long moment, thinking she was going out on a limb here and he wanted to use it to his advantage. "Have you ever been married?"

"No."

"Ever want to?"

"Yes." Her monotone responses were clipped, as if she didn't want to embellish a single syllable, so he couldn't make something out of her reply.

"Ever come close?"

"Yes."

"Who was he?"

"A man I met in college."

"What went wrong?"

"We went to premarital counseling and realized we had different values."

"And they were?"

"Sorry. Too personal."

"Understood." Kyle had his own past demons, and only people he deemed trustworthy knew the facts.

He drank his coffee, looked out at the twinkling city lights, then inhaled deeply. "What do you do for fun?"

She smiled briefly. "You're sounding like a first date now."

He rested his foot on the lower railing, trying to keep his heart from beating faster. The way she said it had his mind running in the opposite direction he'd intended. "Honey, I haven't been on a date in a while."

"Why not?"

"Nobody out there will put up with me for the long haul."

Her lips quirked sardonically. "Oh, I find that hard to believe. Lots of women would forgive workaholic tendencies in exchange for your smile."

After she'd spoken the compliment, she blushed—something he found endearing.

"I really don't have an analytical personality."

"But you do have a smile to die..." She let the sentence drop and he could almost hear the thud of it seventeen stories below. So she was more than a little attracted to him. That made him glad.

"So do you," he said softly.

He watched her blink her long lashes and cast her eyes downward, then glance once more at the view. He suspected she might not have gone out much with the opposite sex. Call it a hunch. Why, however, he couldn't understand, since she was gorgeous and smart.

"What do you do for fun?" he repeated. "And give me the real answer. Not the first-date answer that's supposed to impress me and make me think you're all put together—happy and single."

"Actually, I was going to give you an honest answer." She bit her lush lower lip, letting it rest beneath her teeth for a long second that had his body heat ratcheting up like a firestorm. "I like to draw. I've never watched an episode of the reality shows that everyone talks about. In fact, I hardly ever turn my television on. I like to ride my bike to Hyde Park and have an ice cream, or a glass of wine at Harry's. I'm a people watcher. Sometimes I'd rather watch the world go by than join in the rush. It seems ridiculous to try and keep up with everyone. Nobody knows where they're going, anyway. At least it seems that way."

She finished her coffee and he took her cup from her, setting both their empties down. "I like to go out with my girlfriends and hear about their lives and what they're doing," Franci added. "We laugh a lot, we sometimes cry. I like to go to my parents' house for Sunday dinner and listen to everyone interact. We're all very different, yet we love each other so. I wish I could have that in my own life…if I was involved with someone…."

The thought trailed off, and he sensed she'd forgotten where she was and had almost said too much. But he appreciated her candor more than he could say. It was nice to hear a woman talk from the heart rather than from a point of view she assumed a man wanted to hear.

"So that's about all," she said, then let out a sigh. "How about you?"

Kyle scratched the back of his neck. "Golf tops my list. A close second is flying. I have a good friend in

Seattle and he's been a great sounding board. Even us guys have to talk about stuff that's personal sometimes. You know—like what kind of jeans make our butts look better."

She laughed, a reaction he was going for. He liked the sound of her voice.

He mused, "I like ice cream late at night, around two o'clock if I can't sleep. I don't sleep a lot."

"Me, either."

"Stress maybe."

"Maybe." She bit her lip again, her expression contemplative, before asking, "So what about dating?"

"You? That's a possibility." He liked the pleasant flush that worked its way up her neck.

"I didn't mean *me*. I was just wondering if you'd had any bad experiences…or anything." Her backpedaling was kind of cute.

The warmth inside gave him a pleasant feeling that he wanted to revisit over a real dinner with a city view, so he said, "I'll tell you some other time. I gotta get going."

"Oh," she exclaimed, as if she wasn't ready to leave. She did a quick study of the horizon, took a last look at the mountains and the cross that was lit to cast its heavenly glow upon the city. "I have things I need to do, too."

Kyle pushed the button and the elevator gave a lurch. He steadied Francesca's shoulders and a short minute later they were back on the ground.

He hadn't thought about the fact that the structure wouldn't be lit at night, and as they walked back to the trailer, he extended his hand. “Hold on. Look down and watch where you’re stepping.”

Her fingers were warm and slender. He held on to them with a firm grasp, and for a moment, wanted to rub his thumb across her knuckles. But he didn’t. He needed a chance to reconnect the dots in his brain. He wasn’t so sure why he reacted toward her this way, he just did. And maybe he was a bit more analytical than he let on.

“I’ll drive you back to your car,” he said, and she nodded.

Just as they reached his truck, her cell phone rang. Franci gave a quick glance at the number, then picked up with some hesitation.

“Hello?” The tone of her voice was uncertain, as if she hadn’t recognized the caller ID. Whoever replied brought a look of acknowledgment on her face—and surprise. “Hi. Um, can I call you back in fifteen minutes? I’m not at home.”

After a few seconds, she clicked the phone shut.

“Sorry,” she mumbled, the only comment she made about the call.

Kyle knew beyond a doubt it was a man calling her. One who probably wanted to ask her out. Why that bothered him, he didn’t care to contemplate. He simply drove her to her car, opened the truck door for her and said goodbye.

But much later that night, as he stared into the Boise lights from his front room window, his mind drifted to Francesca, and he wondered if she were out there right now having a drink with some guy.

Music played softly in the background. He liked Sinatra. There was something about that voice that made him feel good.

Kyle was just about to pour himself another glass of wine when his cell rang, and for an instant, he thought it might be Francesca.

"Hello?"

"Kyle, it's Mom."

"Oh, hey," he said, careful not to reveal his disappointment. He was always happy to hear from his mother, but since his father had died, things between them had changed. Their conversations just weren't what they'd used to be. Dad had kept the family together, providing a secure anchor and a sense of belonging for all of them.

Kyle had been an only child and raised mostly around adults, which matured him early on. Helene, his mom, had been a foster child, and it wasn't until she married Parr Jagger that she'd finally found a home where she felt loved, just as she was. Flaws and all. And his mom had a few quirks. But that was something Kyle didn't think about now.

This year, his mom had started dating Ralph Gunderson, a man she'd met at the Lutheran church she attended. She'd been seeing him for about eight months. He lived in Ballard, just north of Seattle. Kyle's mom lived in Bellevue in the craftsman-style home his dad had built her. Helene had been left financially secure after her husband's death, but she lived a fairly simple life. Until Ralph.

There was something about the man Kyle just hadn't been able to warm up to.

"How're things going there, son?"

"Good. The project's moving along. No big problems. Just the usual stuff. How's everything? Raining much?"

"Not in the last five days." She sounded a little tired, but her voice had a note of excitement he hadn't heard since she and Parr had taken a trip to Norway for an anniversary. "The rhododendrons are still blooming."

"That's nice," he murmured. Sensing there was more to this call than generalities, he cut to the chase. "Everything okay?"

"Fine." Helene paused for a moment. "Kyle. I have some news."

"Go ahead."

"Ralph has asked me to marry him and I accepted."

Kyle wasn't really surprised, he'd figured this day was coming. He might not think Ralph measured up to his dad, the legendary Parr Jagger, but who could?

The temptation to fly home tonight to sit his mother down and have a face-to-face was strong. But she was seventy years old. She'd made a lot of intelligent decisions in her life, and maybe she'd given this the kind of thought she needed to. Then again, he'd heard her talk about some pretty random things lately that were somewhat out of character for her.

After a moment, Kyle found himself saying, "That's great, Mom." She had mourned a long time after his dad died. Helene had been a widow for close to a decade.

Who was Kyle to tell her she had to remain alone? It wasn't his place. If Ralph made her happy, there wasn't much Kyle could do.

Early on, he'd run a background check on Ralph Gunderson, and it had been clean as could be. Not even a traffic violation. Just because the guy had a weird sense of humor, plus wore a comb-over and partials, didn't make him unsuitable for Kyle's mom.

"I knew you'd be fine with this. I told Ralph you would." Her voice became a bit breathless.

"I want what's best for you."

"I do love him, son."

Kyle moved the phone from his right ear to his left, then gazed out the window at the lights.

"Ralph and I have been talking about getting married almost since our first date, so it wasn't that big of a surprise to me when he asked last night."

"Well, good. I'm sure you'll be happy with him, Mom."

"I know I will, son. He's really a nice man."

Kyle wondered where they'd live—in her house? Or maybe they planned to buy one of their own. The idea of a stranger living in his dad's house bothered Kyle, but it wasn't his place to comment on that.

"Well, good," he caught himself repeating. It felt so lame to be talking in so neutral a manner. Maybe he was more overcome by the news than he thought. He had a hard time imagining his mom with anyone besides his dad. They'd had a really solid marriage.

"Kyle, there's something else. I didn't know when

you'd be back in Seattle so I could talk to you in person. But you need to know this as soon as possible so you can make the arrangements."

A wave of apprehension gripped Kyle. "What?"

"My Legacy stock. I'm going to need to sell it. Now that I'm getting married, I need the money for…well, things. And I'm assuming you'd want to buy my shares, but I'd like the transaction to take place in about thirty days. Sixty at the most."

Kyle tried to digest her news in the short seconds she gave him before she continued on. He heard her voice as if it were an echo in his head.

"If you can't buy them, I have someone interested. Remember Hal Burton—he owns Burton Builders? He'd pick up my shares in a heartbeat."

A chill ran through Kyle's veins. "You haven't told him your intentions, have you?"

"No, but you know how he's always saying he'd buy out Legacy if he—"

"Good. Don't tell anyone anything." Kyle pinched the bridge of his nose and lowered his head, trying to get rid of the headache that was suddenly pounding through his brain.

Technically, the company stock could be sold to anyone his mother chose. It wasn't traded on the open market, but it was the backbone of Legacy's financial structure. Kyle simply could not imagine an outsider owning part of *his* company.

There was something wrong here, something off.

His mother had been part of the corporation for as long as he could remember, and had a vested interest in Legacy Constructors. She didn't need a lot of money to live. She drew a decent check each month, and then there were his father's death benefits and social security. The kind of money she was talking about was quite sizable. Why now?

The only answer that made any sense had to do with Ralph.

Holding his raw emotions in check, Kyle dragged a breath of air into his lungs. Then, as if talking in slow motion, he said, "Mom, don't do anything just yet. Okay?"

"Of course, son. That's why I was letting you know about it now."

"I'm not talking about me. I'm talking about you. Don't go and elope to Vegas or something—"

"I'm surprised you'd suggest it! I would never do that. I want a Lutheran ceremony in the church."

At this point, Kyle couldn't care less what kind of service she was planning. "Mom, listen to me—you don't have to sell your shares. If you need some cash, I can help you out."

"Oh, no, Kyle. It's not that at all. It's another matter entirely. I've already thought this through and I've decided." The vagueness of her response set alarm bells ringing in his head, intensifying his headache.

"Please," he said firmly. "Don't do anything impulsive. You have to promise me."

"Well, all right, but I'm not stupid."

"I never said that."

Ten minutes later, Kyle hung up the phone, trying to make sense out of the conversation and put it into perspective. There was more to what his mother wanted to do than she'd let on, and he was certain it had everything to do with Ralph.

Kyle put in a fast phone call to his P.I. friend in West Seattle, then he poured himself another glass of wine. If it weren't for an OSHA safety meeting for the project first thing tomorrow, Kyle would have been in his plane, flying to Seattle right now.

Legally, there was nothing he could do to stop his mom from unloading her company shares. But he wanted to know her motives for making such a seemingly spontaneous decision. Time…he needed a chunk of it, because this just didn't sound right.

If she pressed the issue, Kyle couldn't let the shares go to an outsider. But it was going to take a lot of money to buy her out.

Under normal circumstances, he'd have access to it. Only his circumstances right now weren't normal. The Legacy credit line was stretched so thin it might as well be tissue paper.

And it was all because of one thing.

The Grove Marketplace.

CHAPTER SIX

GIOVANNI SAT AT THE HEAD of the large dining table, listening to the conversations surrounding him. Throughout his entire life, even before he'd married, Sunday night dinners had been a family event. They usually started with good-natured laughter, everyone catching up on a week's worth of happenings, then moved on to more liberated discussions involving family members' opinions about one another's business. Love flowed, even in the trying times when the mood grew heated. Everyone had two cents to add, and sometimes it felt as if there were a Vegas-style jackpot on the table that everyone was trying to win. Being wrong didn't mean saying you were sorry. It meant you poured the final glass of wine and raised your glass in a toast of goodwill.

For years, Giovanni had been presiding over this weekly tradition. The heavy table at which his children and their children gathered was one he'd made himself. He'd constructed it and the matching Italian-walnut sideboard over thirty years ago, and it bore the scars of use. The black streak of permanent marker where John's poster on George Washington had bled through. A groove at the edge that Robert had made one night while playing with a steak knife. Mark's contribution had been the cloudy pool on the surface the size of a small dinner plate. Model airplane glue had oozed out of the tube and hadn't been discovered until the next morning. They'd been able to remove the glue, but not the milky film that had set into the table's finish. The pink speckles, barely visible, were at the place where Francesca sat. Nail polish.

Of course, Giovanni could have repaired all these things, but he hadn't. The dings and nicks were what made the piece precious and gave it history.

The table seated twenty, and Giovanni liked it best when all the empty chairs were filled. They'd lost John's wife, and in those early months, her place had remained hauntingly vacant. Soon Robert's youngest daughter, Cora, decided she wanted to sit next to her uncle John, so she'd plopped herself in the chair, and that had become her regular spot each Sunday night. Cora was three years old and the pride of her grandfather's heart. Not liking that her sister garnered the attention, Cora's five-year-old sibling, Emelia, had tried to steal the chair, until Robert offered a compromise: they could sit on it together.

Today, after plates of pasta had been devoured, wine consumed, then a dessert of *zuccotto* served with decaf, the conversation turned to the state of John's life—after Robert's four daughters left the table to play. Aged three, five, seven and nine years old, the little girls were disinterested in adult talk and preferred to climb on

Grandpa's monstrous jungle gym and fort that he'd built in the backyard.

Giovanni could see his granddaughters from the dining room window as they played, climbing to the top and lowering buckets to be filled with rocks, dirt, handfuls of grass, and Grandma's clothespin basket. Mariangela had a dryer, but she often hung the bedsheets and towels on the line to get that sunshine-fresh smell.

"You need to insist they come, *mio figlio,*" Mariangela said in a resolute tone, stirring cream into her coffee. She sat at the opposite end of the table from her husband, giving Giovanni a quick glance over the rim of her cup.

John's two children, Zack and Kara, were now eighteen and sixteen—both driving and with their own cars. They'd neglected to come to dinner this week, and hadn't shown at the previous two Sunday gatherings, either.

"What am I supposed to do—drag them over here?" John was having a hard time with the kids, and it tore Giovanni's heart. Being a widowed dad was proving a challenge for John—especially when dealing with his son, Zack.

John had gone through a terrible period after his wife's death. John had barely functioned in the months after, much less taken on the important role of parenting two hurting teens. The truth, as Giovanni saw it, was that his son had been a workaholic in his law practice, and Connie's death was a wake-up call for him, one he couldn't deal with. When he had to become both father and mother, he failed, because he hadn't even been able to handle the father role.

Giovanni had had conversations about it with Franci, and she was of the opinion the two teens were taking advantage of their dad. She, too, hated to see John floundering—with his kids, the house, plus trying to make a living.

To a degree, Giovanni almost wished he'd hurry up and find a woman, marry her and let her take over in the home. John was like a ship without a sail, trying to stay on course.

"I remember what it was like when I was that age," Francesca said now, causing Giovanni to look at his daughter.

He recalled when she'd turned into a teenager, graduated from high school, then made her way to college. There had been a point in her life, after returning from Oregon, when she'd chosen to spend time with her friends and build a life for herself rather than bothering to attend family dinners. Giovanni hadn't pushed her to make an appearance. And over the next year, she'd begun to stop by the house more frequently. Now she rarely missed a Sunday.

Giovanni wasn't so rigid that he imposed his preferences on his wife and children. However, what was being said right now jarred him from his thoughts.

"No," he stated firmly. "That's not the way we do things."

"Sorry, Dad." John slid his now-empty plate to the

middle of the table. "I'm going to see a counselor with the kids next week. I just can't handle them on my own."

A knot formed in Giovanni's stomach and a sharp pain speared his chest. He ignored it. He had his share of stress, but you sure wouldn't find him at any counselor's office spilling his guts. Private—that's how family problems should stay. In the privacy of the home. "The Morettis are a family unit. What happens here stays here. You don't need to talk to an outsider. We can help you."

John closed his eyes. Giovanni could see his son's mind working as he formed a reply. His next words were spoken carefully, like a lawyer hammering home his point. "I understand that, but my way isn't working. I see so much crap all week, people arguing and judges making rulings that I disagree with. The courtroom is a difficult place to be sometimes, and I have to accept my limitations. I want what's best for Zack and Kara, and I'm obviously not giving it to them right now. In fact, I've already found a counselor I like, and I've been seeing him for a month on my own."

Mariangela's cheeks blanched. "You're talking to someone? If you had to, you should have gone to Father Mike."

"No, Mom. Not the church. One of my clients recommended the guy, and I feel like I'm getting somewhere, putting my life back on track." John toyed with his spoon, clearly uncomfortable about being in the hot seat.

Franci licked her lips, then traded glances with Mark,

who had been silent, before saying, "I think it's great, John. Good for you."

Mark nodded, but didn't add anything.

Giovanni acknowledged that Francesca and Mark had always been close growing up, and their relationship was no different today. His youngest son and daughter worked well together, and if they decided on a plan, there was no changing their minds.

Robert's wife, Marie, spoke up. She was the sensible one, the first to admit fault, then ask for forgiveness. "I'll keep you in my prayers."

"Thanks. I'd appreciate that," John stated.

Robert leaned forward, grasped the wine bottle at the center of the table and reached to pour a drink in everyone's glass. He lifted his toward his brother, then said, *"Salute."*

After a long pause, Giovanni finally toasted his son. Only then did his wife follow suit. *"Salute."*

His beloved Angela, a wistful expression on her lovely face, remained quiet for a moment, then blinked and said in an even tone, "More coffee, anyone?"

But the mood at the table had turned pensive and nobody wanted a second cup. Though nothing further was said on the topic, no one made a move to leave. Mariangela picked up stray cake crumbs with the pad of her thumb, then absently brushed them onto her dessert plate.

Leaning back in his chair and knitting his hands over his chest, Giovanni surreptitiously rubbed his fingers against his rib cage in an effort to relieve the pressure.

He didn't understand families today, as hard as he tried. His headstrong children had a new and different approach, while he and his wife were of a generation of Neapolitans who handled things the old way.

You didn't talk about conflict. Not among friends. Not often with family members. You made a toast, a *salute* to life, and you kissed your cousins on the cheeks and all was well. It was okay to speak about personal issues at home, but troubles should stay in the family.

Head shrinkers, Giovanni thought with distaste. He had no use for them—wouldn't set foot in a counselor's office if you tied him up and dragged him in.

Robert drank the last of his Chianti, then announced it was time to round up the girls and head home. John said his goodbyes and left. Franci rose and caught Mark's attention. "I'll walk out with you."

Mark said, "Okay."

In the kitchen, after everyone had left, Giovanni rummaged in the cupboard for the antacids. Pots and pans were stacked in the sink; bowls of extra pasta sat on the counter. The cake was nearly eaten, and the third wine bottle empty. Aromas of garlic still lingered pungently in the room.

"Your stomach again?" Mariangela asked, bringing the last of the dirty plates into the kitchen.

"It's nothing." Giovanni waved off her concern, drank a glass of water and downed a small pill that did very little to soothe the burn.

"Why didn't you have the kids help you with these dishes before they left?" he asked.

"Because I like to do them. I know that sounds ridiculous, but it's relaxing to me to clean my own kitchen."

He turned to his wife and put his hands on her shoulders, and when he brought her close, she melted into him. Even after all these years of marriage, he loved to hold her. He loved to kiss her and smell the fragrance of her perfume.

"I remember the day I first saw you," he said into her hair.

He could feel her snuggle closer, her cheek next to his chest. "I do, too. Just like it was yesterday."

Giovanni, in a moment of sentimental reflection, said, "Have you been happy with me, Angela? All of these years…forty-four to be exact."

"Very much!" she exclaimed. Her eyes met his, with a look that gave him no cause to doubt her for a second. "We've had our difficulties, but, Giovanni, I have loved you every day for the last forty-four years. I can't imagine my life without you."

"Nor I mine, without you."

He kissed the top of her head. "It's been some honeymoon, hasn't it, *bella?*"

"The longest on record, I'm sure." Her smile warmed him to the core.

"We've got fine children."

"The best."

"Even John."

"Yes, Giovanni. Even John," she affirmed, then tightened her embrace and rested her head on his shoulder.

Giovanni spoke loving words in Italian, thoughtful expressions that just didn't translate the same to him in English. She kissed his neck, stroked the nape of his hair, and he listened to her breathing.

He held his wife for the longest time, marveling at how fortunate he'd been to have found her all those years ago.

"ARE YOU AND KYLE JAGGER going golfing?" Franci asked Mark. "I didn't know you were buddies."

"We aren't."

"Aren't buddies, or aren't golfing?"

"We're golfing when we can both get the same time off."

They stood near their respective cars in front of their parents' old house on the Boise Bench. The brick homes were surrounded by large, mature trees that shaded the sidewalk from the blinding glare of the setting sun.

Mark had slipped on a pair of sunglasses, and Francesca couldn't read her brother's expression.

"Well, I think it's interesting that he's barely been in town and you two are planning on doing something together."

Shrugging, Mark said, "He asked me about golfing. You know I took it up this year. I want Jagger to give me a few pointers. So kill me if I hit a few balls with him."

"Dad might," Francesca offered, although that was a

stretch. Their father didn't dictate who they could be friends with and who they couldn't.

"No, he won't."

"Yes…well, I doubt he'd be happy about it."

"That's stupid and you know it. The Morettis have known the Jaggers for years. So what if we never got together socially when they were in town? It's not like we hate them. After all, Moretti got the Grove Marketplace project and they didn't. You don't see Kyle pointing fingers."

"That's what I'm wondering about. Why isn't he? He's fairly determined, and I know it had to bother him not to get that project. I'm just not sure it's a good idea for you to get too friendly with him."

Mark lowered his sunglasses down the bridge of his nose and gazed at her over the rims. He gave her a long stare that left her a little unsettled, then with a half smile said, "This isn't about the project. This is about you. You like him. I can tell. I hear it in the way you're talking about Kyle. Your voice goes funny. It does that squeaking thing."

"It does not!" she declared, but then cursed herself for not having more control over the telltale rise in pitch.

"Hey, I don't care if you have a thing for him."

"I don't!"

"The hell you don't. I've known you all my life. I can tell when you're lying. The guy interests you. When did all this happen?"

"It didn't! I don't even know what you're talking

about. It's ridiculous to think I'd like him. He just happens to be in the same business as us, so I run into him sometimes. Not very often…just sometimes. Like at that stupid historical meeting."

She thought back to Kyle giving her a tour of his job site. She'd tried with little success to stop reliving that evening on the crane, looking at the Boise city lights. She'd really enjoyed herself. Too much.

Tomorrow she was having an early morning coffee with Rick James at Moz's Firehouse Café. He'd sounded pleasant enough on the phone during the short five minutes they'd spoken. Having coffee with a single and available man ought to distract her from thoughts of Kyle. Dating someone would give new perspective to her life and stop this unreasonable preoccupation with Moretti's top competitor.

"I know you saw Jagger at the historical meeting." Mark's comment dragged her back to the matter at hand. "Tony told me he saw you two eating hot dogs on the street corner, then you got into Kyle's truck and took off."

"Darn this stinking small down." Francesca abruptly frowned, ironing out the deep crease in her forehead with the tip of her finger. Tony P. was their electrical contractor.

"I wasn't going to bring it up," Mark remarked, "but you played into it." Her brother touched the key fob for his truck and unlocked it. Reaching inside, he came up with a pack of gum. "Want a piece?"

"No." Francesca was trying to think, trying to make

something sound less than it was—which was the truth. An idea struck her, a good save. "Kyle did ask me if I wanted to check out his job site, and I went—for business reasons." The half-truth rolled easily off her tongue. Of course Kyle hadn't had anything to show her, he'd just made that up as an excuse to get her up that crane elevator. "You're the one who told me to ask him out for coffee to get information from him. So I toured his job site instead." She pursed her mouth. "Did you know they're using that new, lightweight fiber reinforced concrete?"

"So what?" Mark chucked the gum wrapper onto his truck's floor. It disappeared into the pile of crushed fast-food wrappers, soft drink cups and construction debris.

"So, I thought you might like to know. It's good for Moretti to stay on top of this."

"Franci, go home." He slid his sunglasses back up on his nose. "You need to take a chill pill."

Growing up, he was the only brother she would let get away with making such a comment when she was moody. If John had so much as opened his mouth, she would have socked him in the arm. Mark had always been a charmer, and even now, she grew heated around the collar, but didn't go charging after him.

"Ha-ha," she bluntly replied.

Mark rounded the side of his truck. "Are we done?"

"Go on. Take off." She pointed at him, as if her next words were a premonition. "You can't trust the competition. I would not get too chummy with Kyle."

Mark pointed right back, grinning as he turned over the truck's big engine. The passenger-side window rolled down and he leaned toward it. "You better take your own advice. Tony P. said you were staring at Jagger like he was a pair of high-heeled shoes you couldn't wait to try on."

"He wouldn't say something like that."

"Nope. I changed what he said into words you'd relate to. I can't tell you what he *really* said about how Kyle was looking right back at you. It was barroom talk."

Francesca gasped, but had no time to retort. Mark accelerated from the curb and took off.

KYLE'S LONGTIME FRIEND Neil Bevilaqua had always been a good sounding board. Neil lived in Seattle and was the director of NDB Design and Construction.

Moments ago, Kyle had hung up from a very brief phone call with him that resulted in Kyle packing a ditty bag. He was heading for the airport, flying home to Seattle to meet with Neil and talk about the bombshell his mom had dropped. Then he'd go see his mother personally.

The P.I. was still gathering information, but Kyle was seriously concerned. Business like this couldn't be handled in a phone call, nor could a situation involving millions of dollars for Legacy.

Kyle was compelled to sit Helene down and get to the real reason she'd made a snap decision to unload her stock. Things didn't add up, and he wasn't going to let her just act on a whim. This was serious. She'd never been impulsive like this.

For a sinking moment, he had a sour taste in his mouth as he considered the real possibility of his mom having eloped with Ralph Gunderson. Kyle's brain went on overload, and he sucked in a breath of air. Then he shook his head. His friend Neil might be able to offer some solutions where Kyle wasn't seeing any.

Zipping up his leather overnight bag, he shoved the straps over his shoulder, flipped on a few lights in the condo, then took off.

On the drive to the Boise Airport, he called in his flight plan.

Once at the hanger, he checked the Piper Malibu, took a walk around the aircraft, and began his preflight check inspection. But part of his mind kept going over various scenarios that might work for him to fix this huge problem where his mother was concerned.

The bottom line remained constant: he simply didn't have the money to buy his mother out.

Whenever Kyle made a decision, he lived with it; he accepted whatever consequences arose, and felt okay with what he'd done. He didn't look back with regrets, nor focus on the fallout of a bad choice. That just wasn't the way he operated.

But right now, he rued the day he'd made a decision that was now coming back to haunt him.

CHAPTER SEVEN

HELENE JAGGER USED a level voice as she said, "You know, son, I'm seventy years old and you're forty-two. We're both adults. I need the money in thirty days—sixty tops. You own thirty-six percent of the company and I'll gift you fifteen percent. You can retain fifty-one percent, so you have the controlling shares."

"Why do you need the money?" he responded bluntly, feeling as if the cheerily painted walls of her house were pressing in on him.

She sat straighter on the couch, balancing a cup of coffee on her lap. She was clearly in defense mode. "It's not that I'm in dire straights. I just need to consolidate. If you can't buy me out, I'll have no choice but to sell my shares to Hal Burton."

"What's the real reason you need the money, Mom? If I knew, I could help you."

"Kyle, I'm not a child, so please don't talk to me as if I were one."

He hadn't realized he had been adopting that tone, but there was definitely more to the story than she was letting on.

"I told you I won't sell without consulting you," Helene added, "so I don't know why you had to hightail it over here to check on me."

"Can't I come visit?"

"You rarely do."

The comment hit home. Kyle didn't want to admit it, but she was right. His visits over the past few years had grown more infrequent. He'd never been really close with his mother; she was a hard person to warm up to. He loved her, but it was a love born of obligation. They were incredibly different people and looked at things from opposite ends of the spectrum.

Kyle left her house no closer to having answers than when he'd arrived.

A couple hours later, after going to the Legacy office, he met up with Neil for a late-night drink. But their verbal what-ifs? didn't net him any real results or viable possibilities on how to get out of this stock sell-off.

"Kyle, just buy her out," Neil suggested.

"I can't."

"Why not? That makes the most sense. Legacy's got the capacity to do it."

"Not today it doesn't. I've invested heavily in another project as a silent partner."

"Ah." That one syllable spoke volumes. "So who are your partners?"

"I can't say." For the first time, Kyle wasn't able to clue his best friend in on a deal. He'd given his word to the other company that he wouldn't discuss the behind-the-scenes arrangement. It would be breaking news in the industry if the slightest rumor leaked out. Inasmuch as Kyle wanted to tell Neil, he couldn't risk it.

Over martinis, Kyle and Neil kept speculating about Helene's motives, but couldn't figure them out. Their conversation kept coming back to one person: Gunderson.

Kyle left Seattle without any resolution other than a follow-up phone call to the private detective he'd hired. He wanted Ralph Gunderson put under a microscope.

After getting six hours of sleep at his Seattle condo, Kyle headed back to Boise. During the flight, his mind drifted from his financial dilemma to Francesca Moretti.

Dawn was a blur of orange-white light on the horizon as he flew toward Boise. Kyle often did a lot of thinking in the cockpit. High in the sky, with nothing but space surrounding him, his thoughts could go in all directions, like the clouds.

The calmness lent itself to deep soul-searching, and he had made many decisions while flying.

Today, he recalled times he and his father had done things together before his death—working at Legacy and erecting buildings, bidding on projects, dealing with the trouble the company had been in prior to Parr's demise. Kyle remembered his dad as a strong, yet sometimes irresponsible man.

Kyle thought about his marriage, analyzing his ex-wife and what he could have done to make the marriage work if he could go back in time. Then he reflected on his future, where he wanted to be in five, ten years. He didn't see himself a long-term bachelor; he'd like to be in a relationship with someone. But timing was everything, and he'd been so busy with work, picking Legacy up off the ground and getting it running again….

Eight years had seemed to go by in a blur. Kyle realized he was tired of sitting at his dining room table by himself, looking over plans, giving the go-ahead on bids, going through paperwork, and fielding late-night calls from contractors in a panic over materials that hadn't shown up.

In retrospect, he was living out of a suitcase in Boise, a place where he had no roots. He'd bought his condominium as an investment, a large, converted space on the fifth floor of an old downtown warehouse. He had limited furniture and wasn't into decorating. He'd taken on the seventeen-story project himself because he'd needed a break from Seattle. For the most part, he was fine with the gray weather there, but at times it got to him.

He usually stayed in Seattle, where the majority of Legacy's projects were built. Out-of-state jobs were handled by his project manager, Ken West, or a few other good guys he trusted. Boise had just been a place where Kyle sometimes had to fill in—but meeting Francesca Moretti had made him stop and appreciate the City of Trees.

There were very few single, classy women who made him take notice. Everyone he'd dated had been divorced at least once, or had kids with two different guys, and came with enough baggage to fill a 747. Kyle didn't mind if they'd been married before, so had he. But he'd moved on. He hadn't seen Hailey in six years, and only then because he'd run into her at the bar in Palisades. They were finished business.

As Kyle began his descent into the Boise Airport, he wondered how long it would take for the day to be hit with some kind of crisis. And when he would see Francesca again.

HE WASN'T BAD. In fact, Rick James was attractive enough, and so far, he was proving to be a good conversationalist.

Francesca watched as the waitress topped up their coffee cups; then she turned her attention back to Rick.

He wore his blond hair cut short and neatly parted at the side. His aquamarine eyes were bright and attentive behind trendy wire-rimmed glasses. A blue Oxford shirt fit him quite nicely, as did a pair of khaki Dockers. He didn't have a gym physique, but he wasn't soft. Appearance-wise, he was fairly average, but the way he carried himself was above average. He exuded an easygoing confidence she found appealing.

What had begun as a coffee-only date had turned into breakfast. Franci usually skipped it, not being one for a big plate of eggs, bacon and potatoes. But now she ordered an English muffin and orange juice, surprised to find that she was receptive to the idea of extending their first meeting.

"Overall, it's been a good business fit for me," Rick said while pouring cream into his coffee. "So tell me more about you. What have you designed that I'd recognize?"

She appreciated his question and interest. She'd done all sorts of projects—civic, commercial, residential, and a variety of interiors. Choosing her favorite was easy. "The Towne Centre in Meridian."

He nodded, brows raised as if impressed. "The old farm granary that sits on the corner."

"It had to be gutted, and we redid the exterior in face brick and glazed windows. The inside's really great and the balustrade wood is heavy oak. We made the elevator a replica of the old 1916 grain lift. I heard all the spaces have been leased. I think the last tenant to take occupancy in the building was a jewelry store."

"A woman's favorite shop." Rick smiled.

Francesca didn't do a lot of shopping in jewelry stores. She tended to pick one-of-a-kind accent pieces at downtown boutiques—big broaches, sleek bangles for her wrists and chandelier earrings. She hadn't had a boyfriend in so long, she didn't think about treasured gifts, sparkling or otherwise.

For a moment, she thought back to Italy and Eduardo, then quickly quashed those pointless thoughts.

"What kind of jewelry do you like? Emeralds, sapphires, rubies or diamonds?" Rick asked, assessing her as if trying to gauge what kind of woman she was. It felt awkward to her that he would ask.

She thought briefly of that song about diamonds being a girl's best friend. Francesca would rather have a man be her best friend.

"I like costume jewelry."

"Come on." He grinned. "Don't be shy. Tell me what you like and I'll surprise you one day."

On a scale of one to ten, that comment sent the date from an eight to a four. The sudden move from casual friendly to presumptuous was a turnoff. He took a lot for granted in a short span of time.

Maybe she was just too rusty at this to even attempt it. She'd gotten her hopes up that she could date for fun, date to get to know someone and perhaps have it turn into something meaningful.

As she thought about it, she remembered how easy it had been to talk to Kyle. How comfortable she had felt, joking with him about the building industry, the various trades and their quirks. Not just anyone would know that, and it had been nice to share an insider's view with someone. There wasn't a whole lot about Kyle Jagger she didn't like. That was the problem.

She liked him too much.

"I'm not really one for surprises," Francesca said, sneaking a glance at her watch. She'd been here barely twenty minutes and it now felt twice as long.

She wished they hadn't ordered breakfast.

There was something wrong with her. Why else would she be single at thirty-four, with no prospects and no real inclination to be proactive about changing the situation?

Bad habits.

That was the reason. She'd gotten into the bad habit of telling herself that her life was rich, busy, too full to invest the time it would take to get to know someone.

But over the years, it had been the wrong way to go. She'd ended up spending New Year's Eve with girlfriends, and her birthday and holidays with family. That one last part of life—romance—was missing.

Realizing that, she gave Rick her full attention and told herself that he really was a pleasant man and she should give him a chance. So what if he wanted to surprise her with jewelry? It wasn't a crime, even though it seemed like an awfully sudden whim, with a woman he'd only met that morning.

Rick sat across from her in a booth at Moz's Firehouse Café, the sun coming through the slats of miniblinds at just the right angle to accent his features. He looked pleasing and seemed nice, even if he needed some tweaking in the tact department.

Resting his arm on the booth's back, he comfortably settled in. Clearly, he was no novice at this. "So Lily said you haven't been on a date in a long time."

Keeping her smile fixed in place, Franci promised herself she'd settle with Lily later. "I'm pretty busy," she answered dryly.

"I don't do a lot of blind dates. You never know who you'll end up with, but Lily said you were a knockout. And she was right." He took several long seconds to admire Franci. "You're gorgeous."

He leaned over and took her hand, rubbing her fingers with his own. The contact was surprising, yet in spite of herself, Franci didn't pull away. It was flattering to hear he thought she was attractive.

"Thanks." She drank the last of her coffee, and looking for the waitress to refill her cup when the warmth in her veins iced over.

Kyle Jagger was sitting in the back booth, staring at them!

How long had he been there?

She abruptly faced forward, jerking her hand out of Rick's, but her mind raced. Kyle had an open newspaper on his table, a cup of coffee and an empty plate in front of him. He'd definitely eaten breakfast, so must have been in the café for a while.

Instinctively, she shrank into the booth's vinyl cushion, hoping he hadn't seen her until now. Fat chance.

Why she had a sudden rush of guilt, as if she were doing something she shouldn't, she had no clue. But the very real tingles that rose over her skin, signaling that she needed to get out of here, were something she couldn't ignore.

If only she hadn't been holding Rick's hand, she could have pretended this was a breakfast with a contractor. But instead, Kyle would suspect she was on…a date.

As if a bolt of electricity had struck her, she could feel Kyle's gaze on her as surely as if he'd come right up to stand behind her. It was all she could do not to turn around again and look his way.

She willed the waitress to bring them their food so she could eat and leave. Her breath caught in her lungs and the surge of heat that pulsed in her veins was so ridiculous she could barely think.

Rick was saying something, and she saw his mouth moving but couldn't hear what he said, given the buzzing in her ears.

She should have known Kyle might be here. Moz's was a catchall for every contractor working downtown. If you wanted cheap but good food, this was the place to come.

Thankfully, their server appeared, her arms filled with two plates. She left the meals on the table, and Francesca ate quickly. It was difficult to chew, listen to Rick and answer his questions all at once.

Did she like to cook? No.

Did she have any pets? No.

What did she like better—cats or dogs? Dogs.

Did she ski? Yes.

Did she camp? Not if she could help it.

Swallowing her last bite of jam-covered biscuit, taking a fast drink of coffee and leaving the rest in her cup, Franci made an obvious show of checking the time, then exclaimed, "Rick, it's been really great, but I've got a meeting—"

He reached out to her, encircled her wrist with a warm grasp and met her startled, blinking eyes. Her heartbeat thumped madly inside her chest, and her throat went dry.

With a resonant voice, he said, "Francesca, there's something I've been dying to ask you from the moment you sat down."

THE FIREHOUSE CAFÉ was a Boise institution.

Moz Uberuaga's menu listed standard American fare

with a few of his Basque favorites thrown in: *tortilla de potata*—potatoes fried in grease with green peppers, chorizo and onions, and made into a pie with eggs on top. Kyle had never tried it. He was a four-eggs-and-bacon kind of guy.

He felt along his jawline, absently rubbing his chin where he hadn't had time to shave this morning.

He'd brought his laptop with him, but had neglected to check e-mails. He needed thirty minutes to himself to mentally prepare for his 9:00 a.m. meeting. Since he didn't have time to hit a round of golf, breakfast at Moz's had been his second choice.

But when he'd looked up to find Francesca walking into the Firehouse Café to meet some guy, the scene hadn't helped Kyle's mood. He'd sat back and watched her for the past thirty minutes, laughing and smiling, making small talk.

Her body language had gone from nervous to relaxed, then suddenly stiff. A few minutes later, the set to her shoulders had softened once more, as if she'd warmed up again.

And then she saw Kyle.

She did her best to ignore his gaze, but he could tell it unraveled her. Though she was doing her best to remain composed under fire, it was apparent Francesca would rather be anywhere else than in the café.

Kyle didn't let up on his stare. And he didn't realize that he was gritting his teeth until the man reached out and wrapped his fingers around Francesca's wrist.

The pressure in Kyle's jaw grew unbearable and he swallowed.

Everything inside him collided, and he wanted to get up, head for their table and tell Bozo to back off. Kyle's reaction was over the top, he knew, but he couldn't deny the fierceness he felt.

Studying Francesca's soft profile, the shape of her mouth, and even the furrow in her brow as she tried to ignore him while looking at him from the corner of her eye, he questioned if the jackpot could be hiding right in Boise.

Maybe Francesca Moretti was "the one."

When she and the mystery guy were standing to leave, Kyle flipped some bills onto his table, collected his newspaper and briefcase and headed off as well.

They all met in the doorway on their way out, and the guy put his hand on the small of Francesca's back.

The tenseness that bunched Kyle's muscles was immediate.

"Hi, Franci," he said through a tight jaw that he worked to loosen into a casual smile—even though his gaze was pointedly on the man she was with.

"Uh, hi," she murmured, her voice not its usual firm tone.

She had a flush on her cheeks, a blush that made her look very attractive and kissable.

Whether it was intentional or not, she twisted her body enough so that the guy's hold gave way.

"Kyle Jagger," he said to the man, but with the three

of them in the exit area, it was impossible to extend his hand—not that he felt any real inclination to do so.

The man stepped outside and Kyle got a closer look at him. He was nothing great, but maybe he had a winning personality. His chest wasn't filled out with muscle and he looked like he could use a vacation in Bermuda to put some color on him.

"Rick James." The response almost caught Kyle in a laughing response as he pictured the Jerry-curled, soul-singer for a flash of an instant.

Francesca's discomfort was evident in the way she adjusted her purse straps and plastered a false smile on her lips. "We were just having coffee."

"And a really great breakfast," Rick added.

"I've got a meeting," she said stiffly. "Thanks, Rick." Then to Kyle she murmured, "Nice to see you."

"Yeah, you, too."

She bolted off toward the capitol building, wearing heels and a skirt that hugged her hips. She looked lethally hot in that business suit.

Not waiting for the light to change, she crossed against traffic as it cleared, and dashed between two buildings. She hadn't been kidding when she said she had experience running in those shoes. She didn't miss a step.

When Kyle returned his attention to Rick, he saw the heat of appreciation in the man's eyes. He'd watched Francesca with the same interest.

A tight knot formed in Kyle's stomach. He felt

like taking a swing at the man, a reaction that was pure testosterone.

"So what do you do?" Kyle asked, his voice sounding strained.

"Mortgage broker. And you?"

"Construction."

"Is that how you know Franci?"

"You could say that."

"She's beautiful."

"Yes, she is." Kyle's cell phone rang, but he ignored it and let it go to voice mail. "So, are you two dating?"

"This was our first date, but I asked her out again."

That was all Rick offered. Kyle wondered if she'd said yes, but he didn't ask.

Rick slid on a pair of sunglasses, then said he an appointment he had to get to.

As Kyle stood there, he wondered if he really needed this. His life was heading in an unknown direction right now, and he might become even more tangled in Legacy business than usual. Getting involved could be a huge mistake.

Francesca was stunning, sexy and smart. There was no doubt she'd attracted his attention.

He considered the repercussions of what Giovanni would do if Kyle started dating his daughter. It was almost worth tipping the scale to see what would happen.

Kyle took the thought no further as his cell phone rang once more.

It was going to be a long day.

CHAPTER EIGHT

FRANCESCA'S OFFICE LINE hadn't stopped ringing all morning. It was a typical Monday morning in her tall office building on Idaho Street. It seemed as if every problem that could occur must have hit on Friday at 5:00 p.m., and everyone was slamming architects, builders, electricians and plumbers with it-must-get-fixed-asap calls.

She'd just hung up from talking to her dad. Sending over an extra set of drawings to her father's job site was low priority on her list of things to do right now.

A much bigger problem loomed.

She sat behind her desk, her high-heeled shoes kicked off and her bare feet tucked beneath her chair. She rolled backward and, on the off chance a prime set of velum plans had fallen to the floor, poked her head underneath her desk.

Nothing but a half-dozen pair of shoes.

The original set of plans for the Children's Hospital project had gone missing. They were like gold, her only finished drawing, about to be sent to the printer's. This was crazy.

Straightening, she mentally retraced her steps on Friday, trying to recall when she had last seen the transparent roll. She'd had the plans in her car when she'd met her brother John for lunch.

She was quite certain they'd been in her car when she left the restaurant. She'd gone by her father's trailer, talked to Mark about the brickwork and columns. Then she'd headed to her office once more. But she didn't recall the plans still being in the back seat. She'd angled her car in front of her father's meter at the Grove Marketplace.

Builders were given parking meter hoods on a paid basis, so they wouldn't have to compete for parking close to their job sites. Gone only for a minute, she hadn't locked her car. She hadn't thought she needed to.

But nobody would steal a set of plans.

Her desk phone beeped when her secretary forwarded a call, and Francesca temporarily gave up the search.

Thirty minutes later, she ran out to meet a client.

As she walked swiftly across Bannock, she began to panic. She desperately needed those plans. They were her only final copy. Of course she had her notes and drafts, but this was it—the real thing. Her firm was in the running to do the interior build-out for the new neonatal wing.

The hospital was having a huge fund-raiser that Franci was invited to, a black-tie affair. She had no date. In years past for these sorts of things, she'd brought Mark. She hadn't asked him yet, and hoped he was available.

For a brief second, she wondered if she should ask

Rick to go with her. She'd heard from him twice since their coffee date. Once she'd stared at the caller ID and let it go to voice mail; she couldn't really put a handle on why. The second time, she'd picked up and they'd talked for a short time before she had to take a conference call.

The burning question he'd wanted to ask her was if she'd like to go to Sun Valley with him for a weekend sometime. She'd said it was way too soon to even consider.

Lily phoned and said Rick had called her to report in, and he'd raved about their date. While Francesca wanted to find fault with him, she couldn't, aside from the fact he was a little eager.

There had been something missing. An element. A feeling of unquestionable attraction. That flutter and zing in one's heart, the skipping of a pulse, as if the airplane they were riding in had suddenly dipped in altitude and their equilibrium felt off.

Unfortunately, that's how she felt around—

Francesca flipped open her cell phone as it rang.

"Franci, it's Mark."

"Hey, what's up?" She skirted a group of businessmen exiting the Starbucks.

"I'm holding your Children's Hospital plans."

She stopped short, her heartbeat skipping. "You are?"

"They're a little dirty. One of our superintendents found them lying on the curb, and he's had them in his truck all weekend."

"You've got to be kidding me! They must have fallen out of my car, but I never opened the back door."

"Don't know what to tell you, but I figured you'd want to know I had them."

She heaved a relieved sigh. "You just made my day."

"I'll put them on Dad's desk."

"Thanks so much."

After her meeting, Francesca headed back to her office, eating a cup of noodles for lunch at her desk. She wasn't really hungry and needed to reorganize her day after her hectic morning.

She had a corner office with a great view of the city. From her seat she could see the Wells Fargo Bank high-rise and the balcony of the town's most popular nightclub. It was a prime location to do business. Most of the floor belonged to her firm and the handful of employees she had. The other spaces were leased out to offices, notably an interior designer named Suzy Blaire.

The woman was in her early forties, built, petite and fiery, with a great sense of art. Francesca had used her in the past, to decorate her home.

Franci glanced up when Suzy knocked on the open door frame of her office, while her secretary away from her desk on her lunch break.

"Hi," the designer said. "Are you busy?"

"Come on in." Franci leaned back in her big chair, her legs tucked beneath her.

"Healthy lunch?" Suzy looked at the cup of salty noodles in a processed broth.

"It was convenient."

The woman stood near the edge of the desk, wearing a black pantsuit with a black silk blouse and gold necklace. Franci couldn't recall ever seeing her in anything but black. She had shoulder-length, golden-blond hair, which made for a striking contrast. With her smoky eye makeup, she looked incredibly chic.

The two of them had gotten together for an occasional drink after work, but Francesca was a lot more conservative than Suzy. The designer would constantly point out single men in the restaurant lounge or bar, and suggest they approach them. Not into that type of "speed dating," Francesca had kept their association pretty much business from then on.

Sitting on the desk's edge, Suzy folded her arms. "I saw you the other day."

Franci tilted her head. She and Suzy passed each other in the hallway and sometimes turned up at the same places. She couldn't recollect a recent incident, but apparently there had been one.

"Was my head in the clouds?" she replied, trying to conjure up their last meeting.

"Actually, no. It was turned and focused on a hot guy."

Franci's throat went dry and a bad premonition caused her muscles to grow tense. "A hot guy, huh?"

"Who was he? I saw you get into his pickup the other day. He is one fine-looking man. Broad shouldered and handsome, with a behind on him in those jeans that was just too yummy for words."

Kyle's butt was nice, but *yummy* wasn't a word Francesca would associate with it. She debated whether or not to give Suzy the information she was after. There was something about her cat-on-the-prowl delivery that gave Franci pause. But after a moment, she realized she didn't have any reason not to supply the goods. It wasn't as if she and Kyle were a couple.

"Kyle. His name's Kyle."

"Tell me more. Are you dating him?"

"No," she replied swiftly. She wished she could take the word back as soon as she saw lust fill Suzy's almond-shaped eyes. "He's a builder. We know him through the trade. He's friends with my brother."

That wasn't altogether true. How much of a friendship Kyle and Mark had wasn't really clear. But if Francesca made it sound as if there were family ties involved, maybe Suzy would back off.

But Suzy Blaire was a woman with her own agenda and could be as aggressive as a tiger on a hunt. "Who's he work for?"

There was no way out of answering. "Legacy. He owns it."

"Nice." Her perfectly arched brows rose. "Do you know if he's seeing anyone?"

"I have no clue." The words came out in a monotone.

"Well, it doesn't matter. I'll ask him to the black-tie anyway."

"Black-tie?"

"Children's Hospital." Suzy pushed herself away from the desk and walked toward the door with a soft sway of her hips. The very idea of Suzy Blaire hooking up with Kyle made Francesca lose what little appetite she had.

"You're going, right?" the designer asked over her shoulder.

"Yes. I'm bidding the build-out."

"Great! We're bidding the interior." With a wave, Suzy left the office, and Francesca was left to smell the lingering fragrance of expensive perfume that had clung to the woman's skin.

By the end of the day, when Franci finally slipped out of her office and made it to her dad's trailer, nobody was around. He had closed up for the night. A simple row of fluorescent bulbs burned above his desk as she sat behind it, and immediately found her prized plans tucked into a corner for safekeeping.

Francesca glanced at the clutter, her mind frazzled from a long day. She drummed her fingertips on the desk, looked at the wallboard with all of its take-out menus, notes and multitude of business cards tacked up with colorful pushpins.

She noted the card for Legacy Constructors. Kyle Jagger. His cell phone number.

Slowly, Francesca pulled the pin out and held on to the card. She stared at it for a long time, then tapped its corner on the desk, her mind racing a mile a minute.

Losing track of how long she sat there, she took a final look at the card, then pinned it back on the wall, grabbed her plans and locked the trailer behind her.

THE FLYING M on Idaho Street was a landmark in Boise, a coffeehouse that seemed to consistently win accolades from the locals. The gift shop sold one-of-a-kind books, jewelry and countless other things shoppers thought were cool.

Kyle sat at the far corner of the dining room, his back to the wall. He was dead tired. It had been a long day and he'd wanted nothing more than to head for home after calling it quits.

When his phone had rung earlier, he hadn't been surprised to hear her voice. He'd actually been glad she called.

He checked his watch. She was late. She'd suggested eight and it was ten after. The traffic outside was thick with evening diners as the sunset began to creep across the sky. Summers in Boise saw daylight lengthening until almost ten at night. It made for good golf, water sports or rafting on the river.

After another check of the time, Kyle stretched. The coffee he'd ordered was almost gone and he contemplated ordering another.

The coffeehouse door opened and she came inside, her brown eyes scanning the semicrowded room. Spotting him, she gave a nod, then approached with concise steps. She had her brisk walk down pat, and he never tired of watching the way her hips swayed slightly when she meant business.

When Francesca sat down, he scanned her appreciatively, then smiled.

"Sorry I'm late. I couldn't find a place to park."

She smelled like flowers, a light perfume spray that was maybe more of a body splash. It seemed as if she'd run home after calling him so she could take a shower and change. This was the first time he'd seen her in jeans and a simple white tank top. She had a slight tan, the kind that came from being outside just long enough to tour a job site, then disappear inside an air-conditioned trailer.

Her black hair was tucked behind her ears and she wore silver hoop earrings. He liked seeing her hair down. Its length surprised him, cascading well past her shoulders.

The sparkle in her brown eyes seemed brighter, as if she were breathless. Or nervous. To his recollection, she'd never revealed that around him—although he knew he could unsettle her with a simple hot gaze.

She set her purse down, then picked it back up. "I'm going to order a coffee, too," she said.

Franci began to rise to her feet, but he motioned for her to stay where she was. "I'll get it. What do you want?"

"Decaf vanilla latte. Thanks."

"No problem."

He returned with her beverage, sat across from her and waited for her to enlighten him as to why she'd called. She'd simply said she needed to talk to him.

For a moment, he'd wondered if her wanting to see him had anything to do with Giovanni, but when Francesca had walked into the Flying M, he'd disregarded that idea.

A woman ready to kill a guy didn't come dressed in

jeans and a tank top, keep recrossing her legs or lick her lips a half-dozen times as if trying to say something.

No, she doesn't know.

Kyle had successfully put his attraction to Francesca on the back burner after running into her and her date the other day. He had so much on his plate, but he did take time yesterday to hit balls at the driving range. It was his outlet, and he'd needed to expend some energy before digging into the mound of paperwork on his desk. Invoices were coming due and he had to pay bills, his subs were grumbling about delays, and OSHA had shown up with a warning about a possible fine if the safety issue wasn't taken care of asap. Kyle had thrown himself into his work, hardly giving Franci a thought.

Until he'd seen her come through that door, and all over again, she took hold of every inch of his mind, sending his pulse skyrocketing.

Her voice was clear and strong. "Thanks for meeting me on such short notice."

"Sure."

She took a sip of coffee from her mug, then squared her shoulders. "This is a nice coffeehouse," she said, as if she needed time to lay out what she wanted to say. "Have you been here before?"

"Nope."

The generalities continued when she asked, "How do you like living in Boise part-time?"

"It's fine." He folded his arms over his chest, settled in and took a leisurely assessment of her.

She was very feminine, and he liked that about her. Working in a trade where he dealt with a lot of guys and heavy equipment, he found it nice to see a woman take pride in being female. And once again he wondered what perfume she was wearing, as he breathed it into his lungs. Eyeing the bare skin of her arms, he guessed it would feel just as soft as it looked.

Her breasts were on the smaller side, but offered a slight hint of cleavage at the neckline of her top. She wore a cross around her neck and he wondered if she was religious. Kyle himself had been raised a Lutheran.

He knew her family to be Catholic, and he wondered if she wore jewelry of that sort.

She became flustered as he ran an assessing gaze over her, so he smiled to put her at ease.

"Seattle's a nice city," she stated, drinking more coffee.

"It's great." He broadened his smile. "So, honey, I'm thinking you didn't invite me for coffee to ask me about Seattle."

Resolutely, she sighed. "You're right. I didn't."

"What's up, Franci?"

She looked down, then up again, and tried to keep a serious expression on her face. The facade didn't work for very long before she cracked a smile. "This is silly, really. I'm making a bigger deal over this than necessary."

She definitely had his attention, and several scenarios played out in his head. Whatever she was trying to say was something big. Usually when a woman got like this, she was confessing something.

Kyle was curious about what Francesca Moretti could possibly have to confess…either about herself—or maybe him?

"Just talk, Franci. You've always cut to the chase real quick around me and it's something I appreciate." He reached for her hand, took it and felt her knuckles. Her skin was like satin and he loved the soft texture. She had nicely manicured nails, short but feminine.

Francesca froze, as if she weren't sure what to make of him. The silence stretched.

"What's on your mind?" he asked once more.

He was glad she didn't back down, but held his eyes with hers and uttered in a firm tone, "If you don't have plans this Saturday, I'd like you to join me at the black-tie event for the Children's Hospital. I'm doing the build-out bid and my firm, Bella Design, has a table. It's going to be my employees and their significant others. It could be good business for Legacy."

That last comment felt tacked on, as if she felt she needed to convince him.

"Sure."

"You will?" Her response revealed she didn't ask a whole lot of guys out—if ever. He thought it was refreshingly sweet. So many women he'd encountered were bold and too aggressive, not letting a man be a man.

"Yeah. I think it'd be great." He lifted his hand from hers and regarded her. "And not because Legacy could gain anything from it. But because I want to go with you."

She faltered momentarily at his admission, but got

back to business almost immediately. "Well, you may know some people there, so you won't feel out of place."

"It won't matter to me. I'll know you."

She gave him a half smile while shaking her head. "I don't know what to make of you," she said. The blunt statement threw him off a little.

"How so?"

"I can't say." She inhaled, relaxing, as if she'd just taken an examine and gotten a passing grade.

She toyed with the handle of her mug, then shot him a glance. "By all accounts, we shouldn't like each other."

"Why not?"

"We're competitors."

"I don't compete with anyone but myself, Franci. I've been in this business too long to let industry politics get to me."

Although there were those days when he felt like an overloaded circuit breaker box ready to blow. He didn't have a short fuse and, in fact, could keep a pretty cool head. But sometimes he had to put on a poker face just to get through a meeting or an afternoon too jammed with problems to sort out.

Kyle suddenly laughed. "Hey, you just said you liked me, and you took it for granted that I like you."

Her smile faded. She evidently mistook what he'd said. "It's not that I like you or you like me, Kyle. We both happen to work in the same field, and me asking you to the black-tie isn't technically a date—"

He leaned over and cupped her cheek, bringing her

stiff speech to a grinding halt. Her skin was warm and soft beneath his fingers. "Stop. You're processing too much. I want to go with you because I like you. And it's okay if you like me, too."

The urge to kiss her welled inside him, causing his muscles to tense. His insides heated, his body responding to her in a way he wasn't able to tamp down. "You do like me, don't you?"

She slowly swallowed, her eyes never wavering. "Yes."

"Good."

Reluctantly, he lowered his hand and tried to cool down. He willed himself to think of a million other things than the beautiful woman before him, just so he could get up from the table and not look like an idiot. "What time should I pick you up?"

"It starts at seven."

"Where do you live?"

"In the north end off Warm Springs." She took a pen from her purse and drew directions on a napkin, then handed it to him. Her penmanship was clean and concise, perfectly slanted and legible. "The event's at the Boise Centre on the Grove. It shouldn't take us more than ten minutes to get there from my house, but we'll have to contend with parking."

"I'll be by at six forty-five."

"That would be great."

The planning taken care of, Francesca grew introspective, as if wavering between saying something further or not.

"What's on your mind now?" he queried, once more cutting to the chase.

Her response was immediate. "You asked me something that I'd like to ask you."

"Shoot."

"Have you ever been married before?"

Without hesitation, he replied, "Five times."

At the look of dismay that blanched her cheeks, he laughed. "I'm jerking you, honey."

She gasped to get her composure.

"Once," he said firmly. "Is that okay?"

She nodded. "That's fine."

He couldn't fathom what thoughts were going through her head. If he wasn't so beat after this day from hell, he would have to stick around and enjoy her pretty face while drawing her into deep and meaningful conversation.

But as it was, his phone had rung three times on vibrate, and gone to voice mail, since he hadn't picked up. Nobody thought twice about making after-hours calls to a developer.

"I gotta head out. I'll walk you to your car." Kyle stood and let Francesca lead the way.

The evening was warm, and the window lights of businesses lining the street filled the night with a variety of color. Food aromas filled the air—the pungent scents of frying onions and burgers being grilled, reminding Kyle he'd yet to have dinner. He'd pick up a pizza at Guido's on the walk back to his condo.

At the curb where Francesca had parked, he waited for her to unlock the car.

"Thanks," she said as she opened the door. She paused, then added, "And thanks for saying you'll come with me."

He nodded. "No problem."

As she pulled away, his cell phone rang and he unclipped it from his belt. He didn't recognize the number, but took the call anyway.

"This is Kyle," he answered.

"Well, hello, Kyle!" a female voice said in greeting, her tone as bubbly as a busted mainliner. "I've been trying to catch you all night. This is Suzy Blaire."

CHAPTER NINE

"SO DEAN DIDN'T EXACTLY look like George Clooney, but we had a nice time." Jordan sipped on a glass of red wine at Pomodoro.

Lily spread tomatoes on a slice of bruschetta. "Who'd he look like?"

"Nobody in particular. He looked like a Dean."

Francesca spoke up. "What does a Dean look like?"

"Nice. Big brown eyes, short brown hair. Clean fingernails. I liked him."

Erin asked, "Where did you go?"

"We had Chinese for dinner downtown, then saw a movie at the Egyptian. I'd go out with him again. If he calls."

"You could always call him, thank him for the date." Jordan's eyes looked luminous with bronze eye shadow that set off her golden hair.

"I don't call guys."

Erin adjusted the napkin resting on her lap. "Actually, I think it's politically okay to call these days."

Francesca smiled at Robert, who popped his head out from the kitchen, waved, then went back to cooking.

Her heart wasn't in tonight's Wednesday get-together with the girls. Thoughts about this Saturday crept into her head. She'd been temporarily insane to invite Kyle to go with her.

The possibility that Suzy Blaire could have gone with Kyle had provoked her into asking him herself. If Suzy knew what had happened, she wasn't letting on. The interior designer had been as nice as could be the other day in the elevator. Franci had a hunch the other woman didn't know. Suzy could be quite territorial when it came to men.

"Speaking of phone tag, Rick James said he's called you, like, five times, and you've been too busy to set something else up with him." Lily's comment brought Francesca from her thoughts.

"I really am swamped at work," she said, although there were always ways to make allowances for most anything that came up. It was just that Rick wasn't a priority, so she'd been unavailable. She'd have to talk to him soon and simply tell him she wasn't going to go out with him again. To Lily she said sternly, "And I'm still angry with you for telling him I haven't been on a date in a long time. I felt like day-old bread sitting there, my shelf life expired. I *have* gone out in the last year."

"You have? With who?"

"People."

"'People' is not men, Franci," Jordan pointed out.

Francesca bristled. "Why do we do this? Why do we always let our conversations be dominated by talk of men?"

"Because we like them." Erin's statement brought forth a trio of nods.

"Yes, but why can't we talk about our lives, our careers, what's going on with *us* and not the part that's waiting for a guy to validate a Saturday night? I'm perfectly fine sitting home alone."

"I'm not," Lily staunchly declared.

"Neither am I." Jordan's resoluteness shone in her eyes.

Even Erin agreed. "I'd much rather go out on a Saturday night."

Lily fixed her gaze on Francesca. "You mean you honestly like living alone, being alone, staying home alone? I can't believe it. I've known you for years and we've talked about how nice it would be to have a good guy in our lives. Were you just saying that?"

Francesca felt a headache coming on. She hadn't meant to start a debate. "No, I wasn't. I *would* like to have somebody, but it's not the be-all and end-all. I do have a really great life. And so do you three—in case you've forgotten."

"We know." Erin chewed on an olive from her martini. "But I'm like Julia Roberts. I want the fairy-tale ending."

"You'd have to be a hooker first," Jordan teased.

The women laughed and the topic of conversation went from men to when the next cooking class was being held at Berryhill & Company, and if they should sign up. Since Francesca wasn't big on cooking, she didn't add much and her thoughts drifted.

She had to buy a new dress before Saturday. Well, she didn't *have* to—she wanted to. For special occasions, she shopped online, but there wouldn't be enough time. She'd check downtown at some of the boutiques, perhaps Macy's or Dilliard's.

She'd made an appointment to have her hair trimmed this Friday in between her two afternoon clients. Maybe she'd get her nails done. Gazing at her hands and short nails, she rethought that. Maybe not.

"So, what are your weekend plans, Franci?" Jordan asked.

Francesca blinked and returned to the present. She hadn't planned on discussing Saturday with her girlfriends until after the fact. She just didn't want to talk about something in advance that was no big deal. At least that's what she kept telling herself. She was having a hard time convincing herself that the black-tie event was not a date.

"Nothing much," she replied, glad when Robert brought out their orders himself.

"Hello, ladies." He set the large tray holding their dishes on a stand.

Francesca admired her brother for his personable service. He was so sweet to them each Wednesday, always coming out to make sure everything was okay and that they were enjoying the food.

She loved him very much and was proud of him.

"The grilled chicken with *gremolata.*" He placed the dish in front of Lily. Then he went for another plate, artistically arranged with bits of fresh basil. "*Polpette* and *spaghett'*."

"Yum," Erin said. "That's mine."

Robert lifted a bowl and set it at Jordan's place. "*Zuppa di pesce.*"

"It looks delish! Thanks, Robert." Then she nudged Franci. "Why does your brother have to be married? He's so cute, and what a sweetheart!"

"We have a brother who's single," Robert interjected. "I think you know him. His name is Mark."

The date squad groaned in unison. They had all tried, at one time or another, to catch the elusive Mark Franco Moretti. But he wasn't a fish to be lured out of his bachelor sea, no matter how appealing the bait.

Robert served Francesca last—fresh fettuccine with roasted chicken and broccoli *rabi.* She realized she was starving, and after giving her brother a hug, she tucked into her dinner with relish.

The subject of this weekend's do-or-die date nights was dropped, much to her relief.

She wasn't ready to share something that could end up being nothing.

That thought sobered her, and she took a sip of wine to soothe her throat.

The truth was, deep down, she hated to hope that this Saturday might be a whole lot more than just a business event. She wanted the real thing. The romance. The courtship.

She wanted…a boyfriend.

GIOVANNI FINALIZED the arrangements, a knowing smile crossing his mouth. Just wait until Angela found out what he'd done. She'd blow a gasket, but in a good way.

She deserved this and more. It was about time, and he wanted to make sure she had the best anniversary present ever. He paid the clerk, and left the building feeling as if he'd done the right thing.

So often, his wife's wishes had been put on the back burner, as Giovanni focused on Moretti Construction. She never complained, always said she understood, even if she didn't. Once in a while she gave him a disappointed glance, but very rarely. The woman was a saint. A godsend. He didn't know what he would have done without her in his life all these years.

Giovanni got into his pickup and drove to the florist to engage in part two of his anniversary surprise.

He had just finished placing his order when his cell phone rang. He gave his usual greeting: "Moretti Construction, Giovanni here."

"Mr. Moretti, this is Allison Fitzpatrick."

Recognizing the name, Giovanni stopped walking and held the phone securely at his ear. "What can I do for you, Mrs. Fitzpatrick?"

"I'm calling about the Grove Marketplace. There's a problem. Some of the bonding paperwork is missing."

THE BOISE CENTRE on the Grove was a charity organizer's venue of choice when it came to auctions or business functions. Each year, hospitals raised countless dollars there. During the holidays, the Festival of Trees was held, a display of hundreds of decorated Christmas trees that went up for auction at the end of a black-tie evening. In the summer months, the Beaux Arts Society offered wine tasting.

Volunteers for the Children's Hospital had set up dozens of cloth-covered tables in the theme colors of maroon and gold. Lighting was soft and low; the tables glittered with candles, their flames reflected in the mirrored panes that held them. On the bandstand, a local group played oldies.

In the main lobby, a no-host bar was open for business. Many early arrivals had drinks in their hands when Kyle and Francesca walked through the door. Like them, most people had come to lend their support to a good cause, not caring about winning a trip for two to Whitetail in McCall.

The growing crowd was already lively and boisterous, and the room was warm from the presence of so many people. Kyle took her light wrap and gave it to the coat-check girl. Then they stood near the bar, Francesca more nervous than she wanted to admit.

"Can I get you a drink?" he asked.

"Please." Her response came out quicker than she would have liked. But a glass of wine to settle the butterflies in her stomach was just what she needed.

"What do you want?"

"A cabernet would be great."

"I'll be right back."

Kyle stood in the line and Franci took the opportunity to take in deep breaths of air to quell the tingles that had risen on the back of her neck the moment she'd opened her front door.

She'd never imagined Kyle Jagger on her doorstep, and definitely not dressed in a tuxedo. Her breath had been snatched away at the sight of him in a black coat and white linen shirt.

She should have expected he'd look fabulous dressed up, since he looked so great dressed down.

His hair was shorter, as if he'd recently visited the barber. She liked the cropped style. It suited the angles of his face, the masculine lines of his jawbone and the shape of his nose. He had a strong profile and chiseled features that set off his startling gray-green eyes. She could get lost in that gaze, and in fact had, before he'd escorted her to his truck and opened the door for her.

It had felt as if time stood still.

He'd helped her up onto the seat. The cushy leather interior had been cleaned of all job-site dust, plans and construction samples. She'd appreciated his effort, especially since she was wearing black.

Kyle returned to her with two glasses of wine. "Let me know if it's okay," he said, pressing the glass into her hand. "If it's not, I'll get you something else."

She took a sip. "It's good."

Kyle drank, then gazed around at the large gathering. "They really filled the place."

"They usually do. It's for such a good cause."

"So tell me about this bid you're doing for them."

She proceeded to talk about the build-out and design work she hoped to secure. She was fairly certain she could land the project, but it wasn't a given.

Coming tonight was important, and as she and Kyle circulated through the room, she paused often to converse with influential people. She would introduce Kyle, and was thankful she didn't have to worry about whether or not he'd fit into the conversation. He knew enough about almost anything to add his views. He was neither arrogant nor opinionated, but gave thoughtful comments, often adding just the right touch to the conversation.

Eventually they ran into her parents and Mark. Francesca was on her brother's short list of "inquiring minds want to know." He'd made a phone call to her last week asking what time she wanted him to pick her up for the black-tie. She'd told him she'd already made other arrangements. When she hadn't been forthcoming as to who her date would be, he'd been hounding her nonstop.

Mark raised his chin a notch when he saw who she was with. "Good to see you," he said to Kyle.

Francesca stood taller, determined not to be intimidated by any family teasing. This had been a business date, nothing more.

Although, as she thought that, she knew immediately that she was kidding herself.

"Hey, Mark." Kyle was gracious and shook her brother's hand. "Next weekend. Golfing. You ready?"

"Sure. We'll have lots to talk about."

With that Franci frowned, not liking that her brother might be grilling Kyle about them as a couple.

Her father looked dapper in a tuxedo that strained a little at the midsection. He'd put on a bit more weight this year, but still seemed to be healthy. His energy level hadn't diminished in the slightest.

Her mother wore a long burgundy dress with a jacket that fit her nicely in the shoulders. She carried a black evening bag and wore diamond chandelier earrings.

"Franci," her father said, leaning forward to give her a hug. "I didn't know you'd be bringing Kyle." His voice was low, for her ears only.

In an equally soft voice, she replied, "I didn't think I had to tell you about it, since it's no big deal." She hoped the comment came across as light and breezy.

Standing back, he gazed at his daughter and the man with her, a look of concern in his eyes. Giovanni appeared as if he wanted to take Kyle away and have a private word with him.

Franci didn't think he'd have an issue with her choice in company tonight. After all, he'd invited Kyle to the Grove Marketplace party at Pomodoro's.

Mariangela was gracious, as always. "Kyle, we still miss your father. He was a good man."

"Thanks, Mrs. Moretti."

The four of them engaged in topical conversation

ranging from construction talk to speculation over the aromas coming from the kitchen and what would be served for dinner.

Mark stood with a beer in his hand, his posture casual, but his quizzical eyes often directed at Franci. She could only guess what he was thinking. Of her three brothers, he knew her the best, and it galled her that he could read her so well. She did her best to act cool and casual, as if completely disinterested in Kyle as anything more than a business associate. But she wasn't very successful, and in the end drank half a glass of wine in a short span of time just to settle her nerves.

Franci was more than ready to sit down and attempt to relax when the crowd finally started heading into the ballroom for dinner. Bella Design had bought a table, and she'd seen several of her employees and their respective dates throughout the cocktail hour.

"I'm sorry," she murmured as she and Kyle settled in their seats.

"For what?" He leaned close, and she could smell his aftershave, a masculine, musky scent that captured her senses.

"I don't know what got into my father."

"I didn't notice."

Kyle was being gracious. How could he not have noticed how her father had stared at him, as if trying to figure out a way to get him alone and tell him something…such as "stay away from my daughter."

Francesca could only speculate. But something had happened to make her dad suddenly focus on Kyle.

She was saved from further thoughts about that when a voice came from behind. Both she and Kyle turned their heads at the same time.

"Well, I wondered why you turned me down," Suzy Blaire said to him in a fluid tone that suggested she'd been enjoying her predinner drinks. "I sure as hell didn't think it would be because of *you.*" She stared at Franci.

KYLE DIDN'T RECOGNIZE the woman before them. She was tiny, but her voice packed a wallop. He guessed she smoked cigarettes, given its husky inflection. She had blond hair she'd twisted into an up-do. An extremely low cut gown hugged her figure, and when she leaned forward, he got an eyeful.

Francesca greeted the new arrival stiffly. "Hi, Suzy."

Suzy Blaire. That interior designer who'd called last week and about squeezed the balls right off him.

He hadn't known her from jack, and she'd gone on about how she'd heard so much about him, how much she wanted to meet him, insisting he come with her to the black-tie event for the Children's Hospital. He'd told her he planned on attending, but had already made his own arrangements.

Artful pleading and purring on her part hadn't caused him to change his mind. She'd finally hung up, but with a sensual note in her voice that said she'd see him here and show him just what he was missing.

"Kyle Jagger. It's nice to meet you," she said in her kittenish voice. "I saw you once with our friend Francesca, and I told Little Miss Franci-Pants that I was interested in you." She gave Francesca a scowl. "I had no idea she had her sights already set on you, darlin'. She sure didn't tell me that."

"Kyle's in the same business as my father, and it's inevitable we end up at the same places." Francesca's civil tone was stretched to the limit.

"I don't think you two ran into each other tonight. This was planned," Suzy declared.

Kyle had been ready to stand so he could formally introduce himself to the woman, but now he remained firmly in his chair. "Miss Blaire." He spoke her name with forced politeness. "I told you I had made plans for tonight. I'd already asked Francesca to come with me."

Franci glanced at him briefly and he saw the grateful light in her eyes. He gave her a smile, then rested his arm on the back of her chair.

"She didn't mention it to me," the blonde said bluntly.

"I asked her to keep it low-key because of some business I still had to finalize with her father." He brushed his fingertips over the exposed skin on the nape of Francesca's neck, feeling her warm body shiver in response. "I didn't want Giovanni thinking I was only asking his beautiful daughter out as a corporate strategy."

For the first time since she'd approached them, Suzy had nothing to say. "Well, have a nice night," she murmured at last. "I'll give you a call next week and we can go out for a drink. I'd like to get to know you while you're in town." She disappeared into the crowded room.

Kyle felt Franci tense. Beneath her breath, she said, "Even when she's been put in her place, she has to have the last word. I cannot believe her nerve."

He laughed. When Francesca frowned, he said in a soothing voice, "I'm not laughing at you. I'm laughing at her. I've met her kind before. It's nice to have a woman pursue you once in a while, but the Suzys of the world are downright scary."

Francesca made a face.

"So how do you know her?" he asked.

"She has an office in my building. She certainly doesn't do my interior work, but we've been acquaintances for years. Her client list is huge, and she's got influence. The designers I do use are really great people, very grounded and honest. I love working with them." She tucked a stray curl behind her ear.

Kyle had watched Francesca's lips move, noticing the soft color of her lipstick against her white teeth.

He liked this woman. He liked her more than he had a right to, in light of his recent business dealings.

As if she were reading his mind, she shifted gears and asked in a serious tone, "*Are* you working on something with my father?"

Kyle smiled in a noncommittal way as the announcer approached the podium and got the evening started.

Throughout dinner, he chatted with the various employees who shared the table with them. The Morettis were sitting at their own table, so Kyle had no opportunity to ask Giovanni if there was a problem. He, too, had noticed the guarded, yet anxious look in the older man's eyes when he'd spotted them. For a moment, Kyle had wondered if Giovanni wanted his hide for taking Francesca out.

They were served the standard fare for a charity event—not great, but not bad, either. A waiter busily kept the plates moving and water glasses filled.

Over the course of the meal, Kyle came to realize that Francesca Moretti had done well for herself, building a company that could competently handle large projects. The people who worked for her seemed to idolize her and respect her. They seemed to appreciate her input, and the way she thoughtfully responded to their questions and comments throughout the evening.

When the dessert plates had been cleared, the auction winners began to be announced.

Earlier in the evening, Kyle had laid out a sizable amount for a weekend getaway at Whitetail up in McCall. The lodge was right on the lake, and in all his travels to Boise he'd never been up Highway 55. His odds of winning were slim, but he'd wanted to contribute to a worthy cause.

Francesca had turned her chair a little to view the stage better. He admired the lines of her back, the bare skin at her neck. The baby fine hairs there looked soft and silky, so he reached out and touched her, stroking a finger over the golden skin of her shoulder.

She shivered, a soft moan escaping her lips. For an instant her eyelids closed, as if she was reveling in the feelings.

When applause broke out as a winner was announced, she sat taller, glancing toward the table where the ticket-holder had just risen to his feet to go collect his prize. Kyle studied her clean profile, finding the fullness of her mouth almost too tempting.

Francesca turned back to him and smiled. "I never win anything."

"Yeah," he said with soft exhalation. "But you're lucky."

She slanted her gaze at him. "How so?"

The smile he gave her was deliberately loaded with charm. "You're here with me." He tucked her hand inside his tuxedo jacket so she could feel the steady beat of his heart.

It was more than he should have let her know about him, but he wasn't into games. He liked her. He'd already told her as much.

Franci's palm rested against his chest, slender and warm. She looked into his face, a hundred questions dancing in her lovely eyes.

He wanted to be alone with her, to take her someplace private and hold her. Kiss her.

The weave of his tuxedo felt heavy in the crowded room, where body heat kept the temperature stifling in spite of the air-conditioning units churning out a flow of ventilation. “You want to step outside?” he asked. “It’s warm in here.”

“Sure, that’d be great.”

They walked through the ballroom and then through the lobby. Kyle held the door open for her and, even though the summer evening was warm, the fresh air felt wonderful.

He unbuttoned his tux. Slipping his arms out of the sleeves, he tossed it over his shoulder as he walked toward the large fountain spurting water from the brick pavers in front of the Qwest Arena and Centre on the Grove. When they’d arrived, hours before, little kids had been running through it to cool off. Now only a couple of teenagers rode bikes through the ten-foot-tall jets of spray before pedaling up to Eighth Street.

Kyle and Franci walked to one of the trees and he gazed skyward. “It feels great out here. I love summers.”

“Me, too. We used to go up to Lucky Peak when we were little. Dad had a boat. I miss those days. My brothers were pretty wild.” A far-off look filled her brown eyes, obviously spurred by loving memories.

“So how was it growing up the only girl with three brothers?”

“I learned to be tough,” she said with a smile. “I couldn’t even think about crying if I scraped my knee or took a header off the sofa. If I bawled, I was considered a baby.”

“I wouldn’t mind if you cried, if you had cause.” His comment made her grow quiet, reflective, and as she dipped her head, her sparkling earrings caught the light. "I think it's okay for a woman to show some emotion," Kyle added.

Francesca shrugged. "I can show emotion just fine if I have to. I just don't like to. It's one of those things my dad instilled in me. Better to keep things like that inside and deal with them."

"Is that a Moretti way or the Italian way?"

"It's just…I don't know. The way my family is. We're very private. We keep things to ourselves. If there's a problem, we figure out how to handle it without help from anyone else."

"Sounds kind of limited."

"Not really. It's always worked in the past."

Kyle thought about Giovanni, but only for a moment before he refocused on Francesca.

She sighed, the low neckline of her dress revealing golden skin that looked so soft, so feminine. He felt himself responding to her, wanting to be closer. He wanted to discover how she would fit in his embrace. Acting on impulse, he put his arms around her and drew her nearer, gazing into her upturned face.

If she was wishing he hadn't cradled her in his arms, she didn't show it. Anticipation shone in her eyes and her lips parted in a soft sigh.

Lowering his head, he said, "I've been wanting to do this all night."

Then his lips touched hers and he kissed her, exploring the taste and texture of her mouth. She sighed again and rose up on tiptoe to meet him. Her arms came around his shoulders loosely, as if she weren't quite sure whether or not to fully welcome him.

He felt a tangle of emotions. Fear, matched by unbound desire for a woman he hardly knew. There was a sense of the forbidden he hadn't anticipated, because of a secret only he knew about. But he would never hurt her, Kyle vowed, not for the world.

Franci's breasts flattened against his chest as they stood in the shadows. The taste of her lips was sweet, their slant erotic and warm. He loved how she felt, how she kissed.

The steady beat of her heart thudded against him, and he fought between keeping her close or setting her away again.

When she drew back, he was glad one of them had the resolve to break the kiss, or else he would have pulled the pins from her hair and taken things further.

Francesca licked her lips and shut her eyes for a moment before she said, "I…that was nice."

Her honesty warmed him more than the evening air, touching a part of him that had been empty for a long time. The very sight of her did things to him, made him wonder and fantasize.

"It was," he agreed, though it was unlike him to be sentimental about a mere kiss.

But it hadn't just been any kiss. He'd felt a connection to her he'd never felt toward another woman in all his life.

"There you are!" Giovanni's voice came from the building behind them.

Kyle turned in that direction as Franci's father bore down on them.

"Dad, is everything all right?" Francesca asked, raising a hand to her hair to smooth a wisp at her temple.

"Fine. I just need to steal your date for a minute." Giovanni's gaze wasn't hostile; in fact, he looked worried. "We'll be right back."

Kyle said, "Why don't you go back inside and I'll see you at the table?"

Francesca nodded.

The older man led the way to the railing by the Brick Oven Beanery.

Kyle beat him to the punch, "Look, Giovanni, I like your daughter and there's no ulterior motive for me—"

But the contractor cut him off. "Jagger, I got a call about the bonding paperwork."

Kyle's face was a mask of neutrality, although he was quite familiar with the Grove Marketplace paperwork. So this had nothing to do with Francesca.

With his heartbeat still in overdrive after kissing Franci, he waited for Giovanni to elaborate.

"Some of it's missing. We've got a problem we need to sort out as soon as possible."

CHAPTER TEN

ROBERT FLIPPED THE turn signal on the Suburban and drove down a tree-lined street to his parents' house. His wife sat next to him, and their four daughters were belted in the back seats, watching a DVD. Their intermittent laughter at certain scenes in the movie warmed his heart, and he thanked the Lord for his good fortune in having a wonderful wife and kids.

"So when was the last time you saw your great-aunt Romilda?" Marie asked, studying the homes as they drove by.

"Back in the seventies. She came over with my grandparents for a visit. I have a vague recollection of her. She pinched my cheeks and didn't speak a word of English."

"Your dad's going to be to surprised to see her."

Robert smiled, thinking the plans for the surprise anniversary party were coming along great. His mom had booked Pomodoro for a special forty-five-years-of-marriage celebration, inviting all the family and some close friends without alerting Dad.

His mom had been wondering what she could give Giovanni for a gift. She'd wanted something he wouldn't remotely expect. Both Mom's and Dad's parents had died over the years, but Great-Aunt Romilda, his dad's aunt, was very much alive.

Romilda Tullia Moretti was eighty-three and still lived in the same apartment in Ravello she'd had for the past sixty years, the last seventeen on her own, after the death of her husband.

Robert couldn't imagine living in one place for so long, much less sixty years. He and Marie were already outgrowing the house they'd bought in Meridian two years ago. He wanted to build in Eagle, but prices had gone up so much.

For now, they'd stay put and make do with cramped quarters so Marie wouldn't have to get a job. He liked that she was a stay-at-home mom. So did she.

"My dad's not going to have a clue," Robert said, turning right onto his parents' block. "My mom's been planning this forever, and I can't wait to see the look on his face. He's not going to know what hit him. Mom's picking up Romilda at the airport on Friday, then taking her to Franci's to stay for the night before the party."

"How long's it been since your sister used her Italian?"

"Not since she was out of college. But she said she can pick it up again. She understands it better than she speaks it. Franci had the extra room and wanted to hide 'the surprise' at her house."

"This is going to be a really great party," Marie said. The girls giggled, and she glanced over her shoulder at them. "Do you like *High School Musical?*"

Emelia, who was only five, said, "Troy is cute."

Lord help him, Robert thought. How was he going to manage raising four girls without pummeling the punky teenage boys who would inevitably start coming to the door?

His musings went from Disney movies to the restaurant.

Weeks ago, Robert had began preparing the traditional red peppers the Morettis loved. They were so hot, and he'd Americanized the name for them—Dante's Inferno. He'd had to wear hospital gloves while seeding the peppers, then he'd hung them on a makeshift clothesline in the back room of Pomodoro to dry. This week, all he had to do was roll them in anchovies, then green and black olives, and soak them in olive oil. He planned on making two huge crocks of them.

Fond memories of eating them caused him to smile. When he and his brothers and sister had been little, the other Italians from their church had gotten together for celebrations. The Morettis had always contributed cheese and sausages to eat with the fiery peppers. White towels had been passed out and draped over shoulders, like a dishcloth waiting to dry hands.

Then the eating began, and facial pores opened and sweat ran down the faces of those indulging. They literally dripped from the food's heat.

When Robert had been about seven, curiosity won out. He'd always thought the peppers smelled bad, but figured if everyone was eating them, they must be good.

One bite and his throat had caught on fire, and he'd spat out the offending mouthful as fast as possible. He could remember his father's hysterical laughter to this day.

As the years passed and Robert refined his palate, from boxed macaroni and cheese to pasta and tomato sauce, he gained an appreciation for the traditional peppers and began to make them for the family. Now he served Dante's Inferno on holidays and special occasions, and always with a crisp white hand towel.

He pulled the Suburban into his parents' driveway, noting that John's car wasn't here yet, but Francesca's and Mark's were. Robert made a quick check of the time.

Two o'clock. Dinner would be almost ready to be served.

As he got out of the SUV and went around to open the door for his wife, he hoped his oldest brother would show up, with Zack and Kara.

He felt a moment's sadness that times had changed and things weren't like they used to be, with all of them at the big table for an evening of stories and wine, good food and laughter. While none of them said it, after Connie died Sunday night at the Moretti house just wasn't the same.

IF YOU COULD SNEAK into Mariangela's kitchen, get to the gravy on the stove and dunk a slice of bread into the thick tomato offering without having a spoon thrown at you, you were doing a good job of playing commando.

Too bad Giovanni always got a large serving spoon chucked at him, his bread never reaching the big pot on the front burner with the steam wafting up from under the lid. His successful forays were few and far between; in fact, he was sure he hadn't managed a sampling since 1999.

"*Shooo!* Get away from that pot, *lei il ladro,*" his wife scolded.

Giovanni backed away in a leap, as if he'd been confronted by a watchdog. Why his wife felt she had to guard that gravy, and not let a drop be tasted until serving time, was a mystery to him.

The front door opened, distracting Giovanni. Robert and his crew came inside, and thoughts of sampling the sauce were forgotten.

"Umpa!" Cora declared with a squeal as she ran up to him, and he swung her into his arms. "I'm at Umpa's house!" She laid her cheek on his shoulder and he breathed in her little-girl smell, of candy and sunshine.

Cora was a three-year-old doll with curly black hair and blue eyes, who'd yet to develop the linguistics needed to enunciate "grandpa." To her, he was "Umpa"—even though it reminded him of those purple dwarfs in the Wonka movie. Cora's endearment was something he cherished.

Thirty minutes later, everyone was seated at the long table as Mariangela passed the macaroni and sauce, salads and breads. She put on a spread like nobody's business. His wife was one great cook.

Giovanni looked out at his big clan, happy beyond measure that Zack and Kara had joined John and were seated next to him. No head shrinker had a part in this,

Giovanni was certain. It was good Moretti genes that put some sense into John, so he would rule the roost with a firmer hand.

Zack's hair was longer than Giovanni would have liked—a little on the rebel side if you asked him. Kara was lovely, dark haired and spirited, though she was wearing too much eye makeup for her sweet face.

As Giovanni poured wine into his glass, it felt like old times.

Where daughters-in-law were concerned, Connie had been the best. John would be hard-pressed to find another woman as good as her.

Giovanni moved his gaze to Francesca. His daughter was the light of his life. The pride he felt in her was immeasurable. He wanted her happy, but it would take quite a man to appreciate every facet of this diamond.

He wondered just how involved she was getting with Kyle.

Giovanni thoughts turned to last night's charity event. He'd been more than surprised to see Franci with Kyle Jagger.

Talking to Kyle on the sly had given Giovanni some comfort, in knowing the matter at hand would be taken care of immediately. Not that things could come apart, but he needed the ducks in a row, and Kyle was the only one who could make that happen.

Sometimes Giovanni lay in bed at night and wondered if he'd done the right thing. Wanting something so badly had caused him to compromise in a way he probably shouldn't have. But he had really wanted to make things work. Nobody outside of a handful of people knew what it had taken to get things rolling. Not even his wife.

For that, Giovanni was riddled with guilt. He was barely able to look at the end of the table where Angela was helping Emelia put meatballs on her plate.

He banished guilty thoughts from his head, feeling the press of heartburn begin. It was no wonder he'd felt lousy these past few months. Maybe he should tell his beloved what he'd done.

"So, are you and Kyle dating or what?" Mark asked, wineglass in one hand and a piece of toast in the other.

Franci groaned and looked at Giovanni—as if he could help her. He was just as curious as his son.

"No," she finally said. "We're just friends. I didn't think there would be an inquisition about it."

"Oh, Franci," her mom said, "you had to know we'd all be wondering. And not because it's Kyle, but because you never go out with anyone. We've been hopeful."

"Dad, were you hoping she'd go out with Kyle?" Mark asked.

The *spaghett'* on Giovanni's fork seemed to unravel. "I can't tell any of you what to do—nobody listens to me."

"That is so not true," John insisted with a grin, while helping himself to more ravioli. "You're like the E. F. Hutton of Italians. When you talk, *we* listen."

Giovanni's grip on his fork tightened. "Listening doesn't mean you're doing what I think is the right thing."

"Everyone has to do what's the right thing for themselves." Of course it was Francesca who offered that.

"Is this Kyle dude the right thing for you?" Kara asked, her mouthful of braces exposed as she grinned. "He must be a hottie if you went out with him."

Francesca groaned. "He's just a businessman I know."

"I know him," Mark added, "but I'm not dating the guy."

"No, you're just hitting golf balls with him," she retorted bluntly.

"We haven't been out yet."

"But you will."

"*Ciò basta!*" Giovanni said firmly "That's enough. It's our Sunday, let's enjoy."

"But Grandpa." Zack laughed, his shaggy hair covering his eyebrows. "At Sunday dinners—we *always* talk about stuff that gets people pissed off in this family."

"Zack," John cautioned.

"It's true. I'm not being disrespectful. Our family gets in each others' faces if we think somebody's doing something they shouldn't be doing."

John slowly lowered his fork. He looked in his dad's direction, and Giovanni felt as if he'd swallowed an olive pit. Without anyone saying it, he was reminded of his opinions about John's desire to seek medical—if you could call a shrink that—help.

Neither father nor son had broached the subject since the last time it had come up at the table. It was over and done, as far as Giovanni was concerned. Let John do as he wished, and fix his life how he saw fit. Lord knew Giovanni didn't always captain his ship the way it should be, and there'd been a time or two when he'd sunk.

Sometimes a man had to fall to the bottom in order to climb to the top. Not that he wanted any of his children to reach low points, but it was humbling how God put people on a path that made them stronger when they least thought they could pull out of it.

Mariangela's sweet voice cut the thick air as she raised the pasta bowl. "There's enough ravioli here to feed the whole state. Eat. Eat up, everyone."

"Giddyup, Umpa! Horsey ride!" Cora's cheeks, smeared with tomato sauce, were like big red apples.

Giovanni laughed, as did everyone else at the table. It was a known fact that Grandpa was the best horse in all of Boise. He would get down on all fours, and every one of his children, every one of his grandchildren, had ridden him around on miles of carpet.

Playing horsey for the kids had always made Giovanni happy, putting a glad feeling in his heart and a grateful smile on his mouth.

"After dinner, Cora, I'll play giddyup with you."

She beamed. "I love Umpa!"

Lifting his wineglass, Giovanni said to his youngest granddaughter, *"Salute!"*

Everyone followed his example, glasses lifted in respect as another Sunday at the Moretti table drew to a close.

THERE WAS AN OLD Italian woman sleeping in Francesca's extra bedroom. Great-Aunt Romilda had arrived this afternoon, and Mom had brought her over for the night. The big reveal was set for tomorrow and the anniversary party.

The evening had passed rather creatively for Francesca. Even though she was rusty, she knew how to speak and understand Italian. But Romilda seemed to have her own version. She spoke in slang, with hand gestures, using a lot of archaic phrases and lengthy, run-on sentences that Franci had difficulty trying to figure out.

So she devised a way to entertain Romilda. She'd shown her great-aunt family photo albums, speaking the names of the people in the pictures, describing where the picture had been taken in her basic Italian.

Half the time, Romilda's response to Franci had been, "Eh?"

Romilda Moretti spoke a regional dialect that Francesca, for all her efforts, just hadn't been able to grasp.

Tired from her trip, Romilda had gone to bed by 7:00 p.m. That gave Francesca the rest of the night to catch up.

The week had gone by at a lightning pace. She'd been going to different showrooms, looking at the latest colors and designs. The core and shell of the Grove had to be figured out, and she'd had a planning and zoning meeting for another project yesterday. She'd met with three different trades this week. Each morning, she took notes on the daily project meetings in her dad's trailer.

All this had given her little chance to think about Kyle. Which was a good thing.

She hadn't heard from him.

She didn't know why she'd been expecting to. On Monday, she'd half hoped each time her office phone rang it would be him. By the day's end, she'd told herself he must have been as busy on a Monday as her. Tuesday, she still waited and wondered each time a call was punched into her phone. By Wednesday, her anticipation had dwindled, and she'd had blocks of hours when she actually forgot about him. On Thursday, a niggling thread of upset had woven through her thoughts throughout the day. Had she done something or said something offensive the night of the charity event, to turn him off her? By Friday, she knew it was most likely a lost cause to ever give Kyle another thought. Clearly, he wasn't interested.

So much for her foray into dating. She'd asked a man out and his response had been to drop off the face of the earth.

Perhaps she shouldn't have told Rick James she wasn't going to be dating anyone right now, with the Grove project under way.

It didn't matter. She didn't like Rick and she really didn't have the time to invest, anyway.

But still…

As Francesca finally crawled into bed after a long day, she wished things had turned out differently. She lay beneath the covers, listening to the hearty snores of an eighty-three-year-old woman in the room across the hall. Even with both doors shut, the nasal gasps were fairly loud.

Francesca rolled onto her side and stared at the clock. She thought about all the times she'd looked at that clock, thinking about what her day would be like in the morning, how many phone calls she had to return, what paperwork she had to complete, how many files would be waiting on her desk. Nothing seemed to really matter in the scheme of things. It became so routine, so nothing.

Not that she didn't appreciate her life and her job. She loved everything she'd become, and she was proud of herself.

But yet again, with the sheets cool around her and nobody in the bed beside her to keep her snug and safe, the feeling of being alone threatened to overcome her.

She wondered what it would be like to sleep next to Kyle. Did he lay on his back or his side? Snore or breathe lightly? Was he a morning person or a night person? Did he like to cuddle or was he a bed hog?

The last thought made her smile. She didn't think he was like that. She sensed he would want lots of physical contact.

She briefly thought about the kiss they'd shared and the warm feelings it had evoked. She hadn't been kissed in a very long time. A part of her figured the reason it had been so great was because it had been forever. But deep down, she knew the kiss was special. The fit of his mouth over hers had been perfect.

Those were her final thoughts as she drifted to sleep, only to be jarred awake by the ringing of her cell phone, which she kept charging on the nightstand.

Francesca glanced at the time—3:02 a.m.

Grasping the phone, she managed to say in a sleep-roughened voice, "Hullo?"

The voice on the other end wavered, and at first she didn't recognize it, until Mark called her a name he hadn't used since they were little and he wanted her to do something for him.

"Franny…"

"Mark? What's the matter?"

There was a pause, a sharp note of nothingness. Then he said, "I'm sorry…I've got some terrible news."

The world around her ceased to exist as Francesca held her breath and waited, the endless seconds ticking off an eternity.

"It's about Dad…they think it was probably his heart."

For a moment, Mark's words didn't compute.

Francesca sat upright in the bed, slipped her legs over the side and went to the window. Only later would she realize she'd gone to look outside to see if Mark was out there in her driveway, playing a cruel joke.

"Franny…Dad died."

The last thing she knew, her knees buckled and she dropped to the floor.

CHAPTER ELEVEN

GOD TOOK Mariangela's husband from her the day he gave him to her in marriage forty-five years ago. She didn't understand why, today of all days, the Lord had set this plan in motion.

Father Mike preached that God had everyone's life chapter written before they were even born. Chance encounters, fatal mishaps, loves and tragedies…all were pieces of a whole that had to fit together. And within that tight puzzle of one's life, little feelers reached out and intertwined in other lives, and then those lives connected.

Except for today. It felt as if a glossy bead on her rosary had gone astray, falling from the chain of Mariangela's life.

She sat on the unmade bed, her hands folded in her lap. Her children and grandchildren were gathered in the living room, but she'd asked for a moment alone.

Behind the closed bedroom door, she stared into space with a chilling numbness spreading through her.

Everyone had come over by noon. Tears had been shed, and Mariangela had relayed what had happened.

In the privacy of the room she'd shared with her

husband, she prayed for strength and the will to go on. Within this slice of time, she merely existed. She breathed and her heart beat. Warm blood flowed through her body, but her hands were cold.

She smoothed her hair, realizing she'd neglected to brush it last night. Or was that today? She'd lost track of time.

Dragging in a heavy breath, she willed the numbness to leave her head. Everyone in the living room spoke as if they were dying, too. Or worse, in a funeral parlor. Whispers. The quiet falling of tears and smothered sobs…

Eggshells. They were all walking on them, and it felt as if Mariangela's bones would shatter and break like fragile white shells if one more person called to ask if she was okay.

She was not okay—because tears would no longer come.

And that scared her.

Slowly, she lay down on the rumpled bed with its duvet and feather comforter. She gently laid her cheek on Giovanni's pillow, where a soft depression had been left by his head. She closed her eyes and breathed in the smell of her husband. She did her best to imprint it in her mind, her heart, forever. She knew his scent by memory, because she'd been able to sleep beside him for forty-five years.

She lost herself in prayer; giving her emotions to God was the only way she could get through this. Peace and comfort came from the almighty truth that Giovanni was resting in heaven.

Allowing herself to think through what had transpired over the last twelve hours gave Mariangela a direction for her thoughts.

They'd gone to bed after the kids had left last night. Giovanni hadn't been feeling well. The stress. That Grove Marketplace project was pressure he shouldn't have taken on.

To this day, she had no idea how he'd gotten the bonding. But he had. He'd only told her, "Trust me, Angela. Just trust me on this one and don't ask me." So she hadn't.

At this point, it was irrelevant. She didn't care.

Fanning her fingers across the duvet, she pretended her hand was gliding over Giovanni's chest. He'd been built like a barrel, wide and stout. She'd never thought of him as heavy, although in recent years the doctors had told him he should lose weight.

Guilt now settled over her. She should have put him on a diet, but what could she do? Follow him everywhere and tell him not to eat that doughnut or have that second helping of ziti?

When she'd met him, he'd been in fine shape. Muscled and broad, but with a little bit of a tummy. Not bad. Throughout the years, his physique gave her comfort and strength. Being wrapped in his arms was better than a box of chocolates on Valentine's Day.

Last night, as usual, Giovanni had turned on the television to watch the news for the first few minutes, to get the weather. The man was always wondering what the next day's conditions would be. Could he get up a certain siding? Would the job site be muddy? Would he have to move equipment from one site to another?

She'd read a book beside him, her eyes not following the words, as she'd been mentally finalizing preparations for today's surprise celebration. She'd already cleaned the spare bedrooms, washed all the sheets, made sure the living room was dusted and vacuumed. The kitchen pantry was brimming with food.

Mariangela had planned the forty-fifth anniversary celebration to be held at Pomodoro, and to end with the party moving to her home, the happy guests converging here. She'd wanted the house to be nice for them all.

As the words blurred on the page, she'd set her book down, just as Giovanni took the remote and shut off the television.

Normally she kissed him good-night on the mouth, but he was up and rummaging through the kitchen cupboards, most likely for a stomach reliever. She wasn't aware when he slid under the covers to join her.

She'd long since fallen asleep.

Hours later, Giovanni's muted cry for help from the bathroom woke her up. At 2:21 a.m., the nightmare had begun.

THE FLAG ON THE CRANE at Grove Marketplace flew at half-mast to honor Giovanni Moretti. The stars and stripes billowed softly in the evening breeze, a single light keeping the colors muted, yet visible.

Moretti Construction had shut down at dusk, the trailer locked and dark. Even though Giovanni was gone, and his funeral arrangements being made, the project continued.

During the day, the noise of jackhammers and nail guns resounded off the walls of steel and the concrete floors. Sparks from welders' tools and the steady hum of compressors were the norm. At breaks, subcontractors wearing hard hats would tell stories about Giovanni and smile. They'd laugh and recall times when he had done this or that. Many had worked for him for years, and sharing fond memories made the days pass a little easier.

It seemed as if everyone knew what had to be done, and they did it. This week's project meeting had been put on hold, and subs with any questions had to table them until it was determined who would step in for Giovanni.

No one thought harder about it than Francesca. The attorney had already called her, and the accounting firm wanted to set up an appointment. But they were last on her list. Priorities were to help her mom and the family, work with the church and get the funeral Mass together.

There had never been any question that the business end of Moretti Construction would fall into her lap. Her mother was vice president of the corporation, but Francesca was the secretary. She liked the challenge of paperwork, of taking minutes and keeping things organized. Her mother hadn't wanted any part of that, but she wasn't ignorant when it came to how things were done.

But none of that mattered right now.

Mourning her father hadn't gotten any easier. The earlier shock had begun to wear off, and in its place, a depth of feelings emerged, more tangible, the grief amplified.

Francesca sat on the patio of her home, a glass of wine in her hand. Crickets chirped and other insects made sounds, too. She'd never paid attention to how alive a night was, how noisy.

The neighbor's back light clicked off, leaving Franci's yard in shadows. Her flower beds were in full bloom. The borders of annuals she'd planted months ago from pony packs were bright and colorful. Scents of roses drifted to her, coming from her front yard. The black lab at the end of the block barked. And in the distance, an air conditioner kicked on.

It was late. She'd just come home from her mom's. Mark had been there, with John. Her brother Robert hadn't been able to get away from the restaurant due to a previous commitment he couldn't break, but there was little more he could do at this point, anyway.

Tonight they'd finalized the funeral liturgy, and tomorrow night was the vigil. The funeral would be held on Wednesday.

A hymn that had always touched her father, "Ave Maria," would be played at the Mass processional. John would be giving the welcome. There had been a moment tonight when all of them had reached out and put a hand on John, remembering his own loss and the Mass for Connie.

Francesca would offer the tribute, a role that was daunting, but necessary. In fact, she'd volunteered.

She'd brought out a notepad to try and collect her thoughts in the dark, but thus far, the yellow lined paper was blank.

Closing her eyes, she leaned her head back in the lounge chair and thought about all the things her father had been to her mother, to his family, to those who knew him.

For Francesca, he'd been a friend, a teacher, a confidant.

A tear slipped from her lashes and rolled in a hot trail down her cheek. Her throat closed and she could hardly swallow. It seemed her breath always caught in her lungs whenever she became overwhelmed with the recollection of her father's death.

Wiping her cheeks with her fingertips, she sat upright just as her phone rang.

She had no idea of the time and really didn't feel like talking to anyone, but it might be her mom. Grabbing for the cell in the dark, where she'd left it on the patio table, she didn't bother to read the caller ID before saying, "Hullo?"

"Francesca, it's Kyle."

The sound of his voice was a distant memory, yet oddly welcoming at the same time—as if they'd never lost touch.

She hadn't spoken to him in well over a week. After her dad's death, Kyle had slipped from her mind. Maybe once, in the middle of the night when she hadn't been able to sleep, he'd crept into her thoughts, but only because she'd been hurting and wanting someone to comfort and hold her.

Francesca's mother had received a sympathy card from Kyle, and a floral arrangement had arrived as well. Franci thought it was nice of him. He'd also sent a lush, greens-filled bouquet of pinks and lavenders to Francesca's office.

The card had been simple: "Thoughts of you."

"Hi, Kyle," she murmured, uncertain what to say.

After the charity event, he'd pretty much made things clear he wasn't interested.

"Francesca, I wanted to call you sooner."

She didn't answer, simply waited for him to go on. Her heartbeat had picked up the instant she heard his voice, and it rather unsettled her that he could affect her so.

"In light of everything, I didn't know how you were coping," he said.

The way he phrased the words made her feel as if there could be a double meaning to them. She didn't ask him to elaborate, brushing off the niggling thoughts. Surely it was nothing.

She'd been under tremendous stress lately and had a skewed perception of the heavy burdens in her life. Her focus was nil and her thoughts were, at best, jumbled, if not completely disordered. Bella Design was being run with brief phone conversations to her secretary.

"I'm coping okay." The short response was all she could manage.

"I'm really sorry about your dad. He was a good guy."

The compliment brought fresh tears to Francesca's

eyes. She fought against shedding them while on the phone with Kyle. Even in a crisis, she preferred to appear strong and unflinching.

"Yes, he was." She took in a gulp of air, struggling to keep her composure.

The line went quiet for a long moment, then Kyle asked, "Would you like some company?"

She waited to feel what her gut reaction would tell her, where her thoughts would lead. Would she withdraw, as she'd been doing all week with her girlfriends, not wanting to talk about her dad just yet?

With some relief, and surprise, she replied, "Yes, I would."

"I can be there in five minutes."

"That'd be great."

FRANCESCA GREETED KYLE at the door with a whisper, ushering him inside and leading him down the short hallway to the kitchen.

"Sorry. My great-aunt Romilda is sleeping in the spare bedroom," she said. "She would have gone to my mom's house, but my mom…she's dealing with a lot right now, so Romilda is staying with me. She sleeps pretty soundly, but I'd hate for her to wake up and see a strange man in the house."

Kyle took the opportunity to say with light humor, "I've never been called strange before."

She smiled weakly, but it was a smile nonetheless. "I didn't mean it that way."

"I know that."

Throughout the day, he'd been struggling with calling her. He was glad he had. When he'd found out Giovanni had passed away, Kyle had wanted to be with Francesca. But he knew that with Giovanni's death, the emotional dynamics between them would be altered forever.

Kyle knew things she did not, but now wasn't the time to address them. It wasn't his place to bring to light certain things, anyway. They would come out eventually, sooner rather than later. And when that moment came, Kyle knew he might never again be invited to Francesca's house.

But for now, he wanted to live in the present. To be here for her because she needed him, needed a friend.

Francesca had candles lit, their softly glowing flames wavering under a ceiling fan in the living room. It smelled nice in the house. Like summer rain.

The room was furnished with antiques, the pieces were simple, not cluttered. The feel wasn't country, but rather sleek and inviting, with a touch of nostalgia.

"Would you like a glass of wine?" she asked.

"That'd be great."

"Red or white?"

"Whatever you're opening."

"I have merlot."

"Sounds good." Kyle didn't sit down. Instead, he remained in the kitchen with her. "Can I open it for you?"

"That would be nice."

She handed him a cork-pull and the bottle while she got down two vintage wineglasses.

She wore a blouse and a pair of stone-washed denims—as if she'd stripped off a business suit, kept the blouse on and slipped into old, comfy jeans.

Kyle poured two glasses, then took them toward the living room.

"Would you like to sit outside?" she asked, pressing her hands to the front of her blouse, as if her palms were damp. She looked tired, worn-out, and the pink blush that usually brought life to her cheeks was missing. But she was still beautiful, her thick hair had been swept into a hair claw, and wisps of black framed her face. She had on diamond stud earrings and they caught the candlelight, sparkling like stars.

"Sure," he replied.

She opened the patio door and led him to the lounge chairs. She had lit more candles outside. They winked and wavered, softly scenting the breeze with an oceany fragrance.

There was a planter at the edges of the patio, made of historical bricks. He studied them in the dim light, noticing they all had BOISE stamped on them.

Glancing over his shoulder, he said, "I guess you already had a few of these." His comment didn't readily register with her and he clarified. "The bricks. I gave you one a while ago."

"I know. I keep it on my desk at my office."

"If I'd have known you had so many, I would have gotten you something different."

"I like what you gave me, because it was from you.

That's why I keep it at work. Are you surprised I'm so sentimental?" she added.

"I think it's nice that you are."

When they'd both settled on lounge chairs, he handed her a glass.

"Thanks."

They sat for a long while without speaking. Kyle wasn't sure he wanted to say anything. It was good to just listen to the night, to let things be and not get deeper into emotional dialogue.

After the black-tie event, Kyle hadn't been sure if it was wise to go forward. So he'd stayed away, keeping busy, and telling himself she was just an ordinary woman. But she wasn't.

He'd wanted to come over and see how she was doing, gauge how she felt and find out if she knew his secret.

He didn't want her to know anything right now. It was best to allow her the time to grieve, then heal. But that healing time would be short-lived, as he'd already received a call from the lawyers. They wanted to set up a meeting for early next week.

It was going to be hell at that conference table.

Funny how a tragedy had put opportunity smack in Kyle's lap. His problem was solved, and yet he didn't see this as a blessing.

Before too long, he would have to call Mariangela. But all of that could wait.

Kyle glanced at Francesca. She gazed skyward, as if trying to map the stars and figure out their formations.

She had a deep look of sadness on her face, the feeling echoed in her soft sigh.

"Is there anything I can do?" he offered, feeling out of his element. Most men approached situations differently from women. They were problem solvers, wanting to dive right in and fix things as soon as possible. But there was no way to fix this.

Giovanni wasn't coming back.

"No. But thanks. Getting through the funeral will be the hardest."

"I understand. When my father died, I had a tough time of it. We weren't as close as you and your father, but he was my dad just the same. I thought back to all the times he and I had shared when I was little."

"I've done that, too." Her words choked in her throat. She was crying softly in the dark, and Kyle wasn't sure if he should go over to her or let her have the moment to herself.

He decided to stay put. He sensed she wasn't a weak woman, and didn't like to feel vulnerable. But he recalled how she'd felt in his arms, how her lips had fit against his. He longed for that now, but the timing was all wrong. Yet Kyle couldn't help himself; it was as if his mind had a will of its own. He felt he could fix the situation if he had her in his arms, if he could caress her and protect her, like a man took care of his woman.

But he had no claim to her, and she was going to hate his guts within a few short days. It was inevitable. He saw it coming like a freight train waiting to derail and wreck.

"What's the best memory you have about your dad?" he asked, wanting her to focus on Giovanni's life and not on death.

She was quiet for a long moment, but then started talking. "He let me sit on his lap and drive our old Ford down the street and park it in the garage. I must have been nine or ten." She grew distant, pensive. "There are so many things. He showed me how to use a hammer and nails when I was probably five. Kind of young, but I followed him all over the house, wanting to be his handy-girl."

"I did pretty much the same thing with my dad. It's nice that they were both successful, yet didn't let it spoil them. Although my dad was no businessman."

Francesca glanced at him. "I heard Legacy was in trouble when your father died."

"All true."

Legacy was in trouble once more, Kyle mused, and the solution to the problem had showed up the moment Giovanni passed away. It was illogical, unforeseen, and not how Kyle had played things out in his mind. This situation was last on his list—if on the list at all. He hadn't seen it coming and wished there was another way.

He had no answer, no fix—even though the outcome was as clear as day. He'd be damned by either choice he made. Nobody would be happy by either decision, as both parties would be fighting to control their destiny.

One way Kyle would swim. The other, he would sink….

"I'm sorry," Francesca told him. "But you really took charge and made it work. That's something."

Something of a mess. "Yeah." It was all he could say.

The light above the kitchen sink switched on and Francesca glanced over her shoulder. Kyle flinched as he looked behind him, through the window. An old woman with black hair ribboned with gray stared out at them, her features showing surprisingly few wrinkles.

Spying him, she began speaking in Italian—then disappeared.

"What'd she say?" Kyle asked, facing forward again.

"I couldn't quite tell."

Within a few minutes, the patio door opened and the woman stood in the doorway wearing a pink housecoat and red lipstick. It made sense she'd put a robe on, but it struck Kyle as amusing she'd put a coat of dark color on her lips.

"Fuori da chi quest'uomo siede nel buio con lei?" she asked in rapid Italian peppered with heat, and with her gaze boring into him as if he were a purse snatcher.

The woman's hair was twisted into a thick bun, her brows arched accusingly. Her nose was on the large side, very defined, and in this light, he couldn't be certain, but it seemed as if she had a mole on her chin.

"Il mio amico, grande zia." Francesca's easy response was spoken in a fluid tone.

The aunt rattled off more lyrical Italian, her dialect

thick and the sentences too fast for Kyle to even phonetically try and follow. It didn't matter, anyway; he couldn't understand Italian.

The two women traded words, and finally the old one made cleared her throat pointedly.

"Kyle, this is my great-aunt Romilda." Francesca gazed at her aged relative. *"Grande zia, questo è il Kyle."*

"Lei hanno fame? Posso fare alcuni pomodori."

Kyle looked to Francesca. "What'd she just say?"

"She asked if you're hungry. She can fix some tomatoes."

Great-aunt Romilda had an expectant look on her face, as if ready to spring into action. The timeless ceremonial passage, of feeding people in crisis.... It had been the same with the Norwegians. Anytime anything tragic occurred, leave it to the relatives to bring on a potluck.

Kyle hated to disappoint Romilda, but he'd already had dinner.

The woman's face was set with lines and planes, signs of age that creased the corners of her eyes. But there was a lot of spunk still left in her, the spark of life gleaming in her expression.

He could just see her strolling through the market, a scarf on her head, basket handle in the crook of her arm, giving the vendors a hard time about their wares.

Kyle had a feeling the old girl could disembowel a butcher with her scowl if he so much as tried to cheat her.

"Tomatoes sound great," he finally said, with false

conviction. He'd never really liked a plain tomato. They were okay in a sauce or cooked, but raw in a salad…

He'd have to force himself to choke a few down.

Romilda went into the house and noises reverberated from the kitchen.

"I hope you don't mind," Francesca said.

"No, not at all."

She grew quiet again, then said, "My great-aunt came to Boise to surprise my father on my parents' forty-fifth wedding anniversary."

It hadn't dawned on Kyle how the woman could have flown in from Italy so soon. Realization struck him, and with it, a heaviness in his chest. "When was their anniversary?"

"The day he died."

"Oh, damn…Francesca. I'm so sorry."

"It was bad timing, huh?" She gave a wry smile. "Good one, Dad." The smile only lasted a second or two before she started to cry again.

This time Kyle set his wineglass down, then hers, and brought Francesca to his chaise longue to sit with him. He settled her between his legs, her back to his chest and his arms wrapped snugly around her. She pulled the claw from her hair and let it drop to the concrete. His chin rested on top of her head, in her soft hair, which smelled of shampoo.

Her hands rose to clutch his forearms, keeping him close as she softly cried and let her sorrow out.

In that span of time, he forgot about the Italian

woman in the house and anything else around them. All that was important was comforting this woman who had lost a big part of her heart.

He'd always suspected Franci and her father were quite close. Just one conversation with Giovanni had cinched that. It was painful beyond words to lose a parent. This, Kyle understood.

Francesca's cheek pressed against his upper arm. He'd worn a pullover shirt with short sleeves, and could feel the satiny softness of her neck against his bare skin, the wetness of her tears.

"I miss him so much," she murmured through her sobs. "I can hardly stand it. I want him back. I…I never got the chance to say goodbye."

She cried harder.

Kyle said nothing.

He smoothed his hand over her shoulder, massaged the crook of her neck. He gently stroked her long hair, the outline of her ear, as she grieved.

When she was finally spent, she lay there quietly, her breathing soft and steady. For a minute, he thought she'd fallen asleep.

"Francesca…?"

"Yes?"

"Your dad knew you loved him."

"I know…."

Romilda found them entwined together in the chaise. She carried a plate of food, her formidable brows inching upward, but she made no caustic comment.

Francesca got up and returned to her chair as her great-aunt set the plate between them on the cocktail table.

The rich aromas of garlic, basil and olive oil curled through Kyle's senses, making his stomach growl. So much for not being hungry.

Romilda was talking, going on about something, and all Francesca did was nod.

"What?" Kyle asked.

"Nothing."

"It didn't sound like nothing."

"She wanted to know if we're getting married."

Kyle shot the old girl a look.

Romilda stood there, arms folded, lipstick reapplied. If a stern look of reprimand could singe hair, he'd be bald.

Kyle shot Francesca a quick glance. "All that because we were sitting in the same chair?"

"You had your hands on me. To her, we're as good as engaged."

The great-aunt sputtered and went on.

Francesca smiled, responded to the elderly woman, then said to Kyle, "She questioned the color of your skin—she accused you of being tan. No respectable Neapolitan browns in the sun. We get our coloring from our ancestry, so that makes you unfit for a Moretti. I said the bloodline was thin, but you had some relatives in Sicily."

"But I don't."

"Trust me, it's better if you do."

Kyle shrugged at Romilda and uttered, "A little *Italiano.*"

"Buono." Then she disappeared inside the house, switching the kitchen light off, only to have the soft yellow light spill out into the backyard again seconds later. Apparently she'd changed her mind about leaving them in the dark.

Kyle glanced over his shoulder to see Romilda staring at him, then nodding sternly as if to say, *Don't try anything, buddy.* She left and the kitchen grew quiet.

"You think she's watching?" he asked.

"No." Francesca held the plate out to him. "Sorry, no napkins, and you'll have to use your fingers."

He looked at what she offered. "Where's the tomatoes?"

"They're under the cheese. She made roasted eggplant with cheese and basil, and garlic tomatoes."

"It smells really great."

He took one and ate it, the flavors exploding on his tongue. "It isn't like anything I've ever had. Can you make these?"

"Yes."

"Then maybe I *will* have to marry you."

She grinned, and he was happy to see laughter in her eyes.

They ate and drank their wine, and finally the long day got to Kyle. He told Francesca he'd better get going. She thanked him for coming over and walked him through the house.

The living room candles had been blown out, and down the hallway, soft snores resounded.

"Out for the night," Francesca stated quietly, wrapping her arms around herself and leaning against the jamb of the front door.

He'd stepped outside, onto the porch, and suddenly felt at a loss over how to leave her. He didn't want to. Thoughts of being with her all night washed through him, making him long for closeness.

She was so beautiful, with her long hair cascading about her neck and shoulders. Her eyes were gorgeous, her lips slightly parted.

He said her name in a whisper, unaware he'd even spoken until the sound reached his ears.

He couldn't resist laying his hands on her cheeks, bringing her forward and kissing her lightly on the mouth. She didn't pull away, the fluid heat where they touched burning an imprint into his heart.

She turned her face, changing the angle, but her arms didn't come around his shoulders.

He ended the kiss. It was enough. For now.

"Good night, Francesca," he said.

"Night," she answered.

He turned and headed for the curb, wondering if he'd ever get the chance to come back.

CHAPTER TWELVE

GIOVANNI MORETTI'S funeral had been beautiful, if one could call a funeral that.

Francesca had dressed in a black suit, dark nylons and pumps, and worn smoky glasses for the internment at the cemetery. She'd cried throughout, flanking her mother on one side while John and Mark took the other. As celebrant, John had the most important of their duties to perform, mostly reading.

The Mass had been officiated by Father Mike; the recessional hymn was "The Old Rugged Cross." Francesca had delivered a tribute, a eulogy that had given her fits as she wrote it, but she'd finally finished it in the wee hours the night before. Expressing how much her father had meant to her, she'd also praised him as a husband and trusted businessman, a moral guide to three sons and a role model for his only daughter.

So now it was done. Over. Her father was buried. It was time to move forward, but how?

The weekend had brought sorrow and sadness, a closeness for the family to share. She'd spent it with her brothers and mother, all of them staying near the house. The old kitchen table seemed to be always filled with plates of food. Grande zia Romilda went into overdrive preparing traditional dishes. Nights had been spent reminiscing over childhood memories that Francesca and her brothers brought forth with fondness and smiles. Mariangela spoke in Italian, her native tongue, recollecting the life she'd had with her husband before they had immigrated to America. Romilda added stories of the old country, many about Giovanni.

It was late in the afternoon on Saturday when the travel agent called, informing Mom that Dad had booked a trip to the Amalfi Coast in Italy for their anniversary. The news had sent Mariangela into a fresh spate of tears. True to form, they'd all rallied around her, and Romilda suggested she go when she felt better—because it was what Giovanni would have wanted. Right now, Francesca's mom couldn't think that far ahead.

By midweek, the numbness for Francesca had lessened only slightly. Tomorrow morning, at 8:00 a.m., the meeting with the corporate and family lawyers, and the accountant, was to take place.

Sitting in the construction trailer, with stacks of files and unopened mail surrounding her, Francesca knew that the meeting was going to be a lengthy one.

Mark sat across from her, his tool belt on the desk. They'd just spent the lunch hour together, talking about what needed to be done with Moretti Construction.

It seemed a foregone conclusion that Mark would

take over, but he didn't want the responsibility of corporate taxes, payroll, bonuses and dealing with employees.

"You know that Dad always hoped you'd change your mind," she said to her brother, closing the lid of her take-out box from the Chinese restaurant up the street. "He wanted you to replace him."

"Nobody can replace Dad," Mark said. His black hair was in need of a trim right now, and he raked his hand through it to push the fringe from his eyes.

"That goes without saying," she agreed softly. She and Mark had been a little at odds with each other all day. Tomorrow was on everyone's mind, although there wouldn't be any surprises. Dad's will had been an open book and known to all the family.

The business was to be owned equally by the four siblings, with half shares in the stock to be given to Mariangela. But determining who would be at the helm of Moretti got complicated. Dad had always said Francesca had a head for figures and paperwork, but she already had her own company to manage.

Giovanni had wanted Mark to take over, since his youngest son was familiar with the nuts and bolts, the hands-on running of job sites. It had been discussed over many a Sunday night dinner, and Franci could only assume that while Mark balked at the moment, he would eventually step up to the plate and do what needed to be done. She'd be more than happy to handle her share of the paperwork, but running a complex project such as the

Grove Marketplace when she had Bella Design to oversee would be a challenge beyond compare.

"I think you should do it, Mark. It's what Dad wanted."

One of the subs opened the trailer door, asking Mark to check out something on the site. While he was gone, Francesca's thoughts went from filling shoes that were too big to fill, to trying to organize the piles of papers on her father's desk.

There was so much to do, so much to catch up on.

She got a lump in her throat when she glanced at the coffeepot and saw it was empty. Her dad had always put on decaf at 3:00 p.m.

In the coming weeks and months, even years, there would be so many other things that would be different. How did a person get through it all without falling apart?

A tear slid down her cheek and she brushed it away.

Her cell phone rang from within the confines of her purse, and she finally answered on the fourth ring, almost letting the call go to voice mail. She really wasn't in the mood to talk to anyone.

"Francesca, it's Kyle."

The resonant sound of his voice seemed to lift a weight from her shoulders. She suddenly was wide-awake and alert. She didn't know how he could do that—fill her when she felt as if she were on empty.

"Hey, Kyle."

"How are you doing?"

"All right."

There was a lengthy pause, then he said, "Let me take

you out tonight, Franci. No street-vendor hot dog or piece of overcooked chicken at a charity event. A real dinner."

Torn, she spoke the first thoughts on her mind, when she'd rather have simply said yes. "I'm knee-deep in work and it's just not a good time. I've got so much going on."

"You need to get away from all that right now. I'll pick you up. Where? The house or your office?"

Guiltily, she looked at all the stacks of files, invoices and mail. She couldn't face it right now. It was too much. She didn't know where to begin.

"My house," she agreed.

"Thirty minutes?"

"See you then."

KYLE WAS TEN MINUTES LATE, which was okay with Francesca. She'd been held up at the trailer by a twenty-minute phone call from a contractor who needed immediate help with a problem on one of Moretti's other projects. Doing the best she could, she'd offered several possible solutions and some phone numbers to the man.

At home, she washed her face and reapplied her makeup. Running a brush through her hair, she left it to flow over her shoulders and down her back. She changed from her skirt and blouse into white capris, a black top and sling-back sandals.

As Kyle rang the doorbell, she realized she was starving. It had been a tiring day and she'd only nibbled at the Chinese food she and Mark had ordered.

"Hey," she said, locking the door behind her. "Thanks

for the dinner invite. I guess with everything going on, I didn't think I had to get out. But I do. I appreciate you thinking of me."

"Honey," he said in a whiskey-soft voice, "I'm always thinking about you."

Pleasant chills tingled across her bare arms, and she was glad she'd grabbed a black long-sleeved sweater.

Kyle opened the truck door for her and they took off through the downtown, cutting across Idaho and Main Streets.

"Where are we eating?" she asked, thinking the majority of restaurants were to their left.

"McCormick and Schmick's."

Puzzled, Franci tried to remember where that was. So many new restaurants cropped up in Boise overnight, especially on Eagle Road, a main thoroughfare she didn't travel often. "I've never eaten there."

"It's really great. They're well known for their extensive fish menu."

"You said you don't eat fish."

"I don't. But you do."

"Oh."

He reached over and took her hand. "Don't worry about me. They have a killer New York strip steak tender enough to cut with a butter knife."

The warmth and caring in his touch was almost unbearable. Franci swallowed tightly, feeling as if her heart had shifted. His kindness brought tears to her eyes, for a variety of reasons she didn't care to examine.

She gazed out the truck window as he headed onto the freeway connector that led out of the downtown. He went toward Broadway, not Eagle.

When he exited at Vista and turned into the airport, she glanced at him with a questioning lift of her brows. "What are we doing?"

"Going to dinner."

"At the airport?"

"No," he replied, releasing her hand and using both of his to steer the truck toward the security gate. "We're using my airplane to get there."

"I didn't know you had one," she blurted.

Reaching into his back pocket for his wallet, he said, "There are a lot of things you don't know about me."

An hour later, they were halfway to their destination. Seattle.

Francesca had been surprised, yet not surprised, that Kyle did things out of the ordinary. He was anything but ordinary.

The noise in the small cockpit of the Piper Malibu would have been deafening had it not been for the Bose communication headsets they wore. Franci looked out the windshield, dead ahead. She still had a hard time glancing down.

She wasn't afraid of heights in a commercial plane—there was a lot more metal and bolts surrounding her and keeping her safe. This was her first time in a small aircraft, and she'd initially worried that she'd panic. But Kyle was patient and explained everything to her.

He made her tour the plane with him for a preflight check, showing her what was what and how it worked. She'd felt somewhat better as she'd sat in her seat and put her belt on.

There wasn't a lot of room in the cockpit, but the leather seat was far more comfortable than she'd anticipated.

He'd brought snack food—raisin bread and American cheese sandwiches with bottles of iced tea. She didn't know what to make of the odd sandwiches, but she was hungry enough to appreciate a bite to eat before dinner.

"These are interesting," she said as she chewed.

"What do you mean? They're good." Kyle popped a quarter of a sandwich into his mouth, then washed it down with a long drink of icy tea. There was a cooler in back filled with pop and bottled water.

"That's the Columbia River." Kyle pointed toward her right. She squinted through the side window and nodded quickly before facing forward again.

"You're all right," Kyle assured her, placing his hand on her knee.

"You'd better drive." Her note of caution was met with a laugh.

"This is equipped with autopilot." He motioned to the broad instrument panel with the GPS and dual control yokes—one for her and one for him—that kept the plane level. "I could keep us going without holding on to anything."

She took his hand and placed it on the yoke. "But don't. Okay?"

He smiled, then spoke into his microphone, his voice clear in her headset. "Okay."

They landed at Boeing Field rather than Sea-Tac, which was always bustling with large commercial airlines taking off and landing, one right after the other.

Two hours after leaving Boise, Kyle taxied the Piper Malibu into his private hanger, where he kept a 1988 GMC pickup. He told her it was his beater truck, the one he ran to job sites, more often than not, with materials stashed in the bed.

After tackling heavy traffic on the freeway, Kyle got off on Sixth Street and turned toward the ocean. He knew exactly where he was going. She was in awe of the ease with which he managed the one-way streets, knowing just where to park.

"Grab your sweater," he said, coming around to open the door for her.

Once there, he didn't readily step aside. He stood blocking her exit, his body tall and broad, his arm raised on the truck's cab.

Looking intently at her, he studied her as if he was trying to memorize her entire face. A furrow marked his brow, and his eyes seemed sad, as if he was conflicted somehow.

"What's the matter?" she asked, her voice on the shaky side. He could make her react strongly to him with just a look.

Kyle leaned toward her, kissed her softly on the mouth, then whispered, "Thanks for coming with me."

Her heart turned over in response, but she had little time to think about that as he locked the truck and took her down the block to McCormick and Schmick's.

A chalkboard menu on the sidewalk listed the fresh catches of the day. The aromas that greeted them were wonderful and made her mouth water. Dark wooden floors ran throughout, with brass accents and cozy booths that were perfect for intimate conversation.

They were seated by a window. Kyle declined wine, since he had to fly back to Boise, but he urged her to order a glass if that's what she wanted. She did.

They talked about mundane things for the longest time, nothing concrete or even noteworthy. Until he brought something up that gave her pause.

"Franci, if things were different I'd fall in love with you."

The wineglass in her hand came to an abrupt stop on its way to her mouth. "Where did that come from?"

"I'm not sure. Only that I've been thinking about how easy it would be to love you."

"Oh." She looked away, trying to rein in her scattered thoughts. Truth be told, she'd had the same thought about him.

Kyle was the kind of man she would love to have in her life on a permanent basis. She wasn't good with coyness, flirtation or playing hard to get, the things the date squad insisted had to be in place in order to land a man. Franci didn't think she'd been any of those things with him—she'd just been herself.

Meeting his gray-green eyes, she dared to respond as honestly as she could. "I know what you mean."

"I kind of thought you would. Which makes the future even harder to predict." He ran his fingertips along his jaw, and for the first time this evening, she noted a stress in him she'd failed to pick up before.

"Now I don't know what you mean," she said.

She waited for his reply, but none was forthcoming. He sat on his side of the booth, adjusting the band of his watch and rolling up his sleeves. He'd worn a white shirt with jeans, and had taken along a leather coat for her to wear as backup, since he didn't want it. He'd said Seattle nights even in summer could be misty and damp.

She watched him with acute awareness, her mind fluttering anxiously. His nostrils flared, and his preoccupied expression changed to a slight scowl.

"I wish I could tell you what's going on."

"Going on? I don't understand."

Their server arrived with their dinner orders just then and Kyle turned the conversation to points of interest in Seattle, asking if she'd been to any of them.

Two hours later, they were in the black sky on their way back to Boise, neither of them talking, both immersed in thought.

More comfortable in the airplane at night, because she couldn't see how far below the ground was, Francesca looked out the window at the intermittent lights that dotted the countryside. They'd travel a fair distance with nothing but inky darkness broken by a light or two, then clusters of lights appeared as towns and cities came and went.

Melancholy overtook her.

Kyle must have been a mind reader, because he said something wholly profound. "This is what your dad's looking at, Franci. He's seeing the beauty of the night, just like you are."

She wiped her cheeks, doing her best to keep herself together. She couldn't trust her voice. All she could do was nod.

She *had* been thinking about her dad and missing him. Kyle's perception astonished her.

They landed in Boise and were soon back at her house. Kyle walked her to the front door and took her in his arms. He held her for the longest time, and she clung to him, unwilling to shed more tears, or to let him go. She welcomed the contact, reveled in the way he felt next to her body.

His fingers caught her chin and tilted her head, and then he kissed her, but without the simple tenderness he had in the past. This kiss was filled with raw passion and need. He ran his hands up her back, into her hair. His mouth crushed hers, and they both moaned.

There was no easing into this. Their passion was driven by fluid heat and attraction, a desire that left her shaken, yet wanting all he offered. And more.

His lips seared hers possessively. She gave freely in return, a fiery need curling low inside her.

If this was lust, so be it.

Maybe she was already in love with him, and just didn't know how to process that emotion. It had been so long. She had to be in love in order to have such a strong reaction toward Kyle.

Just when she thought she was drowning and didn't want to come up for air, he broke the kiss and held her tightly—so tight she thought her ribs would break.

"Sorry," he murmured into her hair, grasping a fistful and burying his nose in it, as if breathing in the scent of her shampoo. "I'm so sorry. I wish I could fix things. I really wish I could."

"Kyle?"

He set her away from him. "You'll know soon enough." A somber tone infused his words, as if he were burdened by some terrible news.

Her earlier thrill over their kiss dissipated. Something was wrong.

"What's the matter?" Franci asked.

"Earlier this evening, I talked with your mom. I told her first, and I asked her to allow me to tell you." The polite, tight tone of his voice was like a fist squeezing her chest.

"Tell my mother what? Tell me what?" Caution caused the hairs on the back of her neck to rise. This was serious.

"Tomorrow, you're going to meet with the lawyers and the accountant."

"Yes, I know." She felt suddenly guarded and cool. It was difficult to evoke warmth when the air around her was suddenly chilly.

"I'm going to be at the meeting."

It took a moment for his words to register. "Why?" she asked.

"I can't get into it now. I just wanted you to be aware that I have some business with Moretti Construction that requires I be there to see how everyone wants to handle everything."

"What 'everything'?"

"That's all I can say, Francesca. I'm sorry." There was a note of remorse in his tone, and she believed he *was* sorry. "I just wanted you and Mrs. Moretti to know, so you wouldn't be surprised to see me. It's purely a business reason and my sympathies for your family are still very much in place. I'm sorry about your dad."

She tempered her curiosity, so she'd sound affable, reasonable. "I know you are."

After all, what could be so traumatic about him being there? Legacy and Moretti had been on friendly terms, albeit rivals for the Grove project. They'd weathered the outcome and had both accepted it.

"I'll see you tomorrow."

He walked to the curb, and she was left staring after him in wonder.

KYLE WORE A SUIT to the meeting, something he wouldn't have normally done, but he felt compelled. The tie cut into his throat, where a knot was already settling, anyway.

He arrived thirty minutes early, sitting in the large room with his briefcase on the table before him. Inside were documents that very few people knew about, and within the hour, everything would be exposed.

It had come to this—something he hadn't anticipated, but at the same time, had landed in his lap.

He didn't know whether to laugh or damn himself. Either way he looked at it, he wouldn't get what he wanted without causing hurt to those he loved.

Did he love Francesca Moretti?

He felt himself falling for her, and hard. For the first time in too many years to recollect, a woman had actually gotten his attention and captured his thoughts on a daily basis.

He caught himself thinking about her constantly—whether on the golf course, drinking a glass of wine and looking at the Boise city lights, or in his construction trailer, in between fielding calls that came in throughout the day. He could be in a boring meeting, driving in his car, even in the shower…and her face and voice would come to him. He'd find himself smiling, thinking of her with fondness and warmth. Recalling the feel of her body, the taste of her lips.

The door opened and the accountant came in, and soon after, the Morettis and the lawyers.

Kyle's gaze followed Francesca as she took a seat. He didn't miss the fluid way she walked in those high heels, her rigid posture, the questions in her brown eyes as they met his.

She was confused and worried, as he'd known she would be. There'd been no way around it, and for that, he was sorry. But he couldn't let her come in here blind, not having any indication that something out of the ordinary would transpire. That something beyond his control would be revealed.

The lawyers were Brown and Holt. They looked like bookends in their dark flannel suits, whiter than white shirts, dull ties. They smelled like drugstore cologne, just the way he remembered them from their previous meeting.

He'd not met the accountant, and assumed it had to be the woman in the tasteful dress. He noted the others addressed her as Mila.

The Morettis sat in a group on one side of the long conference table. Kyle recognized the chef and the older brother from the dinner he'd gone to at Pomodoro. Mark nodded to him casually, as if curious, but not unduly so. Kyle assumed either Francesca or Mrs. Moretti had told the rest of the family that he'd be at the meeting.

Mariangela Moretti looked in his direction once, nodded in polite acknowledgment of his presence, but nothing further. They came bearing the trappings needed for such a meeting—briefcases, notepads and spare eyeglasses required to read fine print.

Mila cleared her throat, poured a glass of water from the icy decanter in the middle of the table, then cleared her throat once more.

A dull ache began to throb in Kyle's head, knocking at his skull. He wished he weren't here.

The accountant had a succinct voice, a no-nonsense

approach to getting things started. "Thank you for coming," she said. "This is a difficult time, I know. We all loved Giovanni and we're so sorry for your loss."

Mariangela gave a wan smile of appreciation. The lines on her face gave away her stress, and a tired look dulled her eyes.

"As you know from Giovanni's will—" Mila glanced to the pair of lawyers, who'd apparently drawn up the documents "—upon his death, the board of directors—that being his wife as vice president—would inherit controlling shares of Moretti Construction. All other family members would remain as shareholders—this being Giovanni, Jr.—known as John—plus Robert, Mark and Francesca."

Kyle studied Francesca's facial expressions and body language, trying to read her emotions. He couldn't. All of the Morettis were a closed book.

The accountant went on. "The company would continue as a corporation and his estate would own his shares—again this being his wife, in accordance with his will. Shares will become part of the estate, a taxable estate, with Mariangela now the main holder unless any of you care to buy her out. Or the funds can go into a trust and be controlled by all. There are different ways to handle this." Mila looked at Kyle, and when she did, the others did as well.

Here comes the bomb, he thought. His muscles tensed and he inhaled a slow and deep breath.

"However," Mila cautioned in a brisk tone, "that being

said, also to be enacted are specified legal agreements. And this is where we have an unusual circumstance."

"What unusual circumstance?" John asked.

John Moretti was a lawyer, but Kyle knew he hadn't handled this transaction, nor a huge majority of the Moretti business. John was a divorce attorney and didn't specialize in corporate law. Even so, he had a distrustful air about him now that Kyle recognized as potentially dangerous. Although there would be no loophole found in this particular clause that involved him. It was airtight.

Kyle thought back and remembered the phone call he'd taken from Giovanni this past spring. Initially, after hearing the man out, he'd declined the proposal. But Giovanni had been convincing. He'd drawn a sentiment card—the past history with Kyle's father, Parr—and if he'd been alive, he would have agreed.

Only now, in light of what had happened, Kyle wasn't so sure Parr Jagger would have made such an arrangement.

There was no point in wondering about it further. Kyle had done what he'd done.

The lawyers, Brown and Holt, stepped in, shuffling through papers like Vegas poker dealers. Brown spoke first. "There was an agreement made between Mr. Moretti and Mr. Jagger that, I am sorry to say, will have to be enacted."

"Yes," Holt concurred. "It was never Mr. Moretti's intention, of course, for us to all be sitting here. But Mila is right, under any normal situation, the will and articles of Mr. Moretti's last wishes, along with tax laws, etcetera, would be in effect, and Mr. Jagger, whom you've all met, wouldn't be sitting here with us."

"Just tell us," Francesca said, her tone brittle.

Frankly, Kyle was tired of the drawn-out affair, too, and if it wasn't said soon, he was just going to spill it and dispense with all this legalese.

Brown took a drink of water, then slipped his glasses onto his beaklike nose.

"An agreement between the parties of Giovanni Moretti and Kyle Jagger was entered into on April 23, that..." He paused as he skimmed the documentation, then lifted his chin. "In layman's terms, Giovanni Moretti used the entirety of his stock as collateral in a deal with Mr. Jagger."

Mariangela's face paled. "And this means?"

"It means, Mrs. Moretti, that while your husband intended for you to carry on with controlling shares of Moretti Construction, that can't be. Mr. Jagger, because of the death of Mr. Moretti, now has the stock in his name and has the majority interest of your company. It's all perfectly legal," he added quickly and in a dry tone, as if that would be the next question brought to the table.

All of the Morettis glared hard at Kyle, as if he were Blackbeard incarnate. He didn't flinch or change his demeanor. "It needs to be said, Brown, that I didn't approach Mr. Moretti with this venture, nor did I embrace it without reservations."

"That is true," the lawyer responded.

Holt added, "I can attest to what Mr. Jagger is saying.

Even up to the date of signing, there was concern on Mr. Jagger's part, but he did allow the deal to happen."

"Why?" Francesca's soft voice broke through the tension, her eyes questioning. He ached for the hurt she must be feeling, wished he could do something. "I don't understand. Why would my father make an impulsive arrangement with you with respect to his collateral?"

"It wasn't impulsive," Brown said. "We counseled your father at length on the pros and cons and, in the end, it was his decision."

"But why?" she asked once more.

Holt started to answer, but Kyle interrupted him. "May I?"

The lawyer nodded.

"I'm sorry, this has to really be upsetting for you. Please know that I didn't look for this, nor expect the outcome to end this way. I thought I was doing your father, and husband, a favor—one that I'd never imagined to be repaid in this manner." Kyle took in a breath. "He had to have bonding in order to get the Grove Marketplace project—"

Mariangela's heavy gasp echoed off the walls. "No..."

"Apparently, the project's cost was beyond his ability to finance so the financial folks balked at his proposals. He came to me and asked if Legacy would put up the money and bonding, and he'd use controlling shares of Moretti as collateral."

Mark folded his arms over his chest, his nostrils flaring. There wasn't the animosity there that Kyle had expected. In fact, it was a tightly reined confidence. "We'll just buy the shares back."

The tension in the room was so thick it was like a veil.

Brown and Holt huddled, then looked at Kyle. "Mr. Jagger, if you don't mind, we need to wrap this up with the family only."

Nodding, Kyle rose to his feet, never more glad to get out into the fresh air than he was at that moment.

CHAPTER THIRTEEN

AT TEN IN THE MORNING, Pomodoro was closed to diners. A cleaning crew was just finishing, the steady sounds of a vacuum coming from the corner.

The aroma of espresso was strong, blending with that of onions and crushed garlic as the cooks began to sauté them in olive oil. Robert had been in and out of the kitchen to give orders to his staff, but now he sat with the rest of the Morettis in the dining room.

Mariangela finished her second cup of coffee, declining one of the Italian pastries Robert had brought out.

It had been a long night of prayer and heartache. Giovanni's death had taken its toll on her, but to have a bomb like yesterday's broadside them all… It had been more than she could bear.

Last night, she'd thrown in the towel and taken two of those insomnia-headache relievers. They had worked only marginally and today she felt punchy.

She would have loved to wake up to a cup of Romilda's espresso, a sure thing to make her instantly wide-awake. But the dear aunt had flown back to Italy early yesterday. As she'd checked her bags, she'd talked nonstop about Mariangela coming to Ravello, because it was as Giovanni had wished.

Right now, she couldn't think that far ahead. She could barely think about the next minute and what was in store for her.

John led the discussion in this morning's gathering, but thus far, it had been mostly a rehash of yesterday.

Mariangela felt tears swim in her eyes. "This bonding contract with Legacy Constructors is probably one of the few things I didn't know about in regard to your father's business dealings. But he wanted the job so badly he made an arrangement he knew none of us would approve of." Looking to her oldest son, she said, "Isn't there any way to fix this?

Her emotional state was fragile, and she hated how weak she felt.

"There's nothing to fix," Francesca interjected. "We're dealing with fact."

Her daughter looked smart and polished for not having slept most of the night.

She wore an ivory business suit, her long hair partially caught in a gold barrette. Her lipstick had been lightly applied and her eyes were made up with a soft taupe shadow, with dark mascara on her lashes.

Robert said, "So explain it to me one more time, Franci. How could this have happened?"

"Kyle Jagger and Dad had a side note, a silent partnership over the bonding for the Grove Marketplace. It's like an insurance policy that doesn't have a buyout value. In essence, they co-joined Legacy and Moretti Construction using stock shares."

"Can't we just buy the stock back from Jagger?" Robert asked.

"If we had the money, but we don't."

"Which is why your father went to Kyle," Mariangela added in a clear tone. She drew her shoulders back, drawing in a fortifying breath. "John, just because Kyle has over fifty percent of the company, that doesn't mean he gets that stock today, does he?"

"No, but he does have controlling interest."

"What does that mean?" Mark asked.

"It means Kyle has a large stake of the company Dad built from nothing," Franci stated with a frown. "There has to be a way out."

John said, "We have to get the Marketplace finished, turn it over to the owner, get paid and then buy Kyle out of the note. We just need to speed things up and bring the job in before schedule."

Mark shook his head. "It's impossible, given the calendar we'd have to keep. And even if we could trim a few weeks off, we're still talking a year or so before we'd be remotely close to completion on a job the magnitude of the Grove. The subs could never do it. And besides, we don't know what Kyle plans on doing."

"That's right, nobody asked him," Robert said, before fielding a quick question from one of his chefs and sending the man back into the kitchen.

"We didn't get a chance to ask him anything yesterday," John said, pouring more coffee. "We were all broadsided."

The group grew quiet, Mariangela pondering the situation as she closed her eyes a moment to think. This grave and surprising turn of events was almost beyond her comprehension.

When she finally spoke, her words were as cool and clear as ice water. "The next obvious step would be to have a meeting with Kyle and ask him what he intends on doing. One of us should talk to him."

"Why not all of us?" Mark asked.

"Because we don't all need to ask the one question. I think it would be less threatening if he had to talk to only one of us rather than an army of Italians ready to go to battle."

"He started it," Robert said.

Mariangela slowly shook her head. "No, he didn't. And I hate to say this, but he helped us out. Without him, your father's dream wouldn't have gotten off the ground. We actually owe Kyle a debt of gratitude."

"But he's ending up with more than gratitude," John pointed out. "He's ending up with us financially in debt to him."

"We send Franci." Mark's statement drew everyone's gaze.

"Me?" she squeaked. "Why me?"

"He likes you and you're pretty enough to talk him into what's best for Moretti."

A few brows lifted in obvious skepticism.

Mark gave a vague smile. "Oh, come on. We need all the help we can get."

FRANCESCA DIDN'T WANT much of anything to do with Kyle.

It all made sense now why he'd been so nice to her, taking her to Seattle for that wonderful dinner. Over the last twenty-four hours, pieces had fallen into place. No wonder he had been at the party at Pomodoro, invited by her father. And of course he'd wanted to get on her good side by taking her for a ride in his plane, by taking her in his arms and kissing her.

She forgot about a lot of things when his mouth closed over hers. Mostly, that it took a long time to truly get to know a man, and even then, when you thought you knew him, you really didn't.

She thought back to Paul DiMarco in college. They'd dated for quite some time, talked about getting engaged, and even went to premarital counseling—only for her to discover the man she thought she knew had answers to the counselor's questions she never would have guessed. They were so far off the same page they might as well have been in different books. So she'd scratched off that romance as a learning experience.

Then there'd been Eduardo. She'd let down her guard and been swept off her feet, falling in love and into bed with him for a whirlwind affair. Huge mistake. It had been a very bad relationship that went nowhere fast.

She'd learned hard lessons and she'd vowed to err on the side of caution where men were concerned. She thought she'd been doing a fairly decent job of it with Kyle, letting him into her life by small degrees, until she realized she wanted to have him be part of her bigger picture. The whole package.

And then yesterday morning had happened.

Kyle should have told her that night on her patio when he'd held her, comforted her, eaten the tomatoes Romilda had offered. Forget timing; he should have spilled everything about the entire sordid deal, and confessed all that he knew.

Why he'd kept silent was something she couldn't reconcile. He'd owed her the truth. He could have given her family clarity, before lawyers and an accountant had to bring the arrangement to light.

But that was water under the bridge and there was nothing she could do about it now. Except pray she could forgive him. And she'd find out about that in the next few minutes, as he was due to meet with her.

Franci waited for Kyle at the reception desk, tracking the time on her wristwatch. It was the end of the day and everyone in the building had gone home. She was alone at Bella Design, staying after hours to catch up with the mountain of work she had fallen behind in.

She heard the elevator ding, the doors opening.

Kyle stepped out and headed toward her, wearing jeans and a polo shirt, sunglasses resting on his head. He was tall and assured and handsome.

She put on an impersonal façade.

"Hi," she said, not spending much time looking at him, just glancing at his shirt and jeans, the way his hair appeared windblown and messy. She ushered him directly to her office. It looked out over the city, where the sunset was washing the buildings with an orange tint.

"Nice," he commented, appreciating the city view.

"Thanks." She'd already cleared a chair for him. It wasn't like her to have clutter, but her secretary had been stacking "to do" piles on one of the plush chairs. Francesca had moved the paperwork to the credenza and now offered him the chair across from her desk.

Even though she was upset with him, she acted cordial. "Can I get you anything to drink?"

"I'm good." Kyle sat and splayed his hands over his knees, settling in.

Franci hoped she came across as matter-of-fact. She had the contract in front of her that Kyle and her dad had signed, but it seemed a moot point now to even show it to him. He'd already seen a copy of it; he'd signed it in front of a notary. There was no purpose in using the document as leverage.

She really didn't have any leverage at all.

She took a sip of her diet cola, the caffeine buzz beginning to give her a headache. She'd been on the go all day, and was on a path to burnout.

Giving Kyle a furtive glance, she shuffled through papers on a ruse. She needed a moment to collect herself. She'd been falling for the handsome man across from her, her emotions tangling in a knot as they'd spent time together.

She never could have predicted this situation—her stomach upside down, her heartbeat jagged. Even after all she knew about him, he still could affect her in ways beyond her control.

Once, she would have welcomed him into her heart. Now she wanted him out of the picture.

He represented everything chaotic in her life. A mixture of the unknown, the hard-to-believe, and yet there was still that draw toward him that baffled her.

"Francesca, I want to apologize for putting you and your family in this position." Kyle's words pulled her from her thoughts.

She gave him her full attention.

"I want no part of owning your company." Removing the sunglasses from the crown of his head, he swept his hand through his hair. "I didn't mean for things to turn out this way."

He grew reflective and she said into the silence, "I believe you."

She did. There was no malice behind the sidebar contract. It had never once occurred to her that Kyle had done the deal to make a personal gain.

If only he'd told her about it sooner.

"I wish you would have told me about this beforehand." Her voice was soft, distant.

"I couldn't," he replied. "I gave your father my word."

"But you could have before Seattle."

"Not true. When I told Giovanni I'd let the agreement stay buried for as long as it needed to, I meant it. It wasn't my place to tell any of you. Giovanni had a contract drawn up that was controlled by Moretti lawyers and your accountant. It would have been unethical of me to talk out of turn about it. That's their job."

Everything he said was the truth. His character was above reproach and, in that moment, she did forgive him.

Had she been in his position, she would have done the same thing.

Even so, she had difficulty letting it go. "I understand. But you have to realize that it was a shock for me to hear about it. You and I have been getting to know one another…beyond business."

"Franci, when I give someone my word, I keep it. When your father and I made that agreement, only the lawyers were privy to the signing. If Giovanni and I could have, we would have simply shook hands and made a gentleman's agreement. But you can't do that and have the contract be legal and binding."

"I understand," she repeated, wishing she didn't. "So what do you want us to do?" She slipped out of her high heels, kicking them underneath her desk.

His response was immediate. "Buy back my stock."

It was the answer she couldn't resolve. "I'm sure you know that it would be next to impossible for

Moretti. Which is why my dad made the bonding agreement with you in the first place."

"I was hoping you might have come into some funding from a different source."

She got his implication loud and clear, glad he had the class not to come right out and ask about a life insurance policy.

Of course her father had had one in place, but the amount her mom would receive wouldn't cover the exorbitant cost of buying the stock from Kyle Jagger.

"We haven't," Francesca said, her voice like brittle glass. This was harder than she'd anticipated.

Kyle sat there looking just as frustrated as she felt. It was as if he had a demon on his back that she didn't know about, something that made him shift in his seat and grow uncomfortable.

"Are you sure? I really don't want the stock, Francesca. I just want my money back."

She licked her lips regretfully. "We can't. So now what?"

He leaned back in the chair, crossed his legs and sighed heavily. "I don't know."

Kyle stared at her for a long time, long enough to evoke shivers in her body. This was no speculative perusal; he was looking deep into her core, trying to read her. She feared her emotions betrayed her, and he could tell she was upset beyond words, that she was torn up inside to have been put in the position of negotiator. Having her family send her to do the dirty work wasn't fair. Just because she knew Kyle better than any of them…it didn't mean she could pull this off and do it right.

She felt unraveled, undressed. She was cold and hot at the same time. She wanted to get up and walk away, not look back. It angered her that she allowed him to get to her.

"I'm sorry you can't help me out," he conceded. "But I have some pressing things going myself, and I may have to make choices I'd rather not."

"Like what?" she asked before she thought better of it.

"Like things I have to figure out." He got to his feet, and she could tell he was very agitated—something she'd never seen in him before.

As he headed toward the door, he said, "Do me a favor—try and get the money. See if you can call a note due, get a loan on a loan. *Anything.* I need out of this deal. I need out of it as soon as possible."

NEIL BEVILAQUA HAD FLOWN into Boise on business. He and Kyle met for dinner at Guido's, a downtown pizzeria. They talked over slices of cheese-and-sausage pizza, and cold beer.

"So it sounds like your hands are tied." Neil had been filled in on the latest with Moretti.

"Seems like it." Kyle took a drink of beer, then said, "If I had known what I would be in for, I never would have made that deal with Giovanni Moretti."

"Not true. I know you, Kyle. You're a good guy and you would have wanted to help him out. The problem," Neil went on matter-of-factly, "is your mom."

"Unfortunately, you're right."

Kyle had caught up with the private investigator via phone, and then perused the printed report that had been overnighted.

Nothing in Ralph Gunderson's personal status had changed. No blaring red flags had been in the P.I.'s files—other than that Ralph was flaky. Gunderson had had quite a few jobs over the years, trying out new ventures or start-up tech occupations, never sticking to one thing. He usually moved on within the first year, either by choice or going belly-up.

On an examination of Ralph's discarded trash, the investigator had discovered Gunderson ate frozen dinners, had charge accounts at Macy's and Nordstrom, three VISA cards maxed out to about $10K apiece, and a staggering vet bill for his dog after it had eaten a bag of Hershey's Kisses with the foil wrappers. Grocery receipts turned up nothing out of the ordinary. Credit reports showed he was in some moderate debt, but was current on all his accounts. There wasn't anything out of the ordinary.

"What are you going to do about her?" Neil asked, folding a slice of pizza and taking a bite out of it.

"My mom?" Kyle thought about it a long moment, then said, "What really sucks is that the value of Moretti's stock would give me more than enough to buy my mom off, keep Legacy in my name and carry on."

"True."

"But if I stick it to Moretti and ask them to sell out their shares to someone else to buy me off, then I screw them."

"You could always sell your shares to an outsider."

"I could. But I won't."

"Anyone else would."

"I couldn't do that to her."

Neil smiled. "Her?"

Kyle didn't like the way Neil was looking at him. "The daughter," he said uneasily.

"Francesca. Met her once years ago at a trade convention. If she's anything like I remembered, I can see your dilemma. A pretty face is hard to ignore."

"I know what you're saying, but that's not what this is about." Kyle poured more beer into his mug from the pitcher on the table. "I've seen how she works, how vested she is in Moretti. I can't just take that away from her, back the family into a corner and put a gun to their heads for the stock buyout."

"Then what are your other options?"

"Not sure."

Neil, who was in construction, paused a moment, then looked up, his eyes glittering.

"What?" Kyle asked.

"It's a no-brainer, Jagger." He took another bite, then stated in simple terms, "You take over the Grove project and get the damn thing done. Turn it over to the owners and get out. You get paid, you pay your mom."

"My mom wants her money in less than a month. There's no way I can get a project the magnitude of the Grove done in that amount of time. It's impossible."

"I hate to agree with you."

The tiny pizzeria was busy with customers, and Kyle tuned out the noise around him as he thought about options. His mind went in several directions, then converged on the only solid option at this point.

After pouring the last of the beer, Neil asked, "So what are you going to do about your mom?"

Kyle snorted. "I think I'll send her flowers and a card telling her how much she's meant to me all my life."

"That'll be good for about twenty-four hours. Then what?"

Sobering, Kyle said, "I know how to get my hands on some money. I can get a couple hundred thou out of the equity on my Seattle place. Not enough to satisfy her, but enough for now."

"Sounds reasonable."

"And I'm going to put in a call to Hal Burton and tell him not to buy the stock from my mom if she goes to him." Kyle spoke slowly, his mind processing as he spoke. "Hal's a decent guy and he'd let me know what's going on if it comes to that. He'd also keep things quiet about the possibility of Legacy stock being put up for sale by a broker."

"You think she'd actually try to sell it before she gives you the chance to make arrangements?"

Drinking the remaining beer in his mug, Kyle said tonelessly, "After the week I've just had, anything's possible."

CHAPTER FOURTEEN

FRANCESCA OVERSLEPT. She couldn't believe it when she glanced at the clock and saw she should have gotten up an hour before.

She made a quick call to Mark to say she was sorry, but she'd miss the subcontractors meeting that morning. He gave her a hard time about no doughnuts. His teasing comment gave them both a moment's pause. Giovanni had always bought doughnuts for the meeting.

After that Franci made a mad dash to the shower to bathe and shampoo her hair. It was thick and took forever to style; she used more than the usual amount of hair spray to tame it into place. She put on mascara and blush, an application of pink lip gloss, then grabbed the first thing she saw in her closet—a floral dress and pink strappy sandals. The heels were high and showed the shape of her calves. She loved this pair, and they were actually fairly comfortable.

Driving to the job site, she checked for phone messages, then made a quick call to Lily.

"Hey, about tonight," Francesca said, clutching the

cell phone as she pulled into a parking spot. "I don't think I can make it."

Lily's response was prompt. "Now, Franci. You've missed the last two, but understandably."

Francesca had been dealing with her father's death and the subsequent transition. The date squad had been supportive, calling her all the time to see how she was doing.

Last week she'd had lunch with Jordan, and Erin had stopped by the house on her way home to give her a hug and see if she needed anything. Her friends had been there for her, but Francesca probably hadn't reached out to them as much as they'd hoped she would.

Grief was a funny thing. You never knew how you'd react to it until you were there in the thick of the emotions.

For a flicker of a second, Francesca thought about how comforted she'd been by Kyle.

"I'm sorry, but I'm just buried with work." She cut the engine and grabbed her briefcase before stepping out of the car. "I overslept this morning and I'm going to be playing catch-up all day."

Lily reasoned in a sensible tone, "Which is why you'll need downtime tonight and a good cocktail."

"A cocktail, yes, but time away from what I have to do, no."

"No?" Lily mimicked. "No isn't acceptable. Franci, you need your friends. We're here for you. We were all looking forward to getting back into the old routine. It's not the same without you."

Francesca selected her footing carefully as she stepped over debris on the way to the trailer. "I'll try."

"Not good enough. You better be there tonight. Pomodoro for some of your brother's *sfinciuni.* You have to eat, you know."

Franci had actually lost a few pounds, and on her, it looked more like ten. She hadn't been eating well, being so stressed.

It would be nice to see her friends…to get back to some kind of normalcy even with all this Legacy and Moretti conflict going on.

Climbing the iron steps to the trailer, she grabbed hold of the doorknob. "Okay. You're right. I'll be there."

"Terrific!"

She cut the call, opened the door and stopped abruptly when she saw who was inside. And where. Slowly, she stepped forward, closing out the sounds of the construction site as she shut the door behind her.

Inside, the hum of the box air conditioner cut the silence.

"What are you doing here?" she asked.

Kyle Jagger sat at her father's desk, as if he'd settled in for the long haul. Its top was organized, the paperwork in neat piles, and a thermos sat on the corner, as well as a beat-up hard hat that had to belong to Kyle. A pair of aviator sunglasses rested near his cell phone, the message light of which was blinking.

He'd made himself comfortable in her father's old

worn chair with the stuck wheel. He leaned back in it now and waited for her to say something.

She was at a loss.

Her gaze swept over him, taking in the clean lines of his face. The fresh soapy smell of his skin seemed to fill the small space. He was wearing a polo shirt with the Legacy logo on it, and faded jeans. His unflinching eyes leveled on her, daring her to make a comment, any comment.

"What are you doing here?" she repeated, letting the straps of her briefcase slide down her shoulder. She set the case on her desk in the corner.

"You're late." His statement galled her, but when he spoke again, his tone was teasing. "But I saved you a doughnut."

She glanced at the pastry box on the filing cabinet next to the coffeemaker. A fresh pot had been made, and through a seam in the box, she could see all but one doughnut had been eaten. And of course it was a plain one. All the glazed doughnuts, crullers and maple bars had been snagged.

She didn't know whether to thank him or hit him.

"What are you doing here?" The third time she asked him she got an answer.

"I work here."

She paused, her heartbeat going into overdrive. "I never hired you."

"I own more than fifty percent interest in Moretti. I'm here to get this project done."

Francesca sank into her chair, her legs feeling wobbly. "You can't wear that shirt in here."

He glanced at the Legacy Constructors logo. "Why not?"

"Because it's not who we are."

"I know that."

"But…you just can't be doing this."

Kyle had Legacy to run, a seventeen-story project to finish. He didn't have time to be in two places at once. His company was huge, with projects bigger than theirs.

But here he was.

"Where's Mark?" she asked, desperation in her tone.

"Been here and gone. Probably up on the sixth floor looking at the layout."

"So he knows you're working in our trailer?"

Kyle slanted her a measured look. "I brought the doughnuts."

She could only think in short, jolting steps. "Who's handling your work?"

"Someone I trust."

"How long are you going to be on this job?"

"Until it's done."

"That's going to be a long time. Really—how long?"

"Until it's done or Moretti buys me out."

"How can we do that?" The family had been making calls to banks and no one was willing to loan them that kind of money.

"Don't know. That's your call. I told you that's what I needed to have happen, Franci." Kyle knitted his fingers together, his brow furrowed. "I don't like this any more than you do, but I now have a vested interest in this project, and it's big. Bigger than anything I've got going right now."

"But it's ours."

He shook his head. "You've given me no choice. I have to be here to make sure things are done right. This is some serious money we're talking about. In all honesty—and I mean no disrespect—I can't say that I trust the next generation of Morettis to pull it off. Mark's great, but he's not your dad. Your other two brothers aren't going to quit their day jobs." His eyes narrowed speculatively, with a flash of warning. "And you… you'll need to show me what you've got."

She stared at him, tongue-tied, anger flaring. She was barely able to control herself. Any romantic feelings she'd had for this man evaporated on the spot. She was stunned by his cool appraisal, and she suddenly wondered where that side of him had come from.

Thoughts of getting him out of here, permanently, superceded all reason.

"You can't do this," she stated hotly. "Moretti won't partner in with Legacy on this project. The Grove was started by my father and it should be completed by family."

His response was cut-and-dried, much like his voice. "Can and already did."

Franci eyed the neat stacks of papers on her dad's desk. "You've looked at private folders and ledgers."

"Not really. Mostly what's here are bills. I put them

in order. You'll have to pay them. One's past due, by the way."

She wanted to scream. "No…no, this won't work out. This isn't acceptable. We've still got time and we never said you could work here."

"Your time ran out and I have every right to take charge. I'm sorry, I didn't want this. I have no choice."

Her jaw ached from clenching her teeth so hard. "Neither do I."

She collected her things and left without another word to him.

Outside, the first phone call she made was to Mark. All he was able to say was "Moretti—" before she blasted him with one simple sentence.

"Thanks for calling to warn me!" Then she hung up.

Her Italian temper didn't show itself often, but when it did, it was like a pot of boiling sauce, ready to spill over and burn anything in its path.

The second call she made was to Holt and Brown, the two lawyers who'd been in on this and would now have to come up with an out.

Because Francesca Moretti would never work for Kyle Jagger, in her father's beloved trailer, on the biggest job site Moretti had ever run. It just wasn't going to happen.

Not in her lifetime.

ROBERT SAW THAT "LOOK" on his sister's face when she came into Pomodoro's kitchen. Growing into a teenager, she'd honed that expression into a real corker. It was a combination of “Don’t mess with me,” “Go ahead and make my day” and “I’m going to cry at any second if you don’t give me what I want.”

Before she opened her mouth, he stepped away from the long, stainless steel counter and steered her to the prep area.

“I heard,” he said, then shoved a glass of his best imported wine into her hand.

She took a sip, then another. “This has been the day from hell and it’s not even over.”

“From what Mark said, there’s no way to get out of it. He even called John about some legal loophole.”

“I know,” she groaned. “I talked to Holt and he said the same thing. It’s within Kyle’s right to exercise a limited partnership with Moretti until the Marketplace is released to the owners and we can buy him out.”

She drank her wine, a crease on her forehead. His sister was tall and pretty. Beautiful, actually. But when she was mad, she got this frown that wouldn’t quit. He knew—he’d lived with her while she went through puberty.

“What’s Mom say?” Robert asked. He’d tried to get hold of his mother today, but she hadn’t answered, and she didn’t carry a cell phone.

“She’s upset. We’re all upset. John’s upset. Well, Mark’s not, and you seem to be doing fine.”

Robert adjusted the damp hand towel tucked into his chef’s apron. “I’m not okay with how things are panning out. I called a family meeting. Tomorrow morning. Here.”

“You did?”

"Yeah. Francesca, I may not be in the construction field, but I run a pretty successful restaurant. I've learned to roll with punches and make them work for me. I'm not saying I like Jagger in the spot he's in. I don't. But I want to see how we can handle things if we have no out—which we don't seem to, not unless I sell my stock, and you sell yours…and John and Mark. And Mom. Is that what you want? For Mom to sell on the open market for God knows who to buy? Because then we tear down Moretti Construction and make it a patchwork quilt of owners rather than a blanket of family."

Franci folded one arm, the wineglass in her hand. "I hate to say it, but you have a point."

"I'm not trying to placate anyone, but we need to look at all the right angles."

She merely nodded, the tension in her face seeming to lessen.

"Go hang with your girlfriends. Dinner's on me—okay?"

She smiled. "Thanks, Robert."

"Sta bene."

After his sister went to join her friends, Robert moved back to the row of boiling pots, the hot flames, the rich simmering sauces.

While he'd never admit this to anyone, there was something about Kyle that he admired. He didn't know the guy, but from comments he'd heard his dad make about the Jaggers, he knew they were ethical.

Ethics was a huge thing to Robert. He dealt with it

on a daily basis in his business. Suppliers, wholesalers, waitstaff. Give him a person with ethics over ambition, any day. But if you threw in ambition with a good moral code, that was a winning combination.

As he tossed basil into a pan, he wondered if Francesca's fiery reaction to Kyle had more to do with the man than the situation.

Robert questioned if she'd ever find someone she could settle down with. He'd known a little history about Eduardo, though Francesca didn't talk much about it. That Italian had done a number on her heart. Ever since, she'd had a hard time trusting a relationship.

Robert had set her up a few times, but nothing panned out. His sister was a woman driven by her career and the nice success story she'd written for herself.

Maybe she didn't know a potentially good thing when she saw it.

Robert wasn't sure about Kyle Jagger, but he had a gut feeling that their dad would never have partnered with a devil. Giovanni had been an all-right guy who chose his friends carefully.

With that thought, Robert grew melancholy, missing his father. Yet at the same time, he wondered if this deal with Legacy and Moretti wasn't some kind of fate thing.

He'd ask his wife about it. Marie had a pretty good intuition about most everything.

"HAVE YOU HEARD FROM Rick James lately?" Lily asked, nibbling on a piece of bread crust.

"No." Francesca hadn't given the man a thought in weeks. "I wish I could have liked him. I'm sorry."

Her demeanor had gone from angry about Kyle's takeover of the job trailer to renewed hope and less stress after a glass of good wine. She wasn't sure what they'd be able to accomplish at tomorrow's meeting, but at least Robert had set something up.

She sure loved her brother. He sometimes took a back-burner in her chaotic life, but when she needed a shoulder, she could count on him to be there.

"It's okay," Lily replied, "if he didn't float your boat." She released a sigh through her glossy lips. "If only I could find someone who rocks my world."

"The Rolling Stones are coming to town. You could see if you could get backstage passes," Erin suggested.

Lily frowned. "I don't want a rock star. Mick never appealed to me. His lips are too big."

"I wonder if he kisses good?" Jordan mused. "You'd think a man with big lips would know how to use them."

"Or not," Francesca said. "I don't think it matters about the size, it's all about the technique."

"Who's the best kisser you've ever known?" Erin asked, taking a slice of cheese from the appetizer plate.

For a moment, Franci thought about Eduardo. He'd been a very good kisser. He'd also kissed her off, after the challenge of seducing her had netted him results and, subsequently, had made her less interesting after the fact.

She shuddered at the thought of how she'd behaved,

the choices she'd made. She'd been young and inexperienced...but still.

That summer had changed her. Until then she'd viewed romance with wide-eyed optimism, and having an affair the way she had had affected her more deeply than she'd realized.

It had been in part due to being raised in the Catholic church. She'd felt such guilt and remorse over things. But as she asked for forgiveness, she realized that God had already forgiven her, and she had to forgive herself.

Eduardo was history, a chapter finished over a decade ago. She rarely gave that summer in Italy any thought, other than it had been a good experience workwise, helping her architectural firm become a reality, and giving her a sense of direction with her own designs. Italy's lush piazzas and palaces, its columns and arches and stonework had seasoned her abilities, and she began to draw wonderful things with her own unique flare.

For that, she would always think fondly of Florence.

"Scott Michaels," Jordan said decisively. "No question about it. That man could kiss."

"Whatever happened to him?" Lily refilled her wineglass, then added a bit more to Francesca's.

"Cross-dresser. He married a stylist from DV8 Hair Salon. I've seen him around town. He actually looks pretty good in makeup."

"Why is it the good ones go bad?" Lily pondered

aloud. "Let's see, my best kisser was…Doug Jensen. Yep. Captain of the swim team at BSU."

"I remember him," Francesca said. "Didn't he have a friend named Mike something?"

"Mike Pendleton."

Francesca felt more languid the more wine she drank, and she was actually enjoying herself and the flow of feminine conversation. "I went out with him once to a movie."

Robert brought their entrées to the table and they continued to talk about life, work and men. That last topic seemed to always creep back into the dialogue. Francesca wondered if they could go five minutes without a testosterone reference.

Once the plates were cleared, and one single dessert shared, with four forks, they decided to go to the Red Feather for a Bailey's.

The evening air was warm and sultry, the leaves from trees along Ninth Street billowing softly. Francesca had a moment's pang, with a sense of loss that assailed her to the point of tears.

Her dad had loved this street, the summer nights, and the sounds of people dining at sidewalk tables.

A sudden and overwhelming wave of grief hit her, and she wanted to go home.

"Franci, sweetie?" Jordan asked, putting her arm around her. "What's wrong?"

She blinked back the tears, brushed at her cheeks. "I miss my dad."

"Oh, Franci," Erin said. She gave her a hug.

Lily closed in and the four of them walked in a tight-knit pack.

"I think I should go home," Francesca said, the weight of the day pressing down on her like steel girders.

"No," Jordan replied empathically. "It's our night. You can't go home and cry. It's not healthy. You need your friends."

Lily smiled. "You need another drink."

"I've had too much already," Francesca protested.

"You need a coffee." Erin steered them to the Red Feather lounge and restaurant. "With a small shot of Bailey's to take the edge off."

Francesca's legs kept moving and the next thing she knew, they were seated along a brick wall in the narrow establishment. Because of its small size and sprawling two-story dining area, the noise level could be intolerable, but tonight it wasn't bad. Tables along the sides were all but full, but conversations were muted.

The Bailey's actually tasted wonderful, and she soon felt better.

The door opened and Suzy Blaire stepped in with one of her friends. Francesca had met the woman once, but couldn't remember her name.

Suzy had been fairly cool ever since the night of the Children's Hospital benefit. Franci had landed the build-out, a major client, but dealing with Suzy on a daily basis had been dicey in the beginning. The woman still had her panties in a twist because Kyle had gone to the benefit with Francesca.

This was why she didn't like dating, didn't like the effort and energy. Something always got messed up. Case in point: she'd really been liking Kyle—not that they'd been officially dating, but still. She had had some nice times with him, and now this. This whole ugly mess with Legacy.

Suzy spotted them, gave a classic smile of indifference, then sat at the bar.

Jordan snorted. "What bee stung her on the butt?"

Francesca slid the cocktail napkin out from under her coffee cup. She wet the corner with her tongue, then wiped underneath her eyes.

She probably had mascara smudges, and while she was beyond caring about her appearance, she didn't want to deal with any inquisitions if the interior designer came to their table.

Without thought, Francesca said, "I asked a guy out before she had the chance, and she's been meowish with me ever since."

As soon as she spoke, three pairs of eyes leveled on her, and almost at once the question came flying, "Who'd *you* ask out and why didn't you tell us?"

Francesca startled, then leaned back in her chair. "Geez, it's no big deal. It happened a while ago and I'm not seeing him anymore. Not that I was even seeing him."

"Who was it?" Jordan asked, brows raised with expectation.

"A guy."

Erin leaned her face closer. "What guy?"

Backed into a proverbial corner. Over dinner, Franci had mentioned Kyle briefly. All right, she'd gone on at length, saying how much she disliked the position he'd put himself into today: her boss. She'd spent all of ten minutes roasting him over the open flames of her ire.

Business being business, the date squad had never assumed he might be young and handsome and someone she'd spent some alone time with. And kissed and held.

Her three girlfriends had listened sympathetically, added the obligatory, "That's awful" or "You must be so upset" and the "You'll be fine" at the right moments—never dreaming the man they were bashing was a good kisser.

Of course, she'd never reveal *that* piece of information.

Glancing at all three of her friends, Francesca admitted after a long moment, "Kyle Jagger."

"What?" Jordan gasped. "You dated the guy who's now your archenemy? Your new boss—well, kind of in a weird way."

"How come you never told us?" Lily's eyes were wide, her lips parted.

"Because he's nothing, no big deal."

Erin pointed out, "No big deal didn't take up thirty minutes of our dinner conversation."

"I thought I only mentioned him for five minutes."

"It was thirty. And I wondered, the way you went on

about him." Jordan folded her arms beneath her breasts. "Whenever a woman has nothing but hideous things to say about a man, she's usually very interested in him."

"Jordan," Erin said with a frown, "that's the stupidest thing I've ever heard."

"Stupid, but true."

Francesca wished she had begged off the coffee now.

And never more so when Kyle entered the Red Feather with another guy, and they slowly approached the bar where Suzy and her friend were sitting.

Francesca wanted to slide under the table. Was he meeting the interior designer for a drink? A date? *Oh, great. Shoot me now.*

"What's the matter?" Jordan asked, sensing the change in the way Franci sat. She slouched, pinning herself closer to the wall as if she wanted to disappear.

"Kyle just came in."

All three women glanced in the direction she was looking.

"Ohmygosh," Jordan said first. "He's hot."

"More than hot." Lily's smile lit up like a Christmas tree.

Erin, usually shy and less forthcoming with her thoughts, said, "He can be my boss anytime."

Francesca couldn't argue. Kyle cut a fine figure. But at this point in her relationship with him, she'd rather cut him out of her life.

"I'm going home," she said, grabbing her purse and standing.

The floral dress she'd had on all day seem clingy and wilted, her light makeup washed away from crying.

She tossed some bills onto the table. "That should cover my drink."

She disregarded her friends' pleas to stay. She was done and needed to leave. Using her purse as a shield, she managed to pass the bar, Kyle and Suzy and the laughing foursome, and make her escape.

Francesca wanted nothing more than to call it a day, pull the covers over her head and forget she'd ever gotten up this morning.

CHAPTER FIFTEEN

THE SEVENTH HOLE was hidden in the shadows of the trees, but Kyle managed a wicked drive, sending his ball sailing toward the cup with a few feet to spare. He should be able to sink it with one stroke.

"The secret to missing a tree," Mark commented from beside him, club in hand, "is to aim right at it."

"I've heard that one."

"Works."

"I've tried it a few times and hit the tree."

"Same."

The two men traded dry smiles, then immediately went back to their reserved expressions.

Kyle waited for Mark to tee his golf ball. Mark made a leisurely study of the target, then swung his body into the shot.

They both watched the blur of white. Nothing sounded better than wood striking a ball, sending it airborne.

They gathered up their bags and proceeded to the next hole.

Many people on the course used carts, or had caddies carry their clubs. That was too old-school for Kyle. He preferred a good walk and longer conversation, getting from one putting green to the next.

Mark's ball landed several yards shy of the green. "I should've taken a few more practice shots," he grumbled.

The sun felt good on Kyle's face and forearms as they walked in cleated shoes over the neatly cut grass. "When I first took up the game, I only had two shots—practice and the ones that sent my balls to the closest sand trap or water hazard."

"Is that supposed to make me feel better? I've been playing for three years."

Kyle shrugged. "Don't ever listen to me."

Mark began to smile, but it faded away. "Moretti doesn't have a choice in the matter right now."

The mood went from light to business in a matter of seconds, and they both knew what Mark had meant.

Moretti Construction had conceded to Legacy. They'd sent Mark out to tell Kyle the news. Over coffee in the clubhouse, Mark had spelled out what they'd like the terms to be—if Kyle could be so accommodating.

As the clouds shifted overhead, Kyle thought back to their earlier conversation.

"We'd like you to oversee the project with the same vision my dad had."

"That can be done."

"And we'd like to use the same subs we've got on the project now. No sense in changing."

"Agree completely."

"My mom's still on the board of directors."

"Of course."

Mark had remained motionless, his gaze intent. "We'd like the option to buy you out at any time—we'd hope that you'd agree to that and not get so dug into this project you don't want out."

"Not a problem."

"You'll sign an addendum to that effect?"

"Sure."

Nodding, Mark was appeased.

Kyle had thought their talk was done, until Mark added, "You'll be working closely with my sister. She's the best person to have in the trailer. She's already set up and knows what's going on. It isn't like we had a choice—she really didn't want to, but she's been in on this since its inception. She knows the job in her sleep. She can get demanding, but she means well."

A long pause followed as Kyle thought through what Mark had just said.

Working next to Francesca every day. It was going to be more than a challenge. She tested his patience, but it went beyond that. She intrigued him, attracted him to the point of distraction.

This wasn't going to be good.

"How come *you* don't do it?" Kyle had asked.

"No head for numbers or construction politics. Paperwork isn't my thing and there's a lot of it passing through that trailer. Franci's good at micromanaging."

"Maybe I don't want her managing me."

"Then you manage her." Mark's last statement had

been the final words spoken. He'd picked up his clubs and said, "You wanna golf, or what?"

Letting his thoughts drift back to the present, Kyle approached the hole, looked through his clubs and selected his Odyssey putter. Before he walked onto the green he turned to Mark. "I didn't ask for this. I really don't want to be telling anyone at Moretti what to do."

"I know."

"Especially not your sister."

"Don't worry, she won't bite."

"You sure?"

"Yeah." Mark adjusted the ball cap on his head, smoothing his hair and replacing the cap backward. "But can I give you a piece of advice?"

Kyle's muscles stiffened. "Go ahead."

"Watch out for Suzy Blaire. She's a real ballbuster."

"Suzy?" The light dawned for Kyle. "The interior designer."

"Francesca said you're dating her and—"

"I'm not dating her."

"My sister said she saw you out with Suzy at the Red Feather."

"I ran into Suzy at the bar. I'm not dating her. And what was your sister doing, anyway—spying on me?"

Mark's expression grew intrigued. "Apparently she saw you."

"Then she should have said hi."

"She's not like that when she's interested." As if he'd said too much, Mark grew quiet. But after a moment, he added, “What the hell. Let me tell you something about Francesca. From the way she’s been talking about you, she’s thinking more about you than she’ll let on. It’s been a long time since she had a boyfriend, so don’t hurt her.” He rested his arms on his club handle. “That didn’t sound right—you may not even like her. But what I’m saying is, if you do like her and want to date her, don’t mess her up. Be sincere about it. Don’t say anything you don’t mean, don’t do anything with her you couldn’t do in front of me. You get my meaning?”

Kyle stood back, let out a long slow breath. “I get what you’re saying.”

“Good.” Mark sorted through his clubs. “I love my sister very much.”

Pondering his shot, Kyle wondered if he loved Francesca, too. Nothing happened fast for him. He took his time about most everything, but looking back to that night on her patio when he’d held her, and the flight to Seattle, he acknowledged he was falling for her.

And that scared the hell out of him.

But as he positioned himself to hit the ball, his form was knocked askew by the mere thought of how Francesca’s breasts had pressed against him. His swing faltered, and for the first time in longer than he could remember, his club didn’t make contact with the ball.

He swung at air and missed.

THE DATE SQUAD CALLED an emergency morning meeting at the Java Café. Gourmet coffees were ordered, flaky pastries nibbled on and cell phones ignored as business calls came in and were sent on to voice mail.

"She's definitely got something for him." Jordan wore her hair pulled back into a hair clip.

Lily nodded. "Nobody gets that worked up over a guy she's not interested in."

Playing devil's advocate, Erin chimed in. "But remember, he did take over her dad's company by default. That's enough to send anyone over the edge in the irritation department."

Jordan brought an acrylic nail to her lips, absently biting on its thick tip. "Maybe we're jumping to conclusions."

"Maybe not." Lily shrugged. Her full breasts strained the row of buttons down her silk shirtfront. "I've never seen Franci act like that around a guy."

"We've never really seen her around a guy." Erin took the lid off her coffee and licked the whipped cream on top. "Let's face it, she's not one to swim in the dating pool."

"No, she's not." Jordan slid her pastry aside, then set her briefcase on the coffee table.

The three women sat on two leather sofas, a low table between them, where they'd set out their coffee and food.

"Which is why," Jordan continued, "I took the liberty of making this for our Franci."

"What is it?" Erin leaned forward, gazing at the neatly typed sheet. On close inspection, she saw several information fields that Jordan had filled in: name, age, height, hair color, religion and more. *"Franciful?"* Erin quizzed, lifting her gaze to Jordan.

"It's Francesca's user name. I'm creating an online dating account for her."

"Is that what this is all about?" Lily straightened her back. "When you called this morning, I thought you'd set your hair on fire with your curling iron, you were so hyper on the phone."

"I was worried," Jordan said defensively. "Franci needs our help."

"She doesn't want our help." Erin's red hair was vibrant in the light flooding in the window. "She's going to kill you if you post that."

"She won't know." Jordan shifted through papers. "Here's what I propose. We write the profile from all our points of view. I've done so already—here it is. 'We are a group of Franciful's close friends—Jordan, Lily and Erin—'"

Erin cut in. "Hey, I don't want my name on this!"

"Me, either," Lily said, her expression alert. "I don't think the Internet dating thing is a good idea, Jordan."

"You need to give it a chance. There are some perfectly fine men online. In fact, I've printed a few for you to check out in case you don't believe me."

Jordan passed around several profiles with photos. The two women studied them, reading the information with discerning eyes.

Erin glanced up. "They actually sound rather reasonable. So how come you haven't snatched one for yourself?"

"Neither are my type, but they're Francesca's. Look at that one—'I enjoy reading on a rainy Sunday morning.'"

Lily laughed. "I know this guy. He works in the building across from mine. There is no way he's 'athletic and toned.'"

Snagging the profile out of Lily's hand, Jordan muttered, "A minor technicality! He can join a gym." She organized the papers and went back to what she'd prepared for Francesca.

"So here's the rest of Franci's profile." Jordan looked closely at the paper and read on. "'Though she will probably not be happy about this, we think she's spending way too much time working. Given the fact that she has threatened us if we try and fix her up, we figured this is different, and hey—what are friends for?'"

Lily grinned. "With friends like us, she won't need enemies."

Surprising them all, Erin said, "How come you never did this for me?"

Jordan let out a sigh. "You never asked me to."

Erin replied, "And neither has Francesca. She's never going to speak to you again, Jordan."

"Of course she will." Jordan reshuffled the papers. "Because she's not going to know what we're doing. We're going to weed out all the duds and only let her in on this if we find someone really great."

"But what about her picture?" Erin slid aside her empty cup. "Someone might recognize her. She's very well known in town."

"I thought about that. Which is why I'm going to be very strict in my preliminary-round process. I'm not going to include a photo of her—but at the end of my ad, I'm going to say 'Photo on request *if* we think you're suitable.' That way, we control who gets our girl's picture. It won't be until we've checked him out."

Erin groaned. "Sounds like a mail-order catalog."

"More like male-order date." Lily's bracelets made a jingling noise as she brushed her hair back.

"I think she's already met someone really great—Kyle." Erin drank the last of her coffee. "Only she doesn't know it yet."

"Maybe. Maybe not. And if that is the case," Jordan said as she closed her briefcase, "this will have a positive-positive outcome. If she realizes she likes Kyle and pursues him, she won't need us. If she doesn't like him, she'll have option two—our Internet ad."

Erin wasn't convinced and repeated, "She's going to kill you."

Lily bit her lower lip. "As much as I like the idea, Erin's right. She's going to kill you."

"If I worried about every little detail," Jordan said as she rose to her feet, "I'd never have gotten as far as I have in my job. When you're a marketing analyst you have to think outside the box and really push things to the limit. What you sell to the public is what they think they don't need—but end up dying to have."

Erin had the last word, which might very well prove to be *each* of their last words if Francesca got wind of

Jordan's plan. "My point exactly. We'll breathe our last breath when she finds out what you've done."

YESTERDAY, a utility crew trenching next to the Grove Marketplace parking lot dug up a wire, which blew a transformer feeding an entire city block.

At 10:08 a.m., Francesca's job had been without power. By 11:23, it had been apparent the juice wouldn't be back up anytime soon. An entire day had been lost.

Coming into the trailer this morning, she hoped things would be better. But as soon as she saw Kyle sitting at her father's desk, she knew it would be just as it had been the day before, wrought with tension. The electricity in the air could have supplied power to all of Boise if she had a way to plug in the current.

"Morning," he said over the wide set of blueprints stretched out in his hands.

"Good morning," she responded politely. She set her purse and briefcase down on the desk in the corner. It was already hot, the early morning temperature in the low seventies.

It was going to be a scorcher.

She'd gone to bed late last night, finishing some work for one of her clients at Bella Design. Up at five-thirty this morning, she'd had two cups of coffee already and was feeling a little buzzed on caffeine, made worse without the benefit of breakfast.

No pink doughnut box occupied her desk today, but there was a brown pastry sack—with her name on it.

Going for the bag, she picked it up and looked inside, to find a flaky croissant.

"It's yours. I put your name on it so nobody would steal it. All the doughnuts were gone before six-thirty. It's a dog-eat-dog-world with the subs coming in and out of here. I said if anyone so much as touched that bag, you'd fire them."

"I would not."

"You sure?" His brow quirked, giving his face a handsome yet devilish charm.

She made no further comment, instead taking the croissant, grateful he'd thought of her. "Thanks."

Settling in at her desk, she ate the pastry, conscious of the way Kyle glanced her way from time to time. The last bite she took got stuck in her throat and she went looking for bottled water.

"Milk's in the minifridge," he said, as if reading her mind.

She opened the white door, and there on the top wire shelf sat a small carton of skim milk. How did he know she preferred nonfat to one percent? How had he had the foresight, not to mention the thoughtfulness to get it for her?

She didn't want to mull that over. She simply said, "Thanks" for the second time within her first ten minutes at work.

The morning inched by at a snail's pace, even though Kyle did little to slow things down. He multitasked at lightning speed, never sitting idle. His hands were always moving, holding a cell phone up to his ear, using a pen in his other. He doodled, he took notes, he leaned back in her father's big chair, gazed out the window through the dusty miniblinds as he discussed a project.

His *real* project.

Most of the morning she had to listen to him talk about that seventeen-story building. The contractors, the costs, the way he wanted things done, needed things finished. He worked very differently from her father.

Dad had loved being in the field. Whenever he got stuck in the trailer, he'd been crabby. Out of necessity, he had to handle the business end of things, but he would rather be outside, with the weather beating him in the face and guys from the job site asking him how things were going. Being at his desk, near the phone, was nothing Giovanni had ever looked forward to.

Francesca attempted to write out payroll checks—a challenge, since the bank was still trying to sort through the estate issues. Most of the problems had been taken care of, but there was some question on one of the business accounts that paid the taxes.

She wasn't even on her third check, and Kyle was now on his third phone call, laughing and joking with one of Legacy's subcontractors. Head down, pen in hand, she gazed at him from beneath the fringe of her lashes.

He had a masculinity about him that was easygoing. It irked her that he could be so secure, so self-confident. But worse, it irked her that she even got irritated. She shouldn't care a thing about him.

He put his feet on the edge of the desk, and she saw he was wearing beat-up Red Wings, the kind that laced up beyond the ankles. The leather was scuffed and worn, and the color of burned butter. His jeans hugged him in all the right places. His polo shirt fit snugly over his chest, a pair of folded Serengeti sunglasses tucked into the collar.

"I know," he said into the receiver. "Supplies are short because China is using more cement and copper than the world can supply." He rubbed his temple, nodding. "Uh-huh. I said that in the last general meeting. It's bullshit the way they're looking at this."

She cleared her throat and he glanced in her direction.

His vivid gray-green eyes conveyed a silent apology—either for swearing or for talking so loud. She couldn't be sure.

Francesca noted the time. Too early for lunch.

Pretending to carry on as if Kyle didn't matter, she resumed her task and went for one of the tax form folders. Pulling it out, she smelled the vague hint of garlic. There on the inside of the manila folder was a splash of her mom's Italian gravy.

Melancholy instantly swept over Franci, bringing an ache to her heart as she thought of her father. The last time this folder had been taken out, he'd been the one doing payroll. He must have spilled his lunch on it.

She fought back the tears that burned in her eyes. It was so difficult to move forward without him. How could she do it? How could Moretti's survive without him, his smile, his laughter?

All around the trailer were memories of him. The scars on the table from his boot heels, the old newspapers piled in the corner, the empty coffee cup on the sideboard that had belonged to Dad.

Giovanni Moretti had had a way about him that everyone loved. He was irreplaceable.

Looking at the payroll checks, Francesca could barely finish writing them out. She had a stack of bills to pay, too. Her father always had a reputation for instantly writing a check to a sub when he was presented with a bill—something unheard of today. The fact that she was late on a few invoices made her feel guilty. She'd have to stay more on top of things.

There was a lot of pressure riding on her to complete this project *and* its complications to the end. More pressure than she could take, but she wouldn't admit that to anyone.

Especially not to Kyle Jagger.

Feeling as if she might buckle, she decided she had to get out of there and regroup. Normally, she managed stress very well, but this was not normal stress. She felt pulled in too many directions and feared she might snap.

A walk on the job site would do her some good, she decided. Seeing the progress, talking to a few of the workers—that would improve her mood and give her the motivation she needed to complete the day without any more weak moments.

Just as she was reaching for her purse, Kyle cut off the call and said, "So what do you think?"

She paused. "About what?"

"About the shortage of cement."

"Oh." Her purse remained where she'd left it. "It could be a real problem. But nothing we can't handle. We need to plan in advance."

He nodded. "I agree."

Her mission to revitalize herself on a walk was momentarily forgotten.

Francesca pursed her lips, sat firmly in her chair and folded her arms beneath her breasts—defense mode through and through. Her action caught Kyle's unwavering attention. She let him look before she said bluntly, "Why are you being so nice?"

A perplexed expression overtook his features. "What?"

"You know what I'm talking about. You're being nice." She motioned to the sideboard. "The croissant, asking me my thoughts on cement. You're up to something."

His ire rose, and she felt a twinge of regret. Maybe she'd misread him, pushed things too far.

"I've always been nice to you, Francesca," he said evenly. "I don't know why I'd stop."

She didn't have an immediate response, feeling guilty that she had labeled him unjustly. It was true—he'd always been kind to her and shown her respect. He'd gone out of his way to be civil, even during a trying time. His sincere compassion had been evident the night she'd been really down and needed a shoulder to cry on.

She unfolded her arms, let her hands fall onto her lap and twisted her fingers together.

Kyle's deep voice cut through the small room. "You

know, it sucks that you lost your dad. I'm sorry. And it sucks that I have to work in here. Trust me—I'm *really* sorry. It's not my idea. But it's the way it is."

"I understand," she stated. "I'm sorry, too."

She felt a bit better for having made the simple declaration. It had been childish of her to be defensive. She was just so frustrated with how things were. Mix that in with missing her dad and the way life was today…

She was reaching for her purse when his voice stopped her cold. "Oh, and honey—I'm not dating Suzy Blaire."

Franci sat upright, too surprised to volley a response.

"She's not even remotely my type." His eyes drank her in as he studied her, evoking a shiver across her skin. "You are."

The trailer door opened and Norm Roberts came in, before she could fully process Kyle's words.

Norm was the Grove Marketplace superintendent in charge of exteriors. Built like a barrel, he was as wide as he was tall.

Talk about a bull in a china shop. His hip grazed the filing tray on Kyle's desk, sending a stack of papers to the floor. "Sorry," he mumbled, bending down to pick up the mess.

Once he had straightened up, he glanced toward Francesca, then back at Kyle. "Hey, Kyle, there's a problem with the siding that needs some input. They delivered the first load of prefab brick veneer, but it doesn't match the architectural design. We started putting it up, but it's not working. I need you to come check it out and give us an alternate plan."

Kyle got to his feet, and Francesca's mouth dropped open.

She was the architect.

"Hey, wait—I'm the one who designed the building," she said in protest. "Let me take a look at it."

Norm glanced her way. "But he's the boss," he said without any hint of apology. "Don't I have to go to him now?"

Kyle's manner was cavalier. "You stay here. I'll take care of it. I'm sure it's no biggie."

The two men departed, and Francesca melted into her chair, feeling put out and snubbed.

She fought the knot of tension straining her shoulders, and the ache that crushed her chest and made it hard to breathe. If her dad had been here, that wouldn't have happened. Norm might have deferred to Giovanni, but Dad would have said it was her headache and not his. End of story.

She'd never get used to this new arrangement. And it wasn't just the way Norm bypassed her. It was everything.

Francesca grabbed her purse, hooked the straps on her shoulder and went outside into the blinding sunshine.

She managed to make it to the curb without sinking her heels in the dry earth.

Unlocking her car, she climbed into the inferno. The leather seats burned the backs of her legs as she turned the key over. She punched the AC up full blast, looked over her shoulder at the Grove Marketplace and frowned.

What was to have been Moretti's crowning glory was more like a dunce cap on her head. She felt as if she'd been left in the corner like an idiot.

And she'd never gotten bad grades in her entire life.

Pulling away from the curb, she vowed to attack the situation with a new strategy—just as soon as she figured one out.

CHAPTER SIXTEEN

LEAVING THE SANCTUARY of the Catholic church, Mariangela declined to continue the afternoon and have lunch with the ladies in her WINGS group—Women in God's Spirit. Instead, she went to Moz Uberuaga's Firehouse Café on her own.

The popular restaurant was familiar and safe, although this would be the first time she'd come here without company. She felt very self-conscious at her own table. She really hadn't wanted to eat by herself, but the alternative was to go home and know that Giovanni would not be there for dinner tonight or tomorrow. The reminder was just too painful to bear.

She'd lost nine pounds since her husband's death, and her clothes were looser than they had been in years. The healthy appetite she'd once had was gone. It was all she could do to finish a meal without feeling sick. Most times, she left half the food on her plate uneaten.

The women in her group were prayerful and loving. Being a part of it was helpful, but good intentions couldn't bring back Giovanni. And how Mariangela wished they could.

She knew Giovanni was with the Lord, and she should feel completely comforted in that knowledge, and yet she couldn't accept it. She had asked God over and over in her prayers why he'd taken her husband so soon.

Had her heart not been so burdened by unanswered questions, she would have gone to Father Mike and talked to him about the way she was feeling. But how could she talk to him about her anger, her misplaced resentment?

As it was, she'd had to politely smile and save face over her faltering faith in God's plan, while Father Mike asked her if Moretti Construction would be able to continue working on the new gymnasium for the school. Of course they would. But Mariangela was out of her element on such a project and Father would have to defer to Mark or Francesca.

Sitting by the restaurant window, she gazed outside and, with a fond smile, recalled the evening she and Giovanni had walked along this street and talked about the Grove Marketplace project.

That seemed eons ago.

A glint of shiny light reflecting off her finger caused her to gaze down at the wedding ring she wore. She didn't think she'd ever be able to take it off. The simple gold band had been there for forty-five years.

"Mrs. Moretti." Hearing her name caused her to come back to the present.

Moz stood before her, his expression solicitous. He had a full head of white hair that needed a trim, black-brown eyes and a dark complexion. He was Basque, that stoic mix of Spanish and French. He'd known her and Giovanni for as long as Mariangela could remember, but they'd never once visited outside of the café.

All she knew about Moz was that he had been a widower for nearly two decades. And he was Catholic, like her.

"Hello, Moz," she said. Nobody called him Mr. Uberuaga.

"I was sorry to hear about Mr. Moretti."

His condolences were appreciated and she'd been expecting them. Everywhere she went, she heard the sentiment. But it was beginning to feel awkward—as if she were living in the past and she was stuck there, unable to get out. Perhaps if people started asking her how she was doing? No, that would be worse. Because she wasn't doing real well.

"Thank you, Moz," she murmured.

"He was a good man."

"Yes."

Moz wore a white apron slightly stained from various kitchen spills. His large, gnarled hands were scarred in places, with one finger bearing the faint traces of stitches most likely having come from an accident with a knife and cutting board.

"Are you waiting for someone?" he asked, as the waiter came to bring her a glass of water.

Suddenly, Mariangela was embarrassed to say she was alone. "I was going to meet a friend, but she had to cancel."

Silently, she asked God to forgive her white lie.

"Well, you sit tight, and anything you'd like to order is on me." Moz's eyes were compassionate, creased deeply at the corners from too many years out in the sunshine. She recalled he liked to fly-fish. She remembered him telling Giovanni about it one time.

"Thank you."

He left her a menu and she gazed at the print, reading her choices but not really taking them in. She looked out the window and had a hard time composing herself.

When would the pain end?

She wanted to be back to normal.

KYLE SPOKE ON THE PHONE to Neil Bevilaqua while leaning back in his chair and gazing at the calendar on the bulletin board. "I don't see how I can make that committee meeting on the twenty-first. I'm buried down here. Even if I flew out right after my morning planning and zoning meeting, I wouldn't make it."

"I'll see if I can get it rescheduled, but it's unlikely."

"I wish I could do something, but I've got too many things going on and not enough time. I put Ken West on as project manager for my Boise seventeen story, pulling him off of my stripmall project in Bellingham."

The Bellingham, Washington, remodel would be ready to wrap up in about six months, but Ken's departure had put a crimp on progress. Right now, Kyle was flying Ken back and forth to run both job sites. Kyle took up the slack on the seventeen story as best as he could.

Overseeing the Grove Marketplace was a ten-hour-plus per day operation. Throw in his own construction projects and the minutes spent on everything didn't add up to enough hours in the day to be there one hundred percent for any of it.

"What are you going to do?" Neil asked.

"Nothing I can do unless the Morettis buy me out."

"Any more news about your mother's stock options?"

"She's contacting a business broker on the first and is going to proceed—with or without me."

Kyle recalled what had transpired between him and his mom when he'd handed her a check for two hundred and fifty thousand dollars. She'd declined his generous offer, saying it wouldn't cover the amount she needed. She still wouldn't tell him the reason she had to have the money. On a whim, it seemed, she was going to break apart the family construction company.

Kyle hated to be ugly about it, but the relationship he'd had with his mom had never been all that solid since Dad died. They'd been politely skirting around one another for years, and the older Helene got, the more eccentric she became. It pained Kyle to think he'd lost his mom, but there really was no other way to look at it.

He'd received another report from the investigator. The P.I. had found something of interest in Gunderson's trash—several portfolios on coffeehouses for sale in West Seattle. None of them showed potential or promise. Kyle had made some discreet phone calls and found out all had been failing for one reason or another.

Maybe Ralph needed money to buy a business. If that

was the case, it didn't sit well with Kyle that Helene would sell her shares of Legacy to buy her soon-to-be new husband a livelihood.

Then again, it was his mother's choice, and there was nothing Kyle could do about it.

He would put in another call to Hal Burton. This time the course of their conversation would be drastically different than the first.

Neil was now talking about Jennifer Vega, pulling Kyle from his thoughts. Kyle had dated her causally last year.

"She asked about you," Neil said.

Kyle formed a recollection of the tall blonde in his mind. She was a gorgeous woman, full of incentive, with a sexy spirit. They'd gone to a few social engagements connected with the trades.

Jennifer was a consultant for a factory he did business with. She was very ambitious, driven and motivated to succeed. Those were attributes that had first attracted him to her, but on closer examination, they were also what turned him off.

Her very identity of "self" revolved around how good she was, not how good it was to be with someone she liked.

Absently laughing, he asked, "Does she miss me?"

"She said for you to give her a call."

"I told her I was going to be in Boise for a while." Kyle absently glanced at his watch. He had to be out of here by 4:00 p.m. to make it to city hall on time.

"She told me to tell you to fly in this weekend and see her."

"No can do." Even if he could, he wouldn't. A woman like Jennifer was the furthest thing from his mind.

Kyle's gaze fell on the vacant desk and chair opposite his. Francesca had been MIA today. Something about plans she had to have redrawn for a client, then lunch with someone, and meetings all afternoon for Bella Design. Unlike Jennifer, when Franci had told him she wouldn't be in, her demeanor had been strained, not vitalized by the prospect of spending an entire day without a second to breathe.

In the trailer these last few weeks, he'd been seeing a side to her that garnered his sympathy. While Francesca Moretti was a polished career woman, she was fairly old-fashioned in her views. She was determined, but not obsessed. She could walk away from a potentially big project and not feel it would make or break her.

She was selective, stretching herself only as far as she thought she could manage without lowering the quality of her work.

Since he'd been running the Grove project alongside her, Kyle had seen Francesca exhausted. Some mornings, they didn't even carry on a conversation until after they'd each had a full cup of coffee. Their cell phones rang constantly, each of them being pulled in too many directions.

Moretti needed someone full-time in the trailer to get the things done that had to be done. The seventeen story needed more than Ken West, a temporary fix.

Kyle thought about how one simple phone call could

make a difference in Francesca's life. Or in his. But who should he sell out? Himself or the Morettis?

Neil's office phone rang in the background. "I gotta grab this. I'll be in touch about that meeting."

"Okay." Kyle ended the call, glanced at the time and began to pack his briefcase.

The door opened, letting in the sounds of construction and a wave of hot summer air.

Looking up, Kyle was surprised to see Mariangela Moretti walk into the trailer.

"Hey, Mrs. Moretti." He rose to his feet.

Her appearance seemed fragile, her shoulders slumped. She was a very attractive woman, but she'd clearly been having a tough time with things. "Hi, Kyle."

"What can I do for you?"

"I was hoping to find Francesca."

"Not here. Sorry."

"Oh." Mariangela pulled out her daughter's vacant chair and sat down, then glanced around the trailer with a wistful expression. To his knowledge, this was the first time she'd come in since Giovanni's death.

Kyle hadn't changed much about the setting; he'd just cleaned the endless clutter of papers, invoices and blueprints. He couldn't work in disorganization, never had been able to get past that. He had to know where things were. His time was too valuable to waste tracking down things he needed yesterday.

Mariangela's eyes veered to Giovanni's large desk. She looked for a lengthy amount of time, undoubtedly remembering how things had been in disorder when her husband had last sat there.

Kyle didn't want to tell her he was on a time crunch. "Is there anything I can help you with?" he asked sincerely.

She gave him a weak smile. "No." Then, after a moment, she said, "Did you get my thank-you card?"

"I did."

"The flowers you sent to the house were so nice. And the wreath of red roses you sent to the church was just lovely. We took them to the cemetery."

All he could do was nod. Things were awkward at best. He'd come into play in the middle of the game, not wanting to be put on the mound any more than the Morettis wanted a pinch hitter.

"Is Francesca getting along all right?" Mariangela asked, her attention directed to the work space Francesca had set up for herself.

"She's doing really great." And that was no exaggeration to soothe a worried mother. Francesca was more capable than several subs he knew.

"I worry about her. This is a huge responsibility."

"And she's handling it well."

"I'm sure you're helping."

"I get on her nerves," he added with a half smile, hoping to pull Mariangela out of her melancholy mood by using himself as bait.

"Francesca is usually very levelheaded. Nothing bothers her."

"Oh, I bother her."

"You do?"

"Plenty." Kyle shoved the last of his papers in his briefcase then folded his arms across his chest. "And not because I'm in the trailer with her. I bother her because I'm a guy."

"She's never been bothered by her brothers."

"They don't talk to her the way I do. Nor do they think about her like I do." Kyle was treading foreign waters here. He was telling a mother that he was interested in her daughter beyond business. He couldn't recall the last time he'd actually spoken to a parent and confessed his attraction to her offspring.

Mariangela's purse rested on her lap, her fingers working over the strap. "Have you asked her out?"

"There hasn't really been a good opportunity for that lately."

Thoughtful for a long moment, Mariangela said, "Make one."

"So you'd approve?"

Slowly gathering her words, Mrs. Moretti said, "Kyle, what deal Giovanni made with you was between you and my husband. I can't blame you for the present situation. You were only helping him out. If it hadn't been Legacy, Giovanni would have gone to someone else, someone less reputable, and we'd be in a far worse position. I'm not saying I'm happy about what's going on, but the fact is, it's how things are. I wish there was a way out of all of this."

"So do I."

She gazed at him, reading his expression. Mariangela

wasn't an ordinary woman. She was sharp and astute, seeing past the veneer of his poker face.

"There's more going on here than we know, isn't there?"

Kyle thought about denying it. He certainly wasn't about to drag his mother's poor choice into the light of day. Her wanting to sell her shares was private and that's how it was going to stay.

In a resonant tone, Kyle said, "There are things I can't explain, but I'm desperate to get out of this."

"I'm sorry."

"Me, too. It complicates everything in my life."

"Including Francesca?"

Kyle laughed, unable to hold back the amusement in his voice. "She's the one complication I'd look forward to."

Mariangela stood, then spoke with conviction. "I'd like for you to join us this Sunday for dinner. It's our weekly family night, so it'll be a full house—my sons, their wives and all of my grandchildren." Her perfectly arched brows rose. "And Francesca."

"I see her here most every day, Mrs. Moretti."

"I know." She walked to the door. "But at my house, you can see what you're getting into. We Italians enjoy the music of life, and there hasn't been any around my table lately. I think you're just the thing we need to add a new note to our song."

"I'M JUST NOT BEING TAKEN seriously," Franci complained to Mark. They sat at an outside table of the ice cream shop in Hyde Park. She'd ridden her bike over at dusk, enjoying the warm wind on her cheeks. It had been far too long since she'd got on her bicycle and worked off a day's stress.

"Then act serious."

"I do," she insisted. "I show up, I'm organized, I pay the bills, I oversee the subs as best as I can with Kyle Jagger there to outrank me." She took a bite of her cone, the creamy taste of chocolate on her tongue. "Just because he's a guy, everyone goes to him for an opinion now. I'm as serious as serious can be. You've even said I wrote the book on 'anal.'"

"You wear skirts and heels to work in a construction trailer." The last glowing ribbons of sunset reflected in Mark's sunglasses. "Wear jeans and work boots."

"But I can't do that. I have to go from Dad's job to my job, and it just isn't practical. I've always worn a skirt and heels to work and it's never slowed me down. When have you seen me not walk on a job site because of my shoes?"

"Almost never. But you weren't in the position you are in now."

Her brows lifted and she made a face. "Kyle thinks he's the boss."

"Only because you aren't being a Moretti. Get in his face if you have to."

The chocolate ice cream went sour in her mouth. "I have to work with him. I don't want undue conflict. You know that doesn't solve a thing. I'm just saying I wish the subs would ask me instead of him when there's a crisis."

"Maybe Kyle's more relaxed than you. Lately, you've been uptight."

"Who wouldn't be?"

"A guy. We aren't emotional about the same things women are. Forget about who you were, and be who you need to be. You're really smart, Franci. Show it or else Kyle will take over everything."

"Whose side are you on?"

Mark wiped his lips with the side of his thumb. "I'm on the side that says let's get this project done, let's get it done right." He got to his feet. "And God help us, let's get it done fast before you and Jagger kill each other."

The next day, Francesca came into work with a pair of steel-toed work boots in her hand. They were high-tops, just like Kyle's, with black laces.

She'd tucked a pair of socks into them and planned to give the boots a try right after she took a look at what was pending on her desk. She would tour the entire job site today, top to bottom, connect with the subcontractors and make sure they were following through on the completion dates they'd promised.

If she was efficient with her time, she could get that done in an hour. She had to. She had clients coming to her firm at ten to go over drawings. Being in top-notch professional mode was a must. Which was why she'd worn a black-and-white lace skirt with a white lace sweater. The boots were going to look ridiculous with a skirt, but she had no other choice.

She plopped the work boots next to her desk, took a

seat and did her best to ignore the curious look in Kyle's eyes as he glanced her way. While he was glancing at her, she found the brown paper sack with her name written on it, resting on her desk.

Why did he have to be so thoughtful?

"Croissant?" she asked.

"Biscuit and honey." Kyle barely met her eyes as he went back to reading e-mails on his laptop. "Coffee's hot."

"Thanks."

After ten minutes, she kicked off her black sling-back heels, slipped on cotton socks and laced up the boots.

"New shoes?" Kyle asked, as she stood and grabbed her hard hat.

"Possibly."

The trailer door opened and Tom, the plumbing contractor, said, "We've got a problem. Somebody cut one of our pipes and I need a shut-off on the main valve."

Kyle went for his hard hat, but Francesca cut him off at the doorway. "I can handle it."

Halfway down the trailer steps, she glanced back impatiently. Tom was still standing there with a questioning look on his face, gazing at Kyle.

Kyle waved him off. "What are you waiting for? She knows what she's doing."

At nine fifty-five, after a phone call to her secretary to say she would be ten minutes late, Franci dashed into the trailer to change shoes. She made fast work of it, gathering her purse and the red bag she used to tote blueprints.

Multitasking, she loaded her purse with papers she needed, while wiggling her foot into her high heel. She almost didn't notice the vase of flowers on her desk, a simple arrangement with two white peonies and a pink carnation.

Even though she didn't have seconds to spare, curiosity made her reach for the card.

It read simply: "You're pretty in work boots."

CHAPTER SEVENTEEN

ROBERT SAT IN HIS DAD'S pickup truck, the keys lying on the dash. The vehicle had been in the garage since his father passed away. With the big door up, sunshine sliced through a quarter of the large garage.

Running his hand over the steering wheel, Robert thought back to the time Giovanni had taught him to drive a car. They'd practiced on the '67 Chevy Malibu that they'd restored together. That car would be worth a fortune today.

He wished he'd held on to it. But when he'd married Marie and started a family, the old souped-up Malibu hadn't been practical. Now he drove a Suburban—large enough to haul four kids, and restaurant supplies from Cash and Carry.

Robert slipped the key into the ignition and turned it backward to supply juice to the stereo. Immediately, Bocelli's whiskey-smooth voice sang through the truck's speakers.

Dad's favorite artist.

Leaning back in the seat, Robert closed his eyes. He listened to the Italian ballad and remembered years past, and the things he hadn't said to his father but should have. It was in life that a man had to live. And a real man, a good man, had to have the courage to discuss deep feelings with those he loved. Or else, one day, it would be too late.

Death had a way of coming out of nowhere, and Robert hadn't been prepared to say goodbye. There were days when he did better, and days when he did worse. For the first week or so, he'd thought he was doing really great. Then, two weeks after the fact, it had hit him.

His father was gone.

He didn't know how John could cope after losing his wife. To lose a parent was bad. But to lose a spouse? It would kill him to go on without his Marie.

Robert thanked God he had a wonderful wife, good kids and a job he enjoyed.

He hoped John would find someone again. Same for Mark and Franci.

Franci, with all her smarts and spirit…it'd be tough to find a man who could make her happy.

He'd asked her how she was holding up, what with everything going on, and she'd said fine. But he could tell the situation was hard on her.

If there was something Robert could do to help, he would have done it for her. But there was nothing.

The music came to a crescendo of orchestral chords as Bocelli belted out the final notes.

Robert must have been smiling, because Marie's voice intruded into the dark corners of his mind.

"Thinking of your dad?" she asked from the truck's open door.

With eyes still closed, he smelled her perfume. He knew her by memory and didn't have to look at her to know that her hair would be touching her shoulders, the left side tucked behind her ear.

"I was," Robert replied, slowly opening his eyes. "But when you asked, I was thinking about how much I love you."

He took his wife into his arms, bringing her onto his lap inside the truck's cab.

"I love you, too."

"We're so very lucky," he said, breathing the scent of her hair into his lungs and holding her tightly.

They sat there for a few minutes, then Marie kissed him quickly on the mouth. "Your mom says it's time to eat."

Getting out of the truck, Robert put his hand on the small of his wife's back, knowing that, like last Sunday, this supper wouldn't be the same, with Giovanni Moretti missing from the head of the table.

FRANCESCA HELD ON TO a bowl of macaroni, bringing it into the dining room as the doorbell rang.

"Francesca," her mother said, "I'll get that."

For a moment, Franci wasn't sure if her mom meant the penne or the bell.

Mariangela dashed toward the front of the house to answer the door.

The dining table was brimming with food tonight.

Not their usual Sunday supper. Mom said she'd invited someone to join them, but no amount of prying had gotten a name out of her. She'd said she could invite anyone she wanted, and didn't need permission.

Franci had been wondering who it was, but then Mom knew a bunch of women through the church who she socialized with. Some were more likable than others—no doubt the reason for the mystery. Perhaps it was one of the ladies who talked nonstop, and Mom felt like filling the table with endless conversation.

Mariangela had gotten out some jars of red peppers to go with the plates of sausages and cheeses, macaroni and gravy, the salads and breads.

Traditional Italian suppers began at 2:00 p.m. Today everyone had come, even Zack and Kara.

The room was in chaos, with grandkids taking seats and the adults choosing which wine to pour first. Cora and Emelia fought over the olives, and Mark and John speculated on the upcoming Boise State football season. Marie stood over her eight-year-old daughter, using her fingers as a comb to rearrange her ponytail.

Francesca took her seat, then glanced at the head of the table, where her oldest brother, John, now sat. She gave him a soft smile, refusing to let her father's absence put a damper on her spirits. She'd actually been feeling better this week about how her crazy life was falling into more of a routine. There still weren't enough hours in the day, but she was managing to keep a balance.

Everyone seemed to be talking over everyone else,

until her mom's clear voice broke through the chatter. "Our guest is here. Kyle, I think you know most everyone."

Francesca's chin shot up.

Kyle Jagger? For Sunday supper?

"Hello," he said, evidently uncomfortable, but making the best of it. He made quick eye contact with her, then gave the bottle of red wine he held to her mom. "It's a merlot. It goes great with spaghetti."

"We aren't having 'ghetti," Cora said in her small voice. "I want pen-ney."

Kyle smiled.

Mariangela ushered Kyle around the table to John's old spot. "Here, you sit and I'll get an opener for this."

Nobody spoke for long seconds, then Mark said, "So, you came to have dinner with us."

It wasn't a question, rather a statement. One that Kyle replied to with ease. "Your mom invited me. No bachelor is going to pass up home cooking for a microwave meal."

Zack laughed, then slouched in his seat.

Mariangela said, "It was the right thing do to. After all, we're all but partners. It's time we got better acquainted."

Mark sat next to Franci and poured more wine into her glass so that it almost overflowed. "You may need this," he said beneath his breath.

She scowled. She didn't need extra wine simply because Kyle had showed up for Sunday supper. It was her mom's house and she could do whatever she wanted.

Trying to read her for clues about the sudden peace treaty with Kyle, Franci leveled her gaze on her, but her mother's features were masked. She took her usual seat on the end of the table, facing John. "Zackary, can you say grace?"

Zack, in typical teenage boy fashion, stammered his way through an awkward grace, then everyone reached for serving plates and began to pass them around the table.

"So how's the project coming?" John's question was thrown out to the room.

Francesca and Kyle both began talking at the same time.

Biting her lower lip, Franci looked to Kyle.

"Sorry," he mumbled. "Go ahead."

"No, you," she countered, then didn't say anything further.

Kyle replied, "It's more your project. I'm just sitting in."

"Actually," Francesca interjected, "I end up just sitting in, and you go out in the field."

"Not every time. It was you talking to the plumbers the other day," Kyle pointed out.

Francesca took a long sip of wine, then another. "True."

Mark intervened. "Things are coming along pretty good. We had some problems this week. Franci took care of a large headache with that busted pipe."

"Good for you, Francesca," her mother exclaimed, in an admiring tone that for some reason made Franci feel like a child.

She dipped a slice of bread into olive oil. "It wasn't any big deal."

Her mother filled her plate, something Francesca

hadn't seen her do since before Dad died. She had a different look about her tonight, almost as if she'd created a distraction for herself. A detour to take her mind off missing Giovanni.

"So, Kyle, how are things going in your life?" Mariangela asked as she circulated the cheese plate.

"Pretty good."

Franci thought he looked more than pretty good. He had worn a button-down, white dress shirt tucked into a pair of Levi's that hugged his long legs. He'd unbuttoned the cuffs and rolled up the sleeves to midforearm. His wristwatch caught the light, contrasting with his tanned skin. He was a fine-looking man, and she had a hard time taking her eyes off of him.

"I got a card from your mother," Mariangela said, spearing a wedge of sausage. "If you talk to her, tell her thank-you."

"I will."

"I lost touch with her over the years. She and I would have a cup of coffee sometimes when your father was in town and off with Giovanni about some business project. After Parr passed away, she and I didn't see each other again. How's she doing?"

Franci detected a hint of displeasure, a crease of annoyance on Kyle's face. Or was that concern marking his brow? "She's fine." He ate a bite of macaroni with sauce, then added quietly, "She's getting married."

"Oh, she is?" Mariangela leaned forward, then sighed. "I just can't imagine."

The mood went from casual conversation to an awkward quiet in a matter of half a second.

Nobody in the Moretti family could think about a replacement for Giovanni. His were impossible boots to fill.

"Well, my goodness," Mariangela said in a lighter tone. "Tell her congratulations for me."

"I will."

Table talk moved to Kara's experiences as a new driver, to Cora's latest finger painting that had Marie put on the refrigerator.

"Kyle, I'll bet you didn't know that when Mark was an altar boy he got into quite a bit of trouble."

"Mom," Mark grumbled. "I didn't."

"Oh, but you did. Altar boys are usually the worst Catholics."

Kyle smiled.

"Are you Catholic, Kyle?" Mariangela asked, fork paused in her hand.

"Lutheran."

"That's nice," she replied, then continued eating.

That's nice? Franci thought her mother was acting as if she were a few stitches short of a seam. What was all this about?

"I don't remember Mark getting into a lot of trouble," Robert commented. "It was John."

John cleared this throat. "No, it was you."

"Not me. Maybe it *was* Mark. In high school, he was always on a luge to hell in chemistry class, trying to blow up the place."

"Dad, you were never in trouble," Zack said, an undertone of accusation in his teenage voice. At eighteen years old, he'd become a daily challenge to his father.

Emelia stated, "Cora's trouble."

"No, she's not." Mariangela beamed at her granddaughter. "She's an angel."

"Just like graw-ma is a angel-la."

Everyone laughed—except Franci's mom, who softly smiled, tears filling her eyes. Giovanni used to call her Angela sometimes.

To Francesca, it was interesting to say the least to have Kyle listen in on family conversations that she wouldn't have necessarily shared with him. These were the details of the Morettis—the good, the bad, the funny and sad.

Supper passed with talk that included Kyle. If he hadn't been invited by Mariangela, it was doubtful the group would have included him on the level they did. Even so, comments were guarded when the topic turned to business.

After the table had been cleared, the grandkids went to play in the backyard. Kara and Zack cut out before dessert. Zack had driven them both over in his own car and John gave him strict orders to go straight home with his sister. Marie and Robert lounged in the living room, talking with Mark and John about the restaurant. Mariangela busied herself in the kitchen, and Francesca would have killed to help—but Mom told her to go out back with Kyle and keep him company while he sat on the patio.

She grudgingly went outside.

Franci found him on one of the chaise longues, a half glass of red wine in his hand.

"Hey," he said in greeting.

She sat next to him in one of the covered chairs. "Hey."

The girls' laughter came to them. "Aunt Franci, watch me!"

Cora slid down the slide, aided by her nine-year-old sister.

Francesca clapped. "Great job, sweetie!"

"Again!" Cora shouted.

Franci and Kyle watched the girls, and then his voice broke into her disjointed thoughts. "It's weird being here."

At that moment, she let out a sigh. "I was thinking that very same thing."

"I probably shouldn't have come, but your mom really wanted me to."

"My mom can be persuasive."

"She didn't have to twist my arm." Kyle flashed a smile. "I wasn't altogether kidding when I said I didn't want to eat a nuked dinner."

This time Francesca smiled. "I hear you. I'm not really into the cooking thing myself. I manage, though."

"I'd say you manage pretty good."

The note with the flowers had said she was pretty. She dared to question, "How come you put flowers on my desk?"

"Because I wanted to and because I do think you're beautiful."

She felt a blush wash over her cheeks. "Well, thanks. It was nice of you."

"I didn't do it to be nice." Kyle's expression grew bland. "I can be a real jerk if I want to. I've come close with you, only you didn't really see me going that direction." His smile resumed. "But I was thinking it."

She had to laugh. "Well, good. I'm glad you're human."

The girls giggled, going down the slide one right after the other.

"They're cute," Kyle commented, staring at the four dark-haired little girls. "You think you'll want to have kids when you get married?"

She lifted her brows. "Who says I'll get married?"

"I don't know. I just assumed."

With another a sigh, she admitted, "Of course I want to get married. One day. When I meet the right man."

Her last words brought a self-conscious heat to her face. "And you? Do you want to get remarried?"

"Yeah, but I really need to make sure."

Curiosity about his former marriage won out over her reluctance to question him on such a private subject. "What happened?" she asked.

"I know it'll sound clichéd, but we were two different people moving in two different directions." Kyle drank the last of his wine. "She and I ended up not being a good fit."

"I'm sorry."

"Me, too. Nobody wants an F on their report card. It's a good thing we didn't have kids." He set his empty glass down. "I noticed how your brother is struggling with raising teens on his own, based on a few of the comments over dinner. And please know that I don't mean that offensively."

"I understand what you're saying. It's a challenge being an only parent. I can't imagine how he does it." She rested her arms on the sides of the lounge chair. "I've never asked you, but I guess I've made the assumption—you're an only child?"

"I always wanted an older brother."

"And I always wanted a younger sister." Franci found she was actually enjoying the easy way their conversation seemed to flow. "So are you very close with your mom?"

His huff of laughter countered any thoughts she might have been entertaining that his family dinners could be just as lively as theirs. "That's kind of a sore subject for me right now. My mom and I aren't seeing eye to eye on something at the moment."

"Is there anything I can do?"

He slanted his gaze at her, chin down and eyes probing. "You don't know the half of it, honey."

Intrigued, she sat taller. "Try me."

For a moment, she thought he might tell her, then he said, "Nope. It wouldn't make a difference anyway." Then he changed gears, startling her with his next words. "Franci, since I'm going to be in Boise for the long haul, I'm going to ask a favor of you."

She stilled, tense and waiting. A favor could mean a

million things. Sign over more duties from Moretti, break a contract, walk away from the project… "What?"

"My condo needs a remodel. It's just a big empty space in a downtown warehouse. I have some furniture, nothing great. But I need a color scheme, some ideas on what I should do, and I need someone to handle it because I don't have time."

"And I do?"

"You've got an eye for this kind of thing and I'll pay great."

"I don't need the money."

"Maybe not, but I need what you've got."

There was a double meaning in his words that evoked a shiver across her skin, and caused the fine hairs at her nape to tingle in response.

Suddenly the late afternoon felt chilly, when in fact it was still rather warm outside.

"But I'm stretched thin as it is," she countered. "I don't know when you think I can get to your job."

"Prioritize me." He grinned. His smile was full of charm, his eyes warm and sparkling. He was handsome, yet boyish. He had a way about him that attracted her like no other.

It would be lunacy to work with him. Even though, as an architect, she had an eye for colors and designs.

"I'm no interior decorator," she said, absently tucking her hair behind her ear.

"Maybe not, but you know how to design spaces and you're the best I've seen. The Grove is state-of-the-art, but it's also warm and functional. I think it's probably one of the best building designs I've ever come across."

Straightening her posture, she murmured, "Flattery doesn't work on me."

His eyes shone like summer leaves catching the sunlight at dusk. "Then maybe this will."

Before she was aware of his intentions, he leaned forward and kissed the corner of her mouth.

A delicious flex of her muscles seemed to loosen all the tension in her body as she focused on his mouth, so close to hers yet just a fraction of an inch off.

She might have moved her head to meet it fully, except for Emelia's laughter and declaration, "Eww! They're kissing!"

Francesca sobered immediately and pulled back. Beneath her breath, she murmured, "No fair."

"Who says I'm fair?"

He had her there, and she was silenced. For the longest time, she tried to think of a really good reason why she couldn't do it, but nothing came to her other than she didn't have time.

But since when didn't she have time for a man like Kyle? She had told herself she shouldn't like him, but she did. She'd talked herself out of being civil to him, but she was.

Everything she'd assumed he'd be, he wasn't.

"I suppose I can fit you in," she caught herself uttering, then a soft sigh escaped her lips. "I really don't have a spare minute in my day, so we'll have to do this at night."

"I'm my best at night, honey." He stood, then announced, "I have to get going."

She followed him through the house as he said goodbye to the rest of her family, taking a special moment to sincerely thank her mom for the dinner.

With her hand on the door frame, Francesca watched him get into his truck and pull away from the curb.

She couldn't help thinking she was out of her mind to make a commitment to help him. There were plenty of other architects in Boise, as well as interior designers—Suzy Blaire for starters.

Perhaps it was the very thought of Suzy drooling over pillows and fabric swatches, while holding Kyle captive, that made Francesca want to keep this project, and the man, to herself.

CHAPTER EIGHTEEN

"SO WE ALL AGREE—Trent Black is perfect for Franci," Jordan said as she stirred sugar into her iced tea.

"I hate to say it," Lily replied in a voice filled with excitement, "but he is." She'd been looking over the man's profile and photos, and the follow up e-mails that he'd been trading with them.

Erin had seen some of the e-mails as well, and nodded as she read the responses Trent had given to the questions she'd fired off at him as to why he wanted to meet "Franciful."

Each of the three women had access to the Internet dating account that Jordan had set up, and all three had been corresponding with Trent Black, a venture capitalist from Eagle.

He was forty-two and a widower. He had a three-year-old little girl *and* he was half-Italian. He'd shared personal photos with the date squad, even given some references, which Jordan had checked out. The gorgeous man was on the upper tier of great catches.

Clean-shaven, six feet four, jet-black hair, clear blue eyes. Very athletic—he ran marathons—and appeared to be financially stable. An added bonus was that he loved to cook.

Lily had written to ask him why he'd chosen to use an Internet dating service when clearly he wasn't hurting in the looks or the "having it all together" department. He'd said after being alone for the past two years, it had been difficult to figure out which of the women friends he'd known were genuinely sincere with helping him get through a rough patch, and which ones had wanted to move in on his wife's grieving husband.

He'd isolated himself for the first year, came out of his shell a little for the second, gone on a few dates, but nobody had captured his undivided attention beyond a second date. His standards were extremely high, and as of yet, he hadn't dated any of the women on the personals. He was fairly new to them, thinking this might be a better way to meet a woman, since his schedule was chock-full, and his daughter was a priority in his life.

The e-mail he'd written to Erin had made her cry. He'd talked about how difficult things had been for him, how he wanted to make a good life for his little girl, but he missed the company of a quality woman.

"Well, you know," Erin said, slipping off her stylish reading glasses, "if Franci doesn't want him, I'd take the guy in a New York minute."

"Me, too," Jordan said, squeezing lemon into her tea.

"Me three." Lily shuffled through the e-mails. "This gives me hope. I think I'm going to put up my own ad."

Gazing at Jordan, Erin asked, "So you finally sent him Franci's photos?"

"Last night. And this," she said, drawing out the last sheet of paper, "was his reply. Ladies, listen to this and weep. 'Thank you for sharing your friend's photo with me, but after what you've told me about her, her outer beauty didn't really matter to me. She sounds like a woman I'd like to get to know. But that being said, I sat back with a big smile on my face as I looked through the photos you attached of Franci-ful. She's better than you described. If I had to get shipwrecked on an island, she's the goddess I'd want to wash up on shore with me. I look forward to hearing back from you to let me know when I can meet your friend.' So there you have it." Jordan set the e-mail on the table.

"Well, when do we make the introduction?" Lily beamed.

Erin suggested, "We should call her now."

"This has to be done in just the right way," Jordan said cautiously. "You know how she gets. She's going to be mad as all get-out at first, but once we present her with Trent's profile in a very supportive and enthusiastic way, she can't turn him down."

"If she does, she's crazy." Lily settled her napkin on her lap.

Since the ad was her idea, Jordan made the final decision. "At our Wednesday night get-together, we spill our guts."

"Problem," Erin said. "I've got a meeting with the accountants that night. Can we do Thursday?"

All of them could, and a quick call to Francesca confirmed she was fine with the change as well.

Everything had fallen into place.

Lifting her glass, Jordan sipped her tea and decided it tasted perfect. She couldn't have been more pleased with herself.

MARIANGELA FLIPPED through the pages of her address book, stopping at a familiar name, remembering the times she and Giovanni had socialized with this couple or that person.

Shoving aside her melancholy, she worked her way to the *J*'s. She found the name she wanted, then picked up the phone and dialed.

A woman's voice answered. "Hello?"

"Helene? This is Mariangela Moretti."

"Mariangela! My goodness, it's been ages."

"Yes, it has." Mariangela settled back on the davenport with a cup of coffee resting on its arm. "I told your son to extend my appreciation, but I wanted to thank you personally for the card you sent."

"I was sorry to hear about your husband. Giovanni was always there for Parr if he needed advice or a friend to talk to. It's not too often businessmen in the same field can lean on each other in such a way. Losing your husband is so difficult. But life does march on, Mariangela. Mine sure has."

"That's what your son said." Mariangela took a small drink of her coffee, waiting to broach a subject she was curious about.

"I'm sure my son says a lot of things."

There'd been something in the way Kyle had mentioned the new man in his mother's life and the relationship he had with his mom. They just hadn't seemed right. Something was going on. Not that Mariangela was a snoop, but she sensed Kyle was struggling about it.

"Have you been doing okay?" Mariangela asked.

"I'm wonderful!" Helene proceeded to deliver a monologue about the past ten years and what had been going on in Seattle.

Mariangela listened with half an ear, her thoughts taking her in a different direction.

Having seen Kyle and Francesca talk and interact over the table, she suspected something was going on in Boise, too. Something with her daughter and Helene's son.

At first, Mariangela hadn't been sure that Franci had actually been flirting with Kyle, until she saw them on the patio and watched through the kitchen window as they'd talked and smiled. The body language had been telling, the mutual interest quite apparent. It had reminded her of her and Giovanni all those years ago.

Kyle was in love with her daughter.

Maybe he didn't know it, maybe he was afraid to acknowledge the feeling.

And even more so…Franci was falling hard and fast for the good-looking owner of Legacy Constructors.

Of course, Francesca would deny it if confronted. Mariangela's daughter was so proud, so independent. All those years ago, Franci had confided in her that she'd lost her heart to Eduardo and would never make that mistake again. She dated selectively, or not at all.

Mariangela's and Giovanni's greatest hope was that their little girl would find a wonderful man and marry him, settle down and have children.

That Giovanni would now miss that part of their daughter's life struck Mariangela hard. She couldn't let the feelings overtake her or she'd start crying on the phone.

Pulling herself together, she asked, "So you're getting married?"

"Oh, my, yes! To a wonderful gentleman I met at my church. He's the icing on my cake."

A pang settled in Mariangela's heart, making her feel hollow and empty. Lonely. Giovanni would be the only icing on *her* cake. She didn't know how Helene could move on so exuberantly, but it had been what—eight or nine years? Maybe she'd feel able to make a new life for herself after that much time had passed.

"I hope you'll have many years of happiness," Mariangela said.

"Oh, we will! Ralph's going to be buying a coffeehouse for us to manage. Well, he'll do the managing. I'm supplying the funding so we don't have to get messy and involve investors. Ralph says he can make Cuppa Joe into a chain and we'll sell stock on the open market and everything."

"Cuppa Joe?"

"I've gone and spilled the coffee beans!" Helene gasped. "I told Ralph I wouldn't tell anyone the name he's chosen for our little venture. You will keep it a secret, won't you?"

"No worries, Helene." Mariangela crossed her legs and tucked them beneath her. The fringe of a pillow spilled across her lap and she absently felt one of the tassels. "I had your son over for supper the other day and I must say, he's turned into a fine young man."

"Isn't he though?" Helene's voice sounded sincere, but vague. "I only wish he wasn't so stubborn. You know how some men are. They get their teeth stuck into something and they'd rather chew than let go."

"I'm not sure I follow you."

"It's nothing, just some family business."

A niggling sense of alarm gripped Mariangela, a feeling she couldn't quite pinpoint, but it was there.

She tested the waters, having a feeling there were other things going on. "In spite of everything, the surprise partnership and all, he's really been an asset to Moretti and our biggest project."

"Partnership?"

"He's helping us with the Grove Marketplace. Giovanni and your son had a private deal to join forces."

Helene's next words were flippant. "I'm sure whatever he's doing is spreading him too thin to deal with me. He didn't return my last call. I've given him a deadline."

"To finish a project for Legacy?"

"Good grief, no. I need him to buy out my Legacy stock, but Kyle isn't being helpful. He keeps stalling and telling me he doesn't have the money, but I know he does." An exasperated sigh came across the line. "Legacy is doing fabulously well."

The missing pieces began to fall into place, and they made a puzzle Mariangela could never have foreseen.

Kyle Jagger needed to buy his mother out so she could give the money to her future husband. Only Kyle didn't have the funds to do so because he'd gotten tied in with Moretti.

Oh, my…

And the man hadn't said a word to her family about how dire his situation was. No wonder he was desperate to get out of the deal he had made with Giovanni.

Helene rambled on, but Mariangela didn't really hear what she was saying. Her mind was elsewhere, her thoughts taking her to a place where questions came faster than she could process them.

FRANCESCA SHOWED UP in the trailer with something she'd never in her life touched, much less bought. The X-rated item was nestled inside her red blueprint tote. Deep in the bottom. The wrapper still on it.

The trailer was empty, but the usual pastry bag sat on her desk, where Kyle had left it. She'd seen his truck outside, but hadn't seen him. He must be on the job site somewhere.

It was amazing how much she'd come to expect him to

be here, at his desk. She grew conflicted over how she'd been thinking of this as his space now and not her dad's.

Kyle had slipped into her life without her being fully aware of the deep impact he had on her. She often caught herself thinking about him, wondering what he was doing when he wasn't here. Where he was or who he might be with.

She lay in bed at night and relived their kisses, smiled fondly when she thought about his mannerisms or expressions. The way he talked on the phone and doodled with a pen, or how he kept his sunglasses on the top of his head. The way he sat and the way he walked. How he could manage to make her heart turn over when she saw him, smelled him.

Especially when they kissed.

She loved the firmness of his mouth, the way he could make her feel all warm and safe. The hard press of his body, his strong arms around her…these were the thoughts that kept her awake. There was no doubt she was falling in love with him.

She was both surprised and excited over the idea. And yet she was also cautious. This was territory she hadn't been in for a long time.

She didn't want to make more out of something than there was. She told herself to go slow. To not let him know what she was thinking. That it was better to feign disinterest.

"We've got a planning and zoning problem." Mark's

raised voice intruded on her thoughts as he stepped inside the office.

"And I've got a problem with the plumbers." Francesca turned to face her brother. "You go first."

"The trees along Main Street. We spaced them wrong."

"Easy fix."

"Something about a fire hydrant and the grates beneath the trees."

She frowned, pressing her fingertips to her forehead. Not even ten o'clock and already the day's issues were piling up. "I'll look at my drawings and see what's going on." She sat behind her desk, moving papers to make room for her red tote.

In what she hoped was a casual tone, she asked, "Have you seen Kyle?"

"Eighth floor. Why, what do you need?" Mark's astute eyes grew hooded. "Or is it Kyle you want?"

Francesca didn't want to get into anything with her brother. There were some topics better left untouched. She didn't feel like having her love life examined. At least not today.

"Never mind." She rose and hooked one of the tote handles on her coat tree, but missed the second, and her bag came crashing to the floor, the contents spilling.

Mark glanced that way, his gaze fixed on what had fallen out. "Since when do you read *Playgirl?*"

Scrambling forward, she stuffed the magazine back inside her tote and secured it to the coat tree. After brushing the hem of her skirt and adjusting her blouse, she sat back down with a ramrod straight back and prim demeanor. When she dared to meet Mark's eyes, she found them brimming with amusement.

"What?" she asked, knowing full well she wouldn't get him to leave unless she told him what he wanted to know. Groaning, she said, "Fine. I bought that to put in the plumbers' trailer. I'm sick to death of them not treating me as if I was their equal."

"You want to be a plumber?"

"No," she huffed. "I want to be taken seriously."

"So buying a magazine with nude men in it is going to help?"

"As a matter of fact, yes."

Mark gave her a slow once-over. "Ya know, Franci, I wish I could have been the store clerk who sold you that. Where'd you get it?"

"At 7-Eleven, and I was mortified, but it had to be done," she said while opening the pastry bag to find a bagel with jelly, butter and a plastic knife. She smiled absently. "Have you noticed that the plumbers' trailer has pinups on the walls?"

"I put up Miss January."

"You did not."

Mark laughed. "I didn't. But she's hot."

"I just don't need to see naked women on the walls of a professional office."

"There's only two."

"Two too many. I've asked them several times to take down those photos and they blew me off. Now I'm going to retaliate."

"So you're going to put more up—new ones of guys? I don't think any of the plumbers are into men."

Francesca rolled her eyes. "I know that. I'm going to sneak in there and put this centerfold up and make a statement."

"A statement that you like naked men?"

"That nude photos on a trailer wall are tacky and I don't feel like seeing that when I go in to talk to their guys about job-related things."

Mark's gaze traveled to the corner of the room where her Red Wing boots sat by the coat tree. She still wore them to get around on the job site, but it hadn't made much of an impact.

"The boots haven't been working out for you, huh?"

Her brother's statement hit too close to home. "Mark," she groaned, frustrated. "Just go do something. I'm busy."

Ten minutes later, Francesca was lacing up her boots to go pay a visit to the plumbers—after she'd seen them all bail for the roach coach and lunch. She'd barely finished tying the second one when her mom came into the trailer.

"Francesca," Mariangela said, her voice tight. "I need to talk to Kyle. Is he here?"

"He's around, but I haven't seen him." She stood. "Why, are you asking him over for supper again?" The latter was said with a teasing tone.

The two of them had had a brief discussion about it after Kyle left last Sunday. Franci had asked her mother why she'd had him over with the family. Mariangela explained it had felt like the right thing to do, to move forward by including Kyle. But when Francesca pressed the issue, her mom had asked her outright if she had feelings for the owner of Legacy Constructors.

That was hard to own up to, especially given her heated reaction when she'd found out Kyle would be stepping into the spot left vacant by her father.

She'd ended up answering truthfully, admitting that she respected Kyle's business-making decisions, and the family did owe him a debt of gratitude.

"I just might ask him again," Mariangela replied now. "He doesn't have anyone in town to take care of him."

"Mom, somehow I think he can manage on his own."

"A man always needs a good woman to cook for him and take care of his needs. Make sure he's cared for, his dry cleaning is picked up—things like that."

Francesca's brows arched. "I'm sure Kyle's needs are simple."

"Men are complicated, Franci. And a good man should be put on a pedestal."

Sometimes her mom's thinking just wasn't realistic. What Franci wanted in a partner was an equal. A man who could do for her what she could do for him. They'd help each other. Of course she wanted to take care of her husband, but not to the degree that she lost herself in his world.

While she loved her mother dearly, she felt that Mariangela had had no real life outside of Giovanni. There were the ladies in her church group, and she was involved in a few organizations through the Catholic ministries, but other than that, Mom and Dad had mostly done things with each other.

Suddenly, planting a *Playgirl* magazine took a back seat in her hectic day. "Mom, sit down. Stay and visit with me for a while."

Mariangela readily sat at Giovanni's old desk, tenderly running her hand over the scarred top. Her simple gold wedding band caught the fluorescent light as she gave a half smile.

"Kyle certainly keeps the desk better organized than your dad did."

"Dad never had it organized," Franci responded, smiling as well.

"I miss him." Her mom's expression grew distant. "He was such a huge part of my life. We were best friends."

Francesca stayed sitting. She didn't want to get up and hug her mom, or they'd both start crying. Now wasn't a time for tears, it was more a moment of reflection.

"Remember that time when you came down and brought Dad his lunch, and he asked you to share it with him on the job site?"

"I do." Mariangela's eyes brightened. "He unrolled a set of blueprints on a stack of pallets and declared it was our picnic blanket. I brought him a warm meatball sandwich with cheese. One of his favorites."

"I know. He spilled sauce all over the folders. I notice them every time I'm looking for an invoice."

"That was Giovanni. Never used his napkin."

Franci softly laughed. "He definitely wore his meals down his shirtfront at times. It was just how Dad was."

"And do you remember that time when we bought our first real good furniture and I wanted to cover it with plastic, and Giovanni said, 'Angela, we're going to spill on it sooner or later, let's break it in sooner.'"

"Oh, Mom. Sitting on plastic would have been awful."

"I suppose. But I was so excited when it was delivered. My house smelled like new fabric and leather for weeks. It's one of those smells you never forget."

"Just like we'll never forget Dad."

"No. We won't. His memory is going to be in these buildings that are going up around us." Mariangela looked out the window to the construction site. "I'm sure my love is in heaven, telling God how we could be doing things better down here. Giovanni was good at telling everyone what they should be doing and how."

"I have no doubt he is watching us, Mom. And he's pleased. Look at how things are working out." Franci felt a pulse-pounding certainty, and along with it, the warmhearted emotion of gratitude. "Kyle's not pressuring us to buy him out anymore. He's going along with everything, trying to help."

"So where is Kyle?" her mom asked. "I really would like to talk to him."

At that moment, he entered the trailer, his boots covered in mud. He wore a hard hat and Levi's. His Blackberry phone was stuck to his ear and he was talking a mile a minute to someone. "I know that, but I couldn't make it over. I'm on my way."

He ended the call, then realized Francesca and Mariangela were in the trailer. "Hello," he said, clearly distracted and in his own zone.

He leaned over the desk, rifled through some papers, and was grabbing a few when his phone rang once more. He looked at the caller ID, ignored the ringing, and shook his head. Murmuring beneath his breath, he said, "It just never ends."

"Kyle, how are you?" Mariangela asked, rising to her feet as if she wanted to hug him.

Franci thought that a little odd, but didn't make anything more out of it.

"I'm okay, Mrs. Moretti." To Francesca he said, "I've got an OSHA problem on my seventeen story and I need to run over there, like, ten minutes ago. After I figure that headache out, I'm on my way to Seattle, and I don't know when I'm coming back. Could be a day or more. Sorry. You'll do just fine without me. You've always been the one who could handle everything—that's why Giovanni had so much faith in you."

Kyle packed up his things, juggling his thermos and briefcase, as well as two rolls of blueprints. Calling over his shoulder, he snorted with a grin, "Hell, you don't even need me around here."

Then he was gone.

Francesca sat there with a disconcerted feeling

washing over her. She almost wanted to go after him and say she did need him. On the job site and in her life.

But she didn't. Too many years of guarding her heart kept her silent.

CHAPTER NINETEEN

IT WAS A DONE DEAL.

Kyle agreed to pay Hal Burton ten percent interest when he was able to buy the Legacy stock back. As of this moment, Burton controlled his father's company, the company that Kyle had built into a success.

And now Kyle had paid his mom, and she was free to do with the money whatever she pleased.

The transaction between Hal and himself had been relatively easy. It was cut-and-dried, both men agreeing the situation was only temporary. The deal that left Kyle with a bitter taste in his mouth had been the one struck between himself and his mother.

Helene had been delighted, finally telling him that she was going to front the money to Ralph—who, by the way, had become her husband over the weekend. They'd had a quiet ceremony at their church with just a few friends.

Even if he'd been invited, Kyle would have declined to attend. He'd told her good luck when he'd given her the multifigure check. Then he'd taken the rest of the day to catch up at his Seattle office, stop by his condo and crash. He'd slept for two solid hours, not moving.

Mentally burned out, he'd succumbed to the pressure of trying to be too many places at once.

After eating dinner at Wild Ginger with Neil Bevilaqua, Kyle spent the night in Seattle, and flew back to Boise the next day.

He was in the trailer by noon. Already a Wednesday, and he still had Monday's work waiting for him.

Francesca wasn't there, but she had been. Cold coffee was left in her mug, her heeled shoes were beneath her desk and her work boots were missing. She hadn't taken her cell phone, and it rang three times. Not his place to answer it.

Leaning back in the boss's chair, he wondered what he was doing here.

This was insanity. He'd just sold stock in his company to pay off his mom, when he should have put his Moretti stock on the market with a business broker and been done with it.

But he just hadn't been able to sell the Morettis out. Or rather, Francesca. The woman had captured his attention and interest in ways he hadn't expected.

He'd had this gut-deep feeling of not wanting to disappoint her. Instead, he'd sacrificed himself.

Life was crazy.

Some days, he didn't want to get on the merry-go-round ride of uncertainties in business. Other days, he grabbed hold and let it take him where it would.

He'd been able to rebuild Legacy and make it a company to be proud of. He would do so again.

Hal Burton would simply be a shareholder. He didn't want to run anything, and they'd signed a deal to that effect. This was only temporary, Kyle reminded himself. A means to an end.

Francesca came bolting into the trailer, breathless and with her cheeks flushed. Seeing him, she stopped short.

"You're back," she blurted.

"You sound like you're disappointed to see me."

"No, not at all. It's just that I...well, I was doing something and I didn't know you were here."

"What were you doing?"

"Nothing much."

Guilt surfaced in the form of a blush that made it from her cheeks to her collarbone, revealed by the scooped neckline of her pink summer sweater. She wore a floral skirt that came two inches above her knees, and looked ridiculously sexy in her work boots, which seemed to emphasize the shape of her calves as much as her high heels did.

"'Nothing much' has you a little shaken up, honey."

She brushed her lustrous hair over her shoulders, then sat resolutely. "How was your trip?" she asked, taking a sip of her coffee, then grimacing over its temperature.

"Fine." His eyes narrowed. "Just what were you up to?"

She met his gaze, folding her arms. "It's that obvious?"

"Something's up with you. Did you have run-in with someone on the job?"

"More like a hit-and-run. Me doing the hitting and the running."

"You hit someone?"

"Metaphorically speaking." She sighed, exasperated. "If you must know, I just hit the plumbers' trailer with the centerfold of Mr. August. I taped him on the wall and ran out before I was spotted. I meant to do it the other day, but I missed my opportunity."

Unbidden, Kyle began to laugh, deeply and long. It felt really good to feel humor for a change, to let himself give way to something so stupidly funny.

"And why did you do that?" he asked with a broad smile.

"They weren't taking me seriously and I got fed up."

"And a nude guy is something serious?"

"It was my last resort." She burst into laughter herself, and her face took on a whole new appearance, softer, and if possible, prettier. "I can't believe I just did what I did! I haven't done anything this juvenile since…never."

"You'll definitely get their attention."

"Well, I just got sick of seeing those calendar women on their wall. It's offensive and I figured I'd make my point."

"You'll have to let them know it was you or else it won't be as effective."

"I know. I'll fess up on Monday at the supers' meeting." She uncapped a bottle of water and drank. Then she put her hands on her cheeks. "Oh, my. What a day so far."

She rose and stood in front of the box air conditioner. Her eyes drifted closed for a moment as the cold breeze ruffled her hair. She sighed and breathed in and out; the slow rise and fall of her breasts heated his body, thickened his pulse. He reacted toward her like a man in lust. Or in love.

It was all Kyle could do to stay sitting, and not take her into his arms and pull her down onto his lap.

"Hey, Franci," he said over the noise of the AC unit.

With her eyes still closed, she responded, "Hmm?"

"Why not take the steam out of your engine and check out my condo tonight?"

"DO YOU LIKE HARD THINGS or soft things?" Francesca asked Kyle as she looked around the vast space of his condominium. The area was nice, bigger than she had anticipated. She'd only seen this building from the outside.

The decor was sparse, the unit cavernous. City views were off to the west, but part of the living space faced east, too.

He couldn't help arching a brow. "That's a loaded question."

She paused, looking at him over her notepad. "Oh, come on. You're being silly."

He broke into a grin. "I'm being bad. Sometimes it just kind of happens."

She smiled. "Well, what's your answer?"

"Hard."

Licking her lips, she said, "Why doesn't that surprise me?"

He walked around her, entering the open kitchen,

where the low countertops were simple slabs of industrial concrete. "Get your mind out of wherever it was," he teased while grabbing a bottle of red wine. "I like rocks. Slate and granite."

"What are your favorite colors?"

"Blue and gray. I guess it's a Seattle thing."

She took notes, her concentration focused. She sensed Kyle was watching her as she moved about the area, assessing this and that.

"Do you prefer the ocean or the mountains?"

"Ocean."

"Your favorite season?

"Summer."

"Cool or hot?"

"Hot all the way." His grin caught her attention, and as he gave her a long appraisal, she tried to see herself through his eyes.

Her hair was swept back into a ponytail. She had on a body-hugging T-shirt that emphasized her breasts, and a pair of low-rise jeans. At the end of a long day, she'd dressed for comfort, not style. But somehow, she doubted he was complaining over her lack of fashion sense.

She continued her questions. "Sweet or sour?"

"Sweet. Always."

"Favorite time of day?"

"Right now." He pulled the cork out of the wine. "With you."

She set her notepad down on the breakfast bar, all the

blood in her body seeming to pool in her heart. The way he talked made romance easy.

She didn't know if she should admit having the same response, or let it go. This present moment was, by far, the best part of her long day. While taping up a cheesy centerfold on the plumbers' trailer wall had been exhilarating in its own way, it didn't hold a candle to how Kyle made her feel when she looked at him.

In the end, she said, "That's not an answer."

"Sure it is." He set a glass of wine in front of her, then turned to the stainless steel fridge. His backside was beyond fine, the muscles in his shoulders hard and defined. She hated to admit that Suzy Blaire had made a dead-on accurate observation about Kyle's physique.

Relaxed, he leaned a hand on top of the fridge, his body weight shifting as he peeked inside to the shelves of food. "So what do you want to eat? I've got steak, shrimp I'd have to defrost—"

"I didn't know I was here for dinner."

"Me, either, but you are now."

She was hungry. Lunch had been six hours ago. A steak did sound good.

Peeking over Kyle's shoulder, but keeping her distance, she gave the refrigerator contents a quick once-over. And quick was the key word. He had about as many groceries as she did.

Skim milk, three Coronas, two blackening bananas, butter, a carton of eggs, and ketchup. An unopened tray of T-bone steaks sat on the top shelf next to the milk.

"Steak sounds good." She stood back, then settled on a bar stool at the breakfast bar. "Need any help?"

"I think I can manage to broil a steak. But it's not going to be as good as what your mom makes for Sunday dinner."

Franci smiled as he took the steaks out. "My mom is the best cook ever."

"Your brother's good, too," Kyle said, while firing up the oven.

"I guess that makes up for me being lame in the kitchen."

"Honey, nobody's ever really lame in the kitchen. Either they want to cook or they don't. I fall into the 'don't' category. Just too much going on."

"I'm the same way." She settled in, enjoying her wine as she watched Kyle cook. Steak was a simple thing to fix, but she did appreciate the way he moved. He used concise motions, was very efficient at everything he did. Just like he was at work.

"When I used to hang out with my dad," Kyle said, "he showed me the best way to get through a day was to map out what you can, then always have a plan for alternate routes."

"My dad was different. He winged it most of the time." Franci grew pensive, feeling a vague smile touch her lips. "I really liked to watch him. He'd start ten different things, go in twenty different directions, and at the end of the day, wouldn't have half of anything completed, but he left with a feeling of satisfaction. I wish I could be more like him."

Kyle met her eyes, holding them and prolonging the moment. "I think you're more like him than you realize."

"Thanks. I'll take that as a compliment."

"I meant it as one."

She couldn't help the warmth that shivered through her body and settled deep in her heart. It felt good to sit and talk to Kyle, to reminisce about Dad and not feel lonely or sad. Kyle seemed to be the only non-Moretti who could truly understand and sympathize with what she was going through.

Just looking at him gave her a familiar shortness of breath, as well as a longing for more out of life. More out of her day-to-day existence. She'd always thought she led a full life, keeping up the pace and doing what had to be done. But she never stopped to enjoy the simple things, she realized now.

Of course her nights out with her girlfriends were great; they kept her grounded in a whirlwind week. But it just wasn't the same as sitting here with a good-looking man, enjoying a conversation that seemed to take its own natural course. Franci didn't feel on guard, or that she had to try to be the kind of woman she thought Kyle might like.

It was really nice.

They ate steak and canned corn, drank wine and looked out at the city lights. The space was fantastic, she decided, and with the right design, it could be a showplace.

In spite of her reservations about taking on such a project, she had to admit that the prospect excited her.

She already had a bunch of ideas about textures she wanted to run together. First off, she'd add a half wall in the entry, to draw the eye toward a focal point before entering the largest space. She didn't want to close off any of this area; she liked it as it was. But it needed warmth, a sense of belonging. Roots. Personal touches.

There were no photos, nothing that seemed to say this was Kyle Jagger's home.

"Do you have anything around that's important to you?" she asked, her mind still focused on the renovations.

"Yeah." His response was quiet, humbling. "You."

She sat across from him at the table by the window. Outside, the moon hung low in the sky, the city lights twinkled.

She supposed she could have been coy or brushed his comment off as flirtatious or insignificant, but she didn't. Instead, she basked in the knowledge that he thought she was someone he could count on, could be with, could talk to.

"Thanks," she murmured softly, finishing the last of her steak and drinking the rest of her wine. Kyle refilled her glass. His movements were casual, his manner soothing and relaxing to be around.

The candles he'd lit around the living room and kitchen area bounced shadows off the bare walls. Kyle was awash in pale light, his face chiseled and handsome. She liked how he looked at her, how he smiled. Her heart turned over in response, and she felt truly happy.

She said, "It's funny how all this happened, isn't it?"

"Maybe not so much funny as destined."

"Destined—how so?"

"I think our dads would have eventually gone into a joint partnership together. Not for every project, but on a few important jobs. My father always said if any man in business could be trusted for his ethics, it was Giovanni Moretti. Those words always stuck with me, and that's why I made the deal with your dad. I knew he was a good guy."

Francesca appreciated the tribute, the affirmation of feelings she had about her father. She missed him terribly, but it was nice to have someone like Kyle think highly of him.

"Maybe you're right," she conceded, wondering if there could be some truth to Kyle's supposition. She was quite certain her dad would be beyond proud of her for carrying on the family business the way she was.

"Come on," Kyle said, standing. "Let's go sit on the couch. I'll get the dishes later."

She wasn't much for cleanup herself, usually stacking dirty plates in the sink and dealing with them in the morning. She preferred to rise early and get her day going before sunrise. The evenings were her downtime, and she didn't like to be bothered with household inconveniences.

"Are you a morning person?" she asked as they took seats on the soft leather sofa that faced the large floor-to-ceiling windows.

"Yep."

"Me, too."

"I do like the nights, though."

"Same here. But it's usually when I'm winding down, and I don't stay up real late."

Kyle settled his arm over her shoulder, absently brushing the sleeve of her T-shirt, then skimming his fingers lower, to her bare skin. "Tired?" he asked.

"Not physically. I'm content." As soon as she said it, she felt that very feeling wash through her. The wine seemed to hit all at once, and she was more at ease than she'd been all week. It was so great to sit here, to have Kyle touch her and rub her skin, raising gooseflesh.

Many times in the past, she would have killed for an evening like tonight. To share a meal with someone special, to talk, to sit beside one another and snuggle.

It was an entirely new experience for her, one she embraced and was glad of.

"Kyle," she whispered.

"Yeah?"

"Thanks for dinner."

"Anytime."

Anytime had a lot of possibilities.

She had known months ago that she was attracted to Kyle. Those feelings had been building, growing and deepening. All of the tense laughter, the sideways glances, the phone calls on the pretense of business. All of them led up to this one night, this one moment. This collision of worlds.

His world.

Hers.

Any reservations she'd had about Kyle Jagger were gone. She wanted to be in love with him, so she let herself fall. Right at that instant, she granted herself the freedom of loving and trusting.

Perhaps Kyle sensed her surrender. He reached over and took her hand, rubbing his thumb back and forth—a very sensuous, very reassuring gesture. She knew how he felt about her. It had been unspoken up until now, yet the gifts, the lunches, the dinners, embraces and kisses, and all of the kindness, spoke volumes about his inner being and what he felt.

He leaned toward her and kissed her cheek, his breath warm against her skin as he rested his forehead against her temple.

And then she knew. He'd fallen in love with her, too. She knew it as surely as if he'd said it. But he was scared. Probably more so than her.

He took her into his arms and gently stroked the small of her back, instantly causing tingles on her arms and legs. Franci let out a sigh, and he eased back, his straight white teeth visible when he smiled.

Now she was a bit scared, afraid that feelings she'd hidden away years ago, pushed aside in pursuit of her career, in keeping Moretti Construction and Bella Design the focus of her life, would come to the surface too quickly and embarrass her.

Francesca feared Kyle could read her thoughts, could tell she'd fallen for him.

As he kissed her, her very center came alive in a way

it never had before. She couldn't recall ever being this relaxed, this excited with a man, this lost to her emotions. They came at her rapidly, and she didn't even care to sort them out and make sense of them. She simply enjoyed, giving and taking in a kiss that all but curled her toes.

His hands splayed across her back, holding her close, stroking and caressing. His tenderness said a lot about who he was, who he could be and what he wanted to share.

Neither of them expressed aloud what they were thinking; their actions spoke for them.

Kyle ended the kiss and tucked her head beneath his chin, and Franci snuggled in, her arms wound tightly around him. She'd never known such a feeling of safety and love.

After gazing out the window at the moon for a long moment, she shut her eyes and gave in, releasing all her cares and concerns.

Silently, the tears fell. Tears from her soul. Her heart.

She was in love.

KYLE COULDN'T RECALL the last time he'd spent the night with a woman in his arms.

It had been beyond incredible to wake with Francesca beside him. Too bad he hadn't been able to enjoy the moment.

After a groggy glance at his watch, he'd been wide-awake in an instant. Francesca stirred when he slipped off the couch, but didn't open her eyes. He figured he'd let her sleep a few more minutes while he got ready for an early morning meeting.

There wasn't time for coffee, just enough to brush his teeth and shave. He finished dressing, then went back to the sofa and knelt down in front of her.

He kissed her awake.

Her eyelashes fluttered open as she licked her lips.

"Hey," she mumbled with a drowsy smile, then grew instantly alert as soon as she saw the wash of daylight inside the condo. "What time is it?" She bolted upright.

"Almost seven. I've got a seven o'clock."

"So do I!"

She jerked to her feet. It was a pretty sight to see her rumpled hair, the sleepiness on her face as she rubbed her fingertips beneath her eyes to wipe away the smudges of mascara. He thought she was gorgeous in the slanting sunlight.

The engine rumble of the Bus drifted through the room as it accelerated down Idaho Street.

"I'm going to be late. I have to go home and change."

"Sorry. I guess I should have woken you sooner. I just got up myself a few minutes ago. You looked like you could use the extra sleep." He snagged his cell phone and briefcase.

"I never sleep this late," she complained, already at the door, her tote bag and purse hoisted high on her shoulder. "I'm a light sleeper. The slightest noise wakes me up."

The elevator ride down was quiet, each of them wrapped in thought.

Kyle wanted to relive last night a hundred times, but he only had time for a once-through.

He'd fallen in love with her. It was that simple. He wanted her in his life, beside him forever.

As the elevator reached the ground floor, he kissed her goodbye. "Thanks for sleeping with me," he said, knowing the teasing would get her to smile, and wipe the frown off her brow.

They passed through the doors and out onto the sidewalk, where the early morning hubbub of Boise enveloped them. People were hurrying to work with cups of coffee and cell phones in their hands.

Franci shook her head, but flashed the smile he'd been hoping for. "Sleeping with you, and now I'm going to be late."

"Better late and—"

He'd been about to say "loved," but a man's voice cut him off.

"Franciful?"

Franci's head turned toward a tall, good-looking guy wearing a Brooks Brothers suit. He was clean-shaven, held a Starbucks coffee in his hand and smiled like a million bucks.

"Excuse me?" she responded.

He grinned. "It *is* you. I can tell by the smile and your hair. I'd know you anywhere."

"Have we met?"

"The Internet dating ad," the guy said. "I'm Trent Black. It's really great to finally meet you face-to-face."

Everything inside Kyle slowed to a crawl, and he felt as if he'd been kicked in the gut.

CHAPTER TWENTY

THE NOISE OF WATER filling the washing machine almost caused Mariangela to miss the ringing of her telephone. Walking swiftly down the hallway while she wiped her hands, she managed to catch the call just as her answering machine came on.

"Hold on," she said while shutting off the recording. "Hello?"

"Mrs. Moretti, L. C. Brown here."

Brown and Holt. The attorneys had been calling off and on for weeks with new developments or questions for her. She tried not to let everything overwhelm her, but there were so many forms and documents to be put in order.

"Yes, Mr. Brown?" Distracted, Mariangela heard the washer start to agitate, and tried to remember if she'd put detergent in it.

"I just hung up from an interesting phone call right now."

"Oh?"

"An insurance agent called me. Herbert Scott with Canadian Mutual Life Insurance."

Puzzled, she replied, "I don't know him."

"You will." Brown's baritone voice was as dry as a legal brief, but there was something more in his tone when he stated, "He's your knight in shining armor."

"I'm sorry, but I'm not following you."

"He faxed me a page from a policy Giovanni took out twenty years ago. Scott just heard about your husband's death and sends regrets that he didn't contact us sooner. It's not customary for the agent to call the client to collect on a death benefit, but given the amount of this one, Scott made an exception."

Mariangela gazed out the kitchen window, her hand resting on the sink's edge. "Giovanni had another life insurance policy? I have no record of it here in the papers. Granted, I haven't sorted through everything yet."

Her kitchen table had been piled with folders and boxes she'd been trying to organize and go over. She gave it a quick glance and wondered if in all that chaos was something from Canadian Mutual.

Mariangela thought of the insurance policy she knew about—one for five hundred thousand dollars. She'd already received the payout on it. She had owed $42,000 on the house, due to a second mortgage Giovanni had taken out several years ago. She'd paid it off, then put the rest in the bank so she'd have money to live on. There was the income that would be generated from the Grove project, but that payout wasn't to come through for at least a year or more.

"I have a copy of it here if you can't find yours. I

guess after Giovanni took it out twenty years ago, he forgot about it."

"He was known to forget at times, but mostly he was on top of things. I'm not sure what happened with this policy. I don't recall him telling me about it, but then again, he may have. It's been a long time since I did the bookkeeping for Moretti and paid the bills. Not since I had the children. He liked to be in charge of it, and that suited me just fine, since I had the house to run." Mariangela turned away from the sink and started looking over the papers on her table, seeing if there was anything labeled Canadian Mutual. "How much is the policy worth, Mr. Brown?"

Without preamble, he stated, "Two million."

Mariangela's heart pumped double time and her legs wobbled. She leaned against one of the vinyl-covered chairs for support.

Two million dollars?

"Scott said he'd have a check drawn up for you within the week. I figured you'd want to know right away."

Swallowing the thickness that made it difficult to breathe, she nodded numbly.

KYLE PUNCHED THE DOORBELL of Mariangela Moretti's ranch-style house, thinking it awkward to come midday with nobody else around. No big Italian supper with a houseful of people. Just him.

Mrs. Moretti had called him an hour ago and asked if he could come by and see her. She'd claimed it was urgent she speak to him without any interruptions, or the chance that anyone could see them having a private discussion. That had piqued his curiosity.

He'd spent the morning at city hall, filing permits and then chasing down an engineer about something on his seventeen-story project. Kyle's phone had rung nonstop, but that was nothing new.

Once, it had been Francesca's number on his call display. He hadn't picked up, and she didn't leave a message.

While his day had been hectic, he hadn't been so busy that he'd forgotten about what had happened this morning with Francesca. He'd thought last night was personal, that he could be someone special in Franci's life. Only to find she was surfing the Internet, looking for guys.

She hadn't struck him as the type to use that format to land a date, but he supposed he didn't really know her. He'd thought he'd seen many sides of her working with her every day for weeks, but he certainly hadn't seen this coming.

Clearly this Trent guy was really interested.

A stab of jealousy had cut into Kyle, but he'd shrugged off the feeling and had left before he had to overhear any of their conversation.

It sucked to know he had competition, and normally he would have given chase. But there was too much history between them for him to get more deeply involved with her. They were already tied up with this

Moretti-Legacy deal, and he couldn't walk away from that. It was a lot easier to walk away from her.

So he had.

But as he stood on Mrs. Moretti's doorstep, he wondered if he'd done the right thing. Franci had seemed surprised when Trent Black spoke to her. Then again, maybe that surprise was due to Kyle discovering her dating methods.

He didn't know for sure.

And right now, he really couldn't dwell on it.

Mariangela opened the door. "Hi, Kyle. Thanks for coming by on such short notice. Do come in."

Following her into the living room, he stood there and waited for her to get to the point. Typically, he was a straightforward person. He wanted to know about a problem as soon as possible so he could start trying to fix it. He assumed there was a problem with something, or else Mariangela wouldn't have been so secretive about their meeting.

"What can I do for you?" he asked, shoving his hands into his jeans pockets. He felt tall next to her, out of place. Too big for this small living room and its furnishings.

Gone was the reception he'd felt when he'd first come here for dinner. There was no laughter in the house now, not teasing or roughhousing. There was just him and Mariangela…and, he sensed, Giovanni.

It kind of creeped him out.

Mariangela seemed calm in spite of her phone mannerism. In fact, she almost seemed happy about something, but at the same time cautious. Her face was lightly made up, her hair brushed away from her forehead. For an older woman, she was attractive, and she wore clothing that suited her figure. She had on a warm-up suit of a jacket and matching knit pants. The olive-green color emphasized her brown eyes.

"Take a seat, would you, Kyle?" She directed him to the wing chair by a long sofa.

He sat, placed his hands on his knees and leaned forward. It was hard to relax.

On the end table to his right was a photo of Francesca wearing her cap and gown. The gilt-framed picture had to be from college. She looked older—more polished and sophisticated—than she would have in high school.

"Coffee?" Mariangela asked.

Between meetings and being on the run, he'd had about four cups. "No, thanks. I've had my quota for the day."

Mariangela sat nearby, crossing her legs at the ankles.

"Again, thanks for coming over. It's been a crazy morning. I've been on the telephone for most of it, making sure that the information I was given was truly correct. I had to ask my attorney a lot of questions, as well as the accountant. I also spoke to the insurance agent, Herbert Scott, several times to confirm everything and get the estimated dates."

She was talking in what sounded like circles, but he didn't interrupt. He assumed there was a point in whatever she was talking about, though at the moment, he didn't see it.

Sitting tall, and with a serious expression, she folded her hands in her lap. "Kyle, I got a phone call this morning from our lawyers, Brown and Holt. I believe you met them at the meeting."

He nodded.

"They told me something quite surprising. Nobody knew about this until today—or rather, Giovanni knew, and people did in the past, but then it was forgotten. Until I got the call." She brushed her hair behind her ear. There was a near-empty coffee cup beside her, as well as a cordless phone. He figured she had been making a lot of calls, as she'd said.

He cut to the chase, not sure what his place in all of this was, but wanting to offer his help just the same. "What can I do for you, Mrs. Moretti?"

"A few days ago, I spoke to your mother."

That news settled over him like a leaden cloud. He supposed Mariangela could talk to whoever she wanted, but Helene wasn't real high on his list of preferred topics. Whatever was between him and his mom wasn't something he wanted to talk about.

Mariangela went on. "She told me something that I wish you had told me."

Kyle tensed.

"She said that she needed you to buy her out, that she had to unload her Legacy stock. It all made sense to me—what you'd said to us over and over. That you needed out of this Moretti deal. As I stated, I wish you had told me why."

"Would it have made a difference?" Kyle asked, acknowledging that she was right in her assumption that he'd needed out of the deal.

"No, but it would have explained so much." Mariangela gave him a warm smile, one of heartfelt compassion. "Your silence says a lot about your character, Kyle. I'm sure your father would be proud to know how you've conducted yourself."

Kyle merely shook his head and smiled.

"He would, Kyle," Mariangela insisted. "You are a fine man and a gentleman. You could have dumped the Moretti stock to save yourself and Legacy, but you didn't." Puzzled, she gazed intently at him, as if trying to read his soul. "Why is that?"

He didn't readily answer. He couldn't. How could he tell her that he loved her daughter, when her daughter had just revealed a different agenda?

"I had my reasons," he said at length.

"And I suspect they have to do with Franci, don't they?"

"The reasons were what they were, and now they aren't. So it really doesn't matter, Mrs. Moretti."

"But it does." She slid the cup away from the edge of the end table, looking away briefly, then directly at him. "The phone call I received this morning was about a life insurance policy that Giovanni had taken out decades ago. It's worth quite a lot of money. Enough to get you out of this deal with Moretti."

Her words didn't register right away, but then their meaning slowly sank in.

Moretti Construction had the funds to buy him out of the contract. It was over. He could walk, free and clear. Money in the bank, money to pay off his mother.

He gave a short, sarcastic laugh, unable to contain it.

The irony was that forty-eight hours ago he'd laid his cards on the table and cashed in his chips.

Exhaling, he shook his head.

"Kyle, are you all right?" Mariangela's voice was soft, soothing.

"I'm okay," he said evenly, though his thought processes seemed slower than he'd like them to be. This changed quite a few things. "It's all good. I hope the life insurance can help you out, too."

"Yes, it does. But there's more to this than you're probably prepared for, and that's why I asked you over here."

The muscles in his body bunched and coiled, and he felt as if he were sitting on the edge of his seat rather than firmly in it. "And that is?"

"It's that I'd like to buy you off quietly, and without anyone knowing." She drew in a breath. "Because I want you to keep on partnering with Moretti and helping my daughter."

Kyle said the first thing that came to his mind. "She doesn't need my help, never has."

Mariangela frowned. "Maybe you're right, but I saw the two of you together and I think you'd be good for one another. I'm sorry…perhaps I'm out of line, but I want you to get to know Franci. I'd bet money it's what Giovanni would have wanted."

This was going further than Kyle wanted. He wasn't sure how to handle it, what to say. He'd thought himself in love with Francesca, but wasn't sure how to proceed if she didn't return the feelings. He had a lot to think over, a lot to consider.

"You bring a great deal of expertise to Moretti. And we're all so very grateful. It was Giovanni's dream to complete the Grove Marketplace, and you've stepped up to the plate, offering your advice and knowledge—all while keeping Legacy in the background and the Moretti name in the foreground. It takes an honorable man to do such a thing, and I commend you."

"I do have my good points," Kyle said, making light of the situation. Otherwise he might just get up and walk out. It wasn't as if he was angry about any of this, or torn up over it. On the positive side, this had been the best news he could have heard. He'd call Burton immediately, draw up new contracts and get his Legacy stock back. It would be as if nothing had transpired.

All that said and done, however, things *had* changed between him and Francesca. He'd seen her apprehension on the street this morning, her nerves and her uncertainty.

"Would you consider staying on with Moretti?" Mariangela asked, her expression hopeful. "I know you've got a full plate with Legacy, but Franci needs you. We all do. I never thought I'd say this, but Moretti can't keep up with its workload without help. The last thing I want to see happen is for the Grove to fail."

"It won't fail, Mrs. Moretti. Your daughter is smart and she has a good understanding of what's going on. Mark, too. Both your son and daughter can do it."

Mariangela sighed. "So that's a no?"

"It's an 'I don't know.'" Kyle ran his hands through his hair, sucking in a much-needed breath of oxygen and then letting it out. "I have to think about it."

"I understand. I'm asking quite a lot from you."

"Mrs. Moretti," he reasoned, "if I weren't onboard, you'd be relying completely on family to see you through to the end. I don't see why this changes now because I'm already here."

"That's the thing. I'm certain Giovanni trusted you enough to have thought everything through. He knew that maybe you'd have to call the bonding note due—for whatever reason. But there was something about you that my husband liked. And I have always trusted my Giovanni's instincts. I feel them now, as if he were in the room."

"I can't really address that," Kyle said, rising to his feet.

Mariangela followed suit. "What are you going to do?"

The answer seemed like a no-brainer to him. "Nothing. I'll stay on the Grove project until you get the insurance money."

"Fair enough. But can you do me a favor? Please don't say anything to anyone about the money beforehand. I'm not going to tell anyone, not even my sons."

"I give you my word." At the door, he turned toward her. "But after you've paid me off, I'm going to be up front with Francesca—the day I have the money in my account."

FRANCESCA WALKED into Pomodoro that evening with purpose in her stride. Seeing the date squad at their usual table, she squared her shoulders and made a beeline for them.

She was going to kill the three of them.

They'd been friends forever, had had disagreements here and there, but had worked out their conflicts. However, this time what they'd done was way out of line.

Anger didn't begin to describe how she felt. She wanted to take a blowtorch to something and set it on fire.

After that horribly awkward meeting on the street with Trent Black, she'd gotten him to tell her all about how he knew who she was—through, of all things, an Internet personal ad that her three best friends had written for her.

Too bad his admission had come *after* Kyle had taken off.

Before leaving, Kyle had studied both of them silently, then obviously concluded he wasn't part of the equation. He'd said a hasty goodbye, then continued on his way.

She'd tried calling him once today, but he hadn't picked up, and she couldn't talk about this in a voice mail, so she'd let it go.

For now.

Seeing her three *best* friends, she wanted to tell each one they were no friends of hers. She was that mad.

She'd contemplated calling them to let them know she'd found out, but she'd opted against that, since she'd be seeing them tonight. She was going to pounce on them like a tiger on its prey.

Sitting, she smiled and set her purse down on the floor next to her chair. "Hi, ladies," she said.

They greeted her warmly, seeming more cheerful than usual. Jordan had tucked a manila folder underneath her big white dinner plate.

No surprise. Not anymore.

Franci could only imagine what, or who, was in it.

They fell into their normal chatter, talking about this and that, and it was all Francesca could do to keep quiet. She didn't want to make a scene in her brother's restaurant, especially when he came to the table and poured them each a glass of wine on the house.

They ordered, and Francesca listened as all of them talked about their week, the mundane happenings. Until she couldn't take it anymore.

"What's that folder, Jordan?" she asked.

Lily perked up like a cat in a canary cage. "We were going to wait until after wine and dessert, so you'd be relaxed."

Right now, Franci was so tense, she felt as if she'd snap in two.

Erin folded her hands together. "Go ahead, Jordan. Let's just show her now."

Jordan got this gleam in her eyes as she lifted the folder. "All right. I've been dying to talk about it since the moment you sat down."

Gritting her teeth, Francesca waited.

Her long-time friend pulled out a piece of paper and handed it to her. The other women tried to read it along with her, but somehow Francesca gathered they'd already been privy to the information.

She skimmed the paper, reading the Internet personal ad. And *personal* was the operative word here. It listed everything from her height to her body type, to her favorite foods and colors, to the ages of men she was interested in.

A sick feeling swooped through her stomach. So this Trent Black guy had read all of this. Franci felt as if she were a zoo animal on display.

How could anyone date so clinically? What about eye contact, an interested smile, a soft touch, a flirtatious move? What about the way a man smelled or the sound of his voice?

This new Internet concept took the romance out of the whole affair. While it might be for some people, it wasn't for her.

Franci said nothing for a long while, then looked up. "How many guys answered?"

"Lots," Jordan said enthusiastically. "Because they know a good thing when they read about one. But we screened them, and you'll be glad to know we have the cream of the crop right here." She tapped the folder.

Franci didn't say anything.

But leave it to Erin to intuitively say with a gasp, "She's beyond upset. She already knew—otherwise, she would have cut our heads off because she'd been taken by surprise."

Francesca drank half a glass of wine, welcoming the warmth that sluiced through her body and took some of the edge off her taut muscles. "Bingo."

Lily blanched, then looked to Jordan for help. "I wasn't really for it at first, but Franci, there are some real quality men. One guy in particular—"

"Would his name be Trent Black?" Francesca inquired.

Jordan's mouth fell open. "How did you know?"

"I met him this morning. He introduced himself to me on the street."

Erin murmured, "What are the odds?"

"Apparently not high enough," Francesca retorted. Then she caved under the stress of the day and moaned, "How could you? How could you do such a thing to me? I was humiliated."

"Oh, Franci," Lily said. "That wasn't our intention at all. We thought you needed help—"

"Help?" she squeaked. "By putting my ad up online? It's embarrassing. And you displayed my picture up there for anyone to see?"

"No, we didn't," Jordan quickly assured her. "We only gave it to the guys we thought were worthy."

"Small consolation," she replied, finishing her wine. She felt the stirring of a headache. Stress and being tired.

While sleeping on Kyle's sofa last night, she'd wakened a few times and been aware that he was next to her.

She should have gotten up and gone home, but each time she woke it had felt so deliciously satisfying to have a strong chest beneath her cheek, she'd fallen back asleep.

"I want you guys to yank this ad ASAP," Francesca grabbed her purse and checked her cell phone to see if she had missed any calls. For some odd reason, she was holding on to hope that Kyle would call to ask her who Trent was and what was going on. Unfortunately, the ID window was blank. Glancing at her friends, she amended, "And I mean like ten minutes ago. I want it erased."

A guilty flush worked over Jordan's cheeks. "I'm sorry, Franci. Truly I am, but I just thought we were doing you a favor."

"I don't need a favor like this. I'm...livid." She ground out the last word, feeling torn up inside.

This was killing her. To be so close to Kyle, then to have him think the worst of her behavior... She had to try and fix things.

"I'm sorry, Franci," Lily said.

"Me, too," Erin added. "We love you, Francesca."

"I understand and I love you all, too—maybe not so much right now. But I don't need any help in the romance department." She looked each of them squarely in the eyes. "I already have a man in my life and I want to keep him there."

"Kyle?" Jordan asked.

"Yes." After leaving a couple of bills on her plate to

cover the cost of her dinner, she stood and took the fat folder with her. "Tell Robert I had to go."

She walked out of Pomodoro with a determined stride.

CHAPTER TWENTY-ONE

THE MUSIC OF Chris Rice filled the condominium as Kyle sat at the table going over a set of drawings. They were for a new building Legacy was doing on Mercer Island in Washington, a small retail complex with retro architecture that Pete Ivy had outdone himself on. The lines and details were amazing. Kyle was excited about doing the job, but he wouldn't be able to check it out on a daily basis—not with the ties that were keeping him here in Boise. *If* he did what Mariangela wanted.

He felt his jaw, rubbing the scruffy beard there. Just over twelve hours ago, he'd shaved, while Francesca slept on his sofa.

She sure was beautiful in her sleep.

Looking down at the blueprints, he felt restless. Pensive. Not angry, just lost. He couldn't keep his focus. His concentration had been poor all evening, and as he noted the time, he decided to call it a night.

He rarely went to bed before eleven, managing fine on five or six hours of sleep. It usually didn't bother him, but today the lack of sleep had caught up with him, affecting his ability to perform. Now he was dead tired, and since he didn't feel like working anymore, he decided to lie on the bed and shut his eyes.

Sleep would probably be elusive, but he'd give it a try.

As he shut off the kitchen light, a knock sounded at his door.

He tilted his head in surprise. Nobody came by his condo—not even anyone from work. A couple of weeks ago, a pizza delivery guy had knocked by mistake.

When Kyle had gotten out of the shower earlier, he'd put on a pair of old cotton pajama bottoms that fit him loosely. He wore a nearly threadbare wife-beater shirt and was barefoot. He debated putting something else on, but it was a moot point.

Whoever it was had most likely gotten the wrong unit.

He answered the second knock and found Francesca on the other side of the door.

She stared at him wordlessly, and he saw the beat of her pulse at the base of her throat.

"I tried calling," she finally said, "but there was no answer."

His response was monotone. "My cell died. I'm charging it."

They faced off, gazing at each other. He couldn't guess what she was thinking, but he'd never seen her look better—even though she appeared rough around the edges. She seemed fired up about something. Spirited and on a mission.

She had on a pair of white slacks that made her look sleek and slim and tall; Kyle felt himself grow instantly aroused. A frilly black top with white polka dots may have looked overdone on another woman, but it looked great on her. The cut was low, showing a chunky, black bead necklace that rested at the top of her cleavage.

"Can I come in?" she asked.

Wordlessly, he stepped aside.

"I'm sorry it's so late. Did I wake you?"

"Nope."

She walked purposefully into the living room, a manila folder in her hand. Setting her purse down, she drew in a breath and sat on the edge of the sofa.

"Can I get you something to drink? Beer, wine?"

"Water would be good," she replied, looking over her shoulder at him.

He could see the glint of hoops at her ears, and decided she looked like an exotic gypsy in the muted light streaming in from the uncovered windows.

The condo was nearly dark, and he opted not to turn any lights on. He did light a candle and bring it to the coffee table, with glasses of water for both of them.

He took a seat next to her, their knees brushing. The drugging scent of her perfume invaded his nostrils, making him want to scoop her onto his lap and kiss her until neither one of them could breathe anymore.

Whatever she wanted from him, she could probably have, if she gave him one of her smiles. It irritated him that he could fall so hard for her.

The two of them walked such a fine line between business and personal. And this morning, with that guy on the street, there had been too much personal for Kyle to deal with.

"You need to know something," Franci began, opening the folder on her lap. "My girlfriends thought they were doing me a favor by placing an Internet dating ad for me. I had no idea. This morning when that guy—"

"His name was Trent Black," Kyle stated. He had a great memory for details, and the man's name had stayed with him.

Kyle hated to acknowledge it, but he'd done a Google search on a Trent Black and had come up with a page of matches for the name in Eagle, Idaho. Trent was some kind of hotshot investor.

"Yes…Trent." Francesca pulled out papers, giving him one that displayed facts about a profile ID named Franciful. "He read my profile and my girlfriends corresponded with him. I guess they sent him some photos of me."

Kyle's body tightened, not liking that news.

Even though what Francesca was saying made sense, he was still curious. He skimmed the profile, then gazed at her. "I didn't know your favorite food was Thai."

Her lush lips turned down in a frown. She reached for the paper, but he pulled back, and she leaned over him, the side of her breast grazing his chest. The contact caused heat to flash through him, and stirred the memory of her pressed against him last night.

She ordered cryptically, "Don't read that."

"Then why'd you give it to me?"

"Just to show you that I didn't do it. Okay, fine then,"

she said as she straightened. "Read the opening part, where it says 'we're three of Franci's friends.'"

He did, then gazed at Francesca. "So they want you to get out there and circulate."

"But that's not what I want."

A smile curved his mouth, a sense of satisfaction skimming through him. His gaze traveled over her face, searched her eyes. He'd known from the moment he saw her at city hall that she was a woman who could capture his full attention. And she sure had it now.

Softly, she spoke. "I didn't want a man to come up to me on the street after you and I had spent the night together."

Kyle caught a lock of her hair and twirled it around his finger.

"I didn't want to have my information posted on the Internet."

The urge to kiss her grew stronger.

"I didn't want you to think that I was interested in someone else. Because I'm not."

He caught her chin in his hand and brought her close to him. The sweet smell of her filled him, and when he finally did kiss her, her mouth was hot and intoxicating.

The silky slide of her tongue, the warmth of her skin, all infused his senses, until she occupied every corner of his mind and heart.

She trailed her fingertips over his ear, down the side of his neck to his bare shoulder, sending a rush of blood to his groin. His pulse lurched as he ran his hands across her shoulders.

He felt the curve of her lips against his when she smiled.

Her breath was sweet when she whispered, "I'm a little…okay, a lot…out of practice with this."

"We've got all night," he murmured. He sank his hands into her hair.

"So are we sleeping on the sofa again?" she breathed.

"We could. But the bed's more comfortable."

Time stood still. Her breathing was rapid, the heat between them palpable. Their fevered groping in the dark was sexy, making him want more. To feel her skin next to his, to give her pleasure…

He changed the angle of his kiss, deepening it.

This wouldn't be a reckless moment, but a slow and drawn-out night where tomorrow would be a new beginning.

As Francesca kissed him back, melting into him, Kyle knew there would be no other love like this in his life.

Francesca Moretti was it for him. Now and always.

ROBERT DIDN'T BURN EASILY, but he slathered on a coat of sunscreen anyway. The day was hotter than a Viking oven left on broil. Insects buzzed in the air, the sound of rapids downriver the music for the day.

Rafting the Payette River was something he didn't get to do often. Marie wasn't one to do anything extreme. She preferred to take the girls to Roaring Springs, and even then she didn't go down the fast rides.

She liked to float the manmade river with its cement sides and trickling waterfalls. And if she got hungry, the snack bar was handy.

When Mark had called him last week to ask if he wanted to do a daylong rafting trip, Robert had been all over it. Especially after he found out that John would be coming. And Francesca.

With a date.

That date happened to be Kyle Jagger.

A brothers and sister reunion for recreation, with a nonfamily member thrown in.

As he walked toward the trash can to chuck his empty pop can, Robert wondered if Franci knew what she'd be getting into.

Mark had been the one to set everything up, renting the raft and getting it. He'd gone down to Banks to pick up Franci and Kyle, John tagging along with him. You had to have a second car at the ending point, and John's Lexus SUV had been it.

Robert had stayed behind at the starting point with the life jackets, water cooler and six-man raft.

Other recreationists milled around the river's edge, launching rafts, their dogs lapping up water. Women in bikini tops talked to one another while guys pumped up rafts and used tie-downs to get the coolers settled.

This was Idaho at its best.

Robert had forgotten how much he enjoyed this, and wished his wife shared the same enthusiasm. But it was okay. He'd given her and the girls some cash to take in the latest Disney movie, buy gigantic Cokes and candies, and relax in an air-conditioned theater. They were happy campers.

Sitting on the raft's edge, his Tevas tracing tracks in the dust, Robert shaded his gaze and watched Mark's club cab come into view.

John reclined in the bed, his arm draped on the side as if he didn't have any worries for the day. It was seldom Robert saw his older brother just get out and chill, shake off thoughts of his job and other responsibilities. Teenagers were a lot to worry about, and both of his were skating on thin ice. John had told him Kara had gone to a beer party, and Zack had been fined for speeding.

Robert felt for his older brother and was glad he'd been able to make it today. If John ever needed help, Robert would be there.

Francesca and Kyle sat in the front of the pickup, and when Mark found a parking spot, the four of them walked over to the water's edge.

Unable to wipe the grin off his face—much to his sister's annoyance—Robert stood and extended his hand to Kyle. "So by the end of the day, Jagger, you may not have any hide left on you—not by the time us Moretti boys get done grilling it off you. First up—just what are your intentions toward our baby sister?"

FRANCESCA WANTED TO DIE.

"Robert, shut up," she snapped. She hadn't been that snippy with her brother in years.

He laughed, a good-natured sound that resonated through the parking lot. And making matters worse, Mark grinned like a field cat stalking a mouse. Even John broke out in a broad smile.

"You guys can ask me anything you want," Kyle replied with an ease Franci wished she felt. "Your sister's amazing, but I think you already knew that about her."

"So are you guys like a couple now or what?" Mark asked, his tone marginally authoritative. He knew good and well that they were—she'd told him the other day when he'd been in the trailer.

"We are." Kyle removed his sunglasses, angling them on top of his head. "Anything else?"

John slipped his shirt off and tossed it into the raft. "I'm good for now. If she likes you and says you're okay, then you must be."

"Yeah, she's pretty selective," Robert added.

Franci knew she'd be up against an interrogation if she came on today's rafting trip, and their prying queries were inevitable. It had been a long time since she'd been involved with someone, and she'd told herself that if she acted as if her relationship with Kyle was no big deal, they'd grow bored with their tactics and leave her alone.

"But I'm telling Mom," Robert teased, his sunglasses keeping his eyes from her view.

"Okay." John played along. "Use my cell phone to call her."

Franci refrained from gritting her teeth, but couldn't

help punching her oldest brother in his upper arm. “Hah, hah. No cell service up here, moron.”

“Mark, she hit me,” John grumbled with a grin.

Mark made a face, then dropped to his haunches to untie the knots on the cooler straps. “You guys are being stupid.”

In spite of her annoyance, Francesca caught herself laughing at the absurdity of their joking. And in front of Kyle. It had been a while since she and her siblings had done something like this together.

She supposed her brothers liked Kyle well enough by now that they could feel comfortable kidding around when he was with them.

Inwardly, she smiled. She was happier than she’d been in a long, long time.

“If I get out of line with you,” Kyle said softly, and only for her ears, “are you going to hit me, too?”

“Only if you deserve it.”

“I could tackle you without any effort.”

“I know you could.” Because he had, the other night on her living room carpet, pinning her to the floor and kissing her until she’d grown dizzy.

Grinning, Kyle put his arm around her waist and drew her close. A public display of affection wasn’t something her brothers saw every day. She waited, holding her breath as she tried to gauge their reactions. None were forthcoming.

The boys had already moved into assembly mode and were getting the raft ready for launching.

An hour later, the flowing river had taken them to a sandy beach. The rapids had been maneuvered by paddling, with everyone following Mark's directions to steer either right or left to avoid rocks. The exercise had been exhilarating, the day glorious.

Once on the beach, Francesca removed her life jacket and got a bottle of water. She went and sat on a boulder to sun herself while Kyle and her brothers leaned back on their elbows in the sand, cold beers in their hands.

She couldn't hear what they were saying, wasn't even sure she wanted to. It was enough to know that Kyle had integrated himself into her life with an ease she hadn't expected.

Looking at him, at the sunlight turning his skin a golden tan, she had a hard time thinking about anything beyond the way he made her feel.

He wasn't wearing a shirt, and sometimes she liked him that way. Other times, she liked him in almost nothing. That wife-beater shirt he'd had on the other night had been more sensual than if he'd been shirtless, the cotton soft beneath her fingers, her palms.

She'd relived that night a thousand times since, savoring the emotions and feelings she'd experienced. Waking up next to him, feeling his warm skin against hers, his breath at her neck, his legs tangled with her own, had been bliss.

Watching him now, casually laughing, she felt a fullness in her heart. A completion she hadn't expected.

This time love was different for her. She was more mature, ready to take on the challenges.

And Kyle was certainly a challenge. He was complicated, yet simple. He liked fine things, but the basics satisfied him. He was good grabbing a pizza from Guido's, or dining by candlelight at the Cottonwood Grille. He loved to fly his airplane, had taken her up yesterday for a flyover of Boise at dusk.

He was reliable, stable. Steady and confident.

She wasn't thinking beyond the Grove Marketplace project when it came to where Kyle would ultimately end up. She knew he had ties to Seattle, and always would. But there was something to be said for the contract he'd made with her father. It would keep him in Boise for a good while.

After that, they could decide what they wanted to do.

Kyle glanced her way, gave her a smile, then got up. He crossed the sand to her, blocking the sun from her eyes.

"You in a bikini top and shorts ought to be illegal," he said as he dipped his head above hers. "You've got legs that just don't quit."

She giggled like a teenager. It was nice to receive compliments from a good-looking man. It made her feel silly and young.

Kyle grinned. "I'm thinking I need to kiss you right now."

She leaned back on her hands. "In front of my brothers?"

"They already told me I should."

"You're kidding me."

The kiss that he settled over her mouth was her answer.

"WE HAVE TO BE ON THE twelfth floor in five minutes," Kyle said as he sorted papers on his desk.

He didn't usually keep the trailer so cluttered, but he'd been doing some material estimates on that Mercer Island project and had drawings and yellow legal pads everywhere. His coffee cup was empty, but the spoon he'd used to stir in creamer lay on a pile of receipts, staining them a murky brown.

Franci glanced up from her desk. "I'll be ready."

"Did you get the improvement list? We've got to modify the corner offices, and the specs have to be exact or we're toast."

"I have them." She held up a sheet of paper.

He took a moment from the craziness to admire the way her hair fell against her neck, the way her eyes shone. When she smiled, he was tempted to forget the twelfth, grab her and settle her on his lap.

"Also, the restaurant needs to have a new vent cut out. I don't know how the original could be off by two inches." Kyle reined in his amorous thoughts, trying to refocus on the matters at hand. There would be time to kiss her and hold her later on this evening.

"I already have Mark on that one." She rolled her chair back and gazed at the calendar on her wall, making a notation in her day planner. "Oh, hey," she said distractedly. "I forgot to tell you—the plumbers took down the pinup girls."

"Win one for Franciful."

That comment caused her to turn toward him with a frown. "Thank goodness that got cleared up. Geez, I also forgot to tell you that Erin is dating the guy."

"All was not wasted."

"I guess not. Lily's going out with one of the backup guys, and Jordan—who knows. She never seems to lack a man of the hour."

Kyle listened to her talk further about how she and her three friends had made amends over the Internet dating thing. As she talked on, his mind wandered and he thought ahead to tonight.

They had an eight o'clock reservation at Berryhill & Company, a small and cozy café. He'd sent a bouquet of flowers over for John, the chef, to have on the table. As well as a bottle of his best wine.

Kyle was finally able to tell Francesca about the payoff.

At ten-thirty that morning, a courier had brought the finalized documents to the trailer, bearing his and Mariangela's signatures, which had been notarized yesterday at the offices of Holt and Brown. The courier also delivered a bank receipt of funds deposited into his Legacy account, from Moretti Construction.

He was free and clear. No more ties to a company that wasn't his. He was back at the helm of Legacy—if he chose to be there full-time. Only he wasn't going to make that decision. He'd leave it to Francesca, let her decide where she wanted him.

Funny how things ended up. Given his options, he'd prefer to be here, with her. Even with the chaos of running two companies at the same time, dashing from meeting to meeting while skipping lunch more often than not, and fielding phone calls for twice the problems.

But it was okay. He was managing, and had actually fallen into a niche that was working for him.

He had help at Legacy Constructors to get their multiple projects completed on time and, just as important, on budget. He'd hired another superintendent in Seattle and assigned Ken West to the seventeen story on a permanent basis.

Kyle grabbed his cell phone and hard hat, brushed a kiss over Franci's mouth and wished he could linger. He cupped her cheek for a second, loving the tenderness in her eyes as she gazed at him. "I've got to get something out of my truck. I'll see you up there."

"Um, yeah." She gave him a quick kiss back. "I'll be there in a sec. I'm looking for the electrician's file. Have you seen it?"

Kyle opened the door, letting blinding sunlight spill into the small trailer. "On my desk."

He went to his truck at the curb, rummaged through it for the tape measure, found it on the floorboard and clipped it onto his belt. A pack of gum was on the dash and he stuck a piece in his mouth.

Striding through the building, he passed drywallers hanging Sheetrock on the first floor. At the elevator, he punched the button and waited, talking to one of the welding foremen for a moment. The construction noise was intermittent—nail guns, then chop saws.

Just as the elevator doors opened, Francesca arrived. Rather than get on the lift with him, she stood there, gazing at him as if he'd two-timed her.

"What?" he asked, but as soon as he said it, he knew.

The legal papers. They were on his desk, in a courier mailer, the return address Holt and Brown. She had to have looked. And he couldn't blame her. They were her attorneys. This was her project. If something was on his desk, it was likely for Moretti.

"How could you—" she demanded. Then the squeal of a screw gun cut off the rest of her words and he couldn't make them out.

"Franci, come here."

She didn't move, so he reached out, grasped her arm and steered her into the elevator.

Rather than hitting the button for the twelfth floor, he selected the rooftop.

She stood away from him, staring out the window. Neither of them said anything as the gears meshed and the elevator climbed higher and higher.

Once at the roof, he fought against wrapping his arms around her and telling her to trust him, so he could talk to her tonight like he'd planned, with the flowers and wine, with romantic words instead of hurried explanations on a construction site.

The warm breeze ruffled the American flag above them as he guided her to the railing, the sounds of the city rising up from below.

"You sold out and you never told me," Francesca

stated flatly. "How did my mom get the money? What did you make her do?"

A light wind blew her long hair across her eyes, catching in her lashes. She tucked the strand behind her ear.

"It's not like that at all, Franci. Your mother came to me with news that your father had a life insurance policy worth two million dollars."

Disbelief blanched the color from her cheeks. "He didn't…"

"It was something nobody remembered until the attorney got a phone call from the insurance agent. All of a sudden, Mariangela had the means to buy me out of the bonding clause, but she asked me not to tell anyone about it."

"Why not?"

"She thought that you and I should keep working together. That if you knew, you might give me the boot. I don't know what exactly she had in mind, but it seems she knew something about us before we did."

He took the next few minutes to tell Franci everything. About the stock he'd had to sell to pay his mom off, and the reasons he'd needed to get out of the Moretti deal early on.

Francesca said nothing as he framed her face in his hands.

Kyle gently rubbed his thumbs over her cheeks, an ache filling him when he saw tears gathering in her eyes. He knew by now it took a lot to make Francesca cry.

He spoke with assuredness, the conviction that he'd done the right thing. "I gave her my word, Franci, but with a stipulation. That I would tell you what happened as soon as the money was put into my Legacy account."

"Today…"

"As of this morning, yes."

"So you're free to go," she stated blankly.

"I am."

He placed his hands on her hips and drew her to him.

Her quiet voice filled his ears. "So are you?"

Closing his eyes, he breathed in her perfume. His heart began to swell, overflowing with love for her. "I can't make that decision."

"Why not?"

Looking into her upturned face, her shimmering eyes, he gave her a tender smile. "Because you're the boss again. You make all the decisions now, not me."

She gave a half laugh, half cry that she smothered by clasping a hand to her mouth. "I see. Well, then. Okay. If you put it that way."

Seconds ticked by as she tried to control her emotions. "Kyle, you could have sold us out to strangers…but you didn't."

"I'm not that kind of guy."

Linking her fingers with his, she kissed him passionately. His blood heated immediately and he offered no resistance. Her body shivered when he crushed her to him. She was warm and willing.

And she was his.

He spoke against her mouth. "Is this job harassment?"

"It's whatever you want to call it." Reaching up and circling her arms around his neck, she spoke the words he wanted to hear. "Stay. Stay with Moretti. Stay with me."

"You've got yourself a deal, honey."

She held on to him, her cheek pressed to his chest, her heartbeat echoing the pounding of his own.

"I love you," Kyle said into her hair, feeling the truth of that to the core of his soul.

He felt the wetness of her tears against his neck. "I love you, too."

They held each other, stroking and caressing, loving with open hearts.

The noise of midday traffic drifted up from below; the clink of metal against the flagpole seemed in sync with it. The construction of the Grove Marketplace continued to progress, leaving a mark in the city's history.

And in the shadows cast by the tall buildings that would stand for years to come, Giovanni Moretti would be remembered.

EPILOGUE

DRY CREEK CEMETERY WAS peaceful and green, its expansive lawn perfectly manicured. In the distance, sprinklers were watering the eastern plots. Bouquets dotted the graves, some with balloons or other mementos. There were ornate markers and plain ones. Loving epitaphs, as well as simple names and dates inscribed on flat slabs of marble, left as tributes to those who'd departed.

Mariangela and Francesca had brought a bouquet of sunflowers with a bright yellow ribbon. Using the spigot by the road, Mariangela filled the urn with water.

The day was gray and gloomy for September, the temperature having turned cool for this early in fall. Clouds hung low in the sky, perhaps holding the threat of rain.

While she'd arranged the long fuzzy stalks, then tied the bow around the urn, her daughter said, "That looks nice, Mom."

Mariangela smiled, feeling close to Giovanni while setting the urn next to his headstone. The words on the marker were basic and true:

Giovanni Moretti
Immigrant, Father, Husband, Builder

"I think he'd like them, *bella mia,*" Mariangela said softly, "even though he wasn't much for flowers. He'd rather have been digging up pipes in the backyard than planting."

The corners of Francesca's mouth lifted. "I'm thinking that, too. But, hey—at least we didn't pick out pink for him."

"Oh, he wouldn't have gone for that. He was very manly, your father." Mariangela rose to her feet. "But he did have a soft heart."

"He did." Franci put her arm around her mother, laying her head on her shouler.

The pair of them gazed at Giovanni's grave, each lost in private reflections.

After a while, Mariangela wiped her eyes with a tissue, then blew her noise. "I'm going to head for the car, *bella.* Are you ready?"

"I'll just be a minute, Mom."

Francesca stayed, knelt down and touched the cool edge of the headstone with gentle fingertips. "I miss you, Dad. But I want you to know that I'm going to get the Grove done. We all are. Me, Mark and Kyle." She brushed a tear from her cheek. "You knew, didn't you? You knew Kyle was a good man. That's why you trusted him, why you went to him when you needed help." She choked on a sob, then composed herself and smiled.

"I'm glad you did what you did, Dad. If it weren't for you, I wouldn't be getting married. I wish..." she gulped "...w-wish you could walk me down the aisle. I know you'll be there, though. I'll feel you just as surely as if you were holding my hand."

She swallowed the heaviness in her heart just as the clouds parted and a slender beam of sunshine touched her. The sun instantly warmed her cheek and the side of her neck, bared by her ponytail.

Drawing a breath, she gazed heavenward.

"Thanks, Dad," she said in awe. "I'll see you in the church."

AUTHOR BIO

Stef Ann Holm lives in Boise, Idaho, with her husband and family. She has two beautiful daughters, and one space cadet dog who will stare for hours at any food substance. She loves hot summers, sunshine and sitting poolside in her backyard. Visit her Web site at www.stefannholm.com to read more about what's going on in her life. Or you can write her the old-fashioned way at P.O. Box 1206, Meridian, ID 83680-1206.